once
upon
a
flarey
tale

To anyone locked in a tower. Of any kind.

1

I was filling out a job application in the Barnes & Noble. Because, you know, that's what you're supposed to do when you are out of work. And broke. And about to be homeless, and everything is random and awful, and the only answers you can see to any of your problems are the dull ones, and no, you don't have magical powers no matter what you might have once believed.

And you know the drill. They keep the applications behind the counter. You walk in and smile sweetly at the nearest counter clerk. You try not to act too eager or too envious of the clerks all happily drawing their regular paychecks and becoming BFFs with the other clerks, plus they'd attended community college and graduated in three years debt-free instead of picking an obscenely expensive private school and then—to top it off—deciding hell yes, why not a master's, too? What could possibly go wrong?

What could possibly go wrong. Other than losing your nerve and dropping out and being single and alone and adrift and the terrifying pile of debt and the cranky creditors and soon, no place to live.

I carried the blank application to the end of the counter nearest to the front door.

My phone buzzed.

I ignored it. It buzzed again.

I filled out the standard bits at the top of the application.

Customers filed past, their plastic shopping bags rattling and bulging.

I pulled a piece of paper from my handbag. I began copying over my somewhat sketchy employment history.

There was a lull in the stream of customers at the counter, and the two clerks nearest to me started chatting. BFFs, clearly.

And at first, nothing they said really broke through the intense level of concentration it takes to copy your employment history from a piece of paper onto a job application neatly and legibly, when secretly you want to just scribble and be done.

And I'm no Rapunzel. I don't even have long hair.

But I heard the word "tower."

• • • • •

It was the clerk with the long, straight hair and the cleavage winking sideways from the scooped neck of her tee. She's the one who'd said it. And as this registered, my brain whirred through its short-term memory bank and retrieved the preceding remark by the other clerk—pink hair, nose ring—and I was ninety-nine percent sure what I'd just heard was something like, "Vicki still hasn't found someone to take her apartment?"

Followed by: "Nope! Can you believe it? A place like that! With a tower?"

And that's all it took.

All those years of trying to be normal? Rational?

Gone.

And instead? I, Marion Flarey, was instantly ensconced in my marvelous Tower.

And it was everything you're thinking. It was a gorgeous, exotic, hallowed place of divine seclusion. I'd been shut into it, of course. Against my will but not really. And I was waiting. Devoted to nothing but thinking and reading and waiting. And—you know what happens next—somewhere out there? My Prince, of course! Thundering over the mountain pass on his white steed. Searching, searching...

And okay, maybe this Prince wasn't a literal Prince. Because that may be too much to ask, considering that I'd already had my shot at not one, not two, but three—yes, three!—flesh-and-blood potential partners who would have made perfectly wonderful modern-day Princes. And how'd that work out for me? News flash—horribly. So at this point maybe I should settle for a metaphorical Prince, say in the form of a wonderful new career.

So, edit my story to: come to me, my sweet, metaphorical Prince. Come to me. Thunder metaphorically over the mountain pass on your white steed, thunder through the forest, come closer and closer and closer and...

And?

Now you know.

That's all it took to forget myself.

The word "tower" is all it took for me to go from normal Marion to kooky Marion, and there I was, darting back down the counter, waving my partially-filled-out job application at the two clerks to get their attention.

"Did I hear you say Tower?" I squeaked. "Where is this Tower, exactly?"

The clerks stared, giving me a who's-this-girl look.

Which—I suppose I should thank them—was exactly the face-slap I needed to bring me back to Reality, and I felt my cheeks go all hot because oh crap, now you've done it, Marion. You've fallen back into a story. The one thing you keep promising yourself you'll never do again.

Be normal for once, Marion!

"I'm, um, I'm sorry to..." I licked my dry lips. "I overheard you talking just now. Did you say your friend is looking for someone to take her, uh, apartment?"

The clerks exchanged glances. But then they admitted that yeah, sure. Their friend, Vicki, was in a terrible spot. And—thank you, clerks—they started sharing, tag-teaming the story about how Vicki was all set to move cross-country later this month and she'd lined up someone to take the place but that person backed out, something about

3

unforeseen circumstances that the two BFFs cluck-clucked about for a bit but I didn't really follow. Because of how hard it was to keep my mind on apartment instead of Tower.

"Where did you say the building is?" I said, and they told me, and I knew the place. I knew, exactly, the place.

Because of course it was a neighborhood I knew and of course I'd notice a house with a Tower.

The neighborhood: enormous old houses built in the nineteen-teens or twenties with hardwood floors and high ceilings and huge, wooden-framed windows. Brimming with old boomers and students and people like me. Ex-students. And super walkable, lots of mature trees, and the residential parts are bordered by commercial streets that keep sprouting new brew pubs and vegan restaurants and coffee shops. Some of the houses are on the blah side, big sprawling boxy things, but others are stunners.

And the Tower?

Don't picture a Rapunzel Tower. It's not ten stories tall and built of stone blocks with a window at the top and no other way to get in. No. This Tower was integrated elegantly into the corner of a gorgeous Queen Anne, two stories plus attic, and sided like the rest of the house with scalloped shingles that were painted white.

And I should just calm down. This was nothing to be nervous about. It was a perfectly normal thing for a perfectly normal person to want an apartment with a Tower.

"So, uh, maybe I get Vicki's contact info?" I asked.

The clerks exchanged glances again. ESP glances about whether it was okay to give a slightly strange-acting, hunting-for-a-job wandering supplicant the phone number of a friend.

"I am really really really interested," I said, "and could move in, like, right away?"

I held my breath.

A mom with a kid in tow walked up to the counter.

Cleavage clerk stepped back to her register and began scanning the mom's stack of kiddie picture books.

I focused my puppy dog eyes on the skeptical face of the nose ring clerk.

Her eyes slid again toward her friend. Her friend was too busy swiping books across her scanner to notice.

"Well," nose ring clerk said, slowly, "Vicki actually works in the Wegmans floral department."

She waved in the general direction of the Wegmans supermarket which happens to be a parking lot away from that exact B&N.

"She's there now."

I felt a sudden clutch in my middle that made me feel almost out of breath.

Because there is serendipity, and there's Serendipity.

And this was an awful lot of Serendipity.

I hovered for a second, looking down at the application.

And then I gave in.

I snatched the application and folded it and shoved it into my bag and darted out the door, and a couple minutes later I'd crossed the Wegmans parking lot.

I stood a moment to catch my breath and tuck my bangs back into their barrette.

And are you kidding me—was that my phone?

Again?

I pulled it out of my bag and swiped at the spiderwebby cracked screen.

And my jaw dropped.

Candace?

A text from Candace?

Who I hadn't even spoken to in, like, seven years?

OMG.

Like I needed a text from Candace at that particular moment!

Make that: any particular moment!

Delete! Delete!

Go away and stay away, Candace!

2

I found Vicki right where the B&N clerks said she'd be. In the Wegmans floral department. So cute, Vicki! So perfectly solid and normal. Standing there surrounded by sprays and ribbons and greenery. Stabbing freesia stalks into a glass vase.

I sidled up to peek at her name tag. Just to be sure.

I wondered how much it paid to be a Wegmans florist. Must be enough to cover her rent.

Mental note. Fill out application for job at Wegmans.

"Hey," I said. "You're Vicki, right?"

"Yuh huh." She looked up from her bouquet.

"Your friends at the bookstore said you need someone to take your apartment?"

She nodded and yeah, she'd had someone who wanted it, but he'd backed out, and her family owned the building, and her dad would kill her if she didn't rent it before she left for Portland.

"I can't even tell you," I said. "This is huge. I'm looking for a place and it sounds amazing."

"It's a studio." She picked up a stalk of miniature roses and gave it a little shake.

A studio.

A studio.

Of my own.

Me. And my books.

And for a glorious moment the story caught me up again, and I didn't even need a Prince. It was my life as a perfect Happily Ever After, me and my books in my apartment in a big gorgeous house in the part of town where the hip people live.

Only something else about apartments in big gorgeous houses with towers in the part of town where all the hip people live.

They aren't exactly cheap.

"When can you move in?" Vicki said. She tucked the spray of roses into position and studied the effect. "We'll need first month's rent, last month's rent, security deposit."

"Uh, no problem," I said, watching her tie a bow around the vase. While trying to muster the courage to ask her how much the rent actually was. And simultaneously dreading her answer. And also trying, very hard, not to think about my checking account balance. Because it was very, very small.

She picked up a length of pink ribbon. "I have a couple other people who are interested in it."

My stomach clenched.

The was no way I was getting this apartment. I was stupid for thinking, for one second, that I was getting this apartment.

But as I stood there trying to get my somewhat food-deprived brain to come up with a way for me to gracefully back out, Vicki gave the bow a final tug and looked up.

"You'll want to see it first, right? I can meet you there around four."

So, okay.

No way was I going to get my Tower.

But at least I'd get to see the inside.

· · · · ·

I avoided the prepared food section on my way out of Wegmans because when you haven't eaten anything since yesterday except coffee it's best not to let yourself be tempted.

I crossed Monroe Ave. and grabbed a bus to Park Ave.

Telling myself, okay, this sort of thing happens to people all the time. They find something they want more than anything, but they can't afford it. And what happens? A miracle. A miracle happens and suddenly they have the money. So think positive, right? Go fill out applications at the restaurants and shops and things near the Tower, because something miraculous will turn up and if I somehow really did end up living there wouldn't it be nice to have a job I could walk to?

I settled into my seat and pulled out my phone.

Teagan would be so excited for me if I got this place...

good vibes needed Tea! Found a maybe apt and omg it is fab!

I hit send.

I waited. And she didn't answer, but Teagan works on a cruise ship and can't always answer texts right away. So I put my phone back in my bag and looked out the window as the bus bounced down Monroe Ave. and turned onto Culver and crossed 490.

Reminding myself to stay positive, Marion. Stay positive and you've maybe got an apartment, now.

All you need to do is come up with first month's rent, last month's rent, and security deposit.

· · · · ·

The apartment was incredible.

Second story. Parquet floors. And because it was a Tower, the exterior wall was a curve with an enormous set of curved windows looking out over the street.

I walked up to the windows.

And that did it. I was completely gone. I'd put my new bed right there by the windows and every morning I'd wake up and open my gorgeous drapes and look out of my Tower, and everything would belong to me, the whole world would belong to me. Everything would belong to me, as far as I could survey.

It's how stories work. They're like an enchantment, almost. And you don't know when you're in one.

I turned around.

8

Vicki's bed wasn't in front of the windows. It was in the middle of the room.

She saw me looking at it. "It's a bit of a pain, placing furniture. Because of the walls."

"Oh, I know all about that," I said. "I grew up in a geodesic dome. You know what they are? My stepdad built it."

Not that I normally like to talk about my crazy family.

"No kidding," she said. "Weren't those big in the 70s?"

And was that a sign? I mean, what are the odds? That she'd even know what a geodesic dome was?

I nodded vigorously. "Yes! Although my stepdad built his in the late 80s. They're very energy efficient. And if you want to push furniture against a wall, you can always put something in the gap. You know. A little shelf or a floor lamp or something."

She led me to the kitchen, which was tiny and dark. But the appliances looked fairly new.

"So your friends said you're going to get your master's?" I asked. "What in?"

"Cultural studies," Vicki said. "I did an undergrad class in folk architecture. That's how I know about geodesic domes. My prof once met Buckminster Fuller. You know who that is, right? The bathroom is over here."

I felt giddy.

Buckminster Fuller is the guy who invented the geodesic dome.

And folk architecture? Really?

Two more signs, right? So a total of three? Three signs?

"I'm working on my master's, too," I said. "Although I'm on a little hiatus." I pushed the shower curtain aside, pretending to check the condition of the bathroom plumbing. "The, uh…the expense. You know. I need to re-fill the coffers a bit."

"Ah," Vicki said.

Yikes. That "ah" sounded…funny.

And I knew why. I'd revealed a tiny bit too much with that last comment. And Vicki was now noticing a flicker of doubt. She was wondering whether this Marion Flarey person was a serious rental prospect or a college drop-out with leaking coffers who might not be in a position to afford first month's rent, last month's rent, and security deposit.

Dang.

Don't get paranoid, Marion… Stay positive. Don't read too much into a little "ah."

We were back in the living-slash-bedroom.

Time to be brave. Time to face the dragon. "How much did you say the rent was?" I said.

"Seven fifty."

That was high for a studio. Even a Park Avenue district studio.

But heroines don't back down just because dragon mouths are smelly and full of fangs.

"And, uh, when do you need the money by?"

And seriously?

Right at that very second? My phone.

Buzzing again.

And again. And again.

Rattling the very innards of my handbag.

"Do you need to get that?" Vicki had seen me glance down. And no doubt about it, her voice was noticeably cooler than it had been a few minutes ago.

"No, no! I'm good! It can wait." While inside I was thinking *that better be Teagan and not freaking Candace.*

And also who was I kidding?

I knew what Vicki wanted. She wanted me to reach into my bag, push aside that stupid buzzing phone, pull out a little drawstring sack and start counting out $2250 worth of gold coins into her hand…

And ugh, was she no longer making eye contact? Was she already thinking about how she was going to have to find someone else, not this so-called Marion Flarey person, to take over her gorgeous apartment?

"When did you say you were leaving?" I heard myself say. "For Portland?"

"I'm leaving town at the end of the month. But I'll have my stuff out of here before that. I'm crashing at a friend's. So if you need to move in sooner, we could work something out."

This could not be happening. "So you're saying I could move in, like, next week?"

"We could work something out, sure."

And maybe it was not eating all day. Or maybe it was my phone, which just then started buzzing again. Maybe my phone, buzzing, addled my brain.

Or maybe it was that I'd let myself fall into a story that ended up with me living in a Tower.

All I know is, I suddenly reached into my bag and grabbed my checkbook.

"Tell you what," I said. "I'll give you a check, right now. To hold the place."

My heart was pounding.

"Only, do me a favor. Don't cash it right away. I just…need a few days."

And without letting myself think about what I was actually doing, I scribbled my signature on my check and tore it off the pad and held it out.

Come on, Vicki… Come on…

Just close your pretty little pollen-stained fingers around my check…

And then she did it. She took the check.

I steadied myself.

"So. This is, uh, fine," she said, and her eyes darted around the room, her words picking up speed. "But how long do you need, exactly? Because I'll need to cash it this week. By Friday. I've got a mover coming for my stuff. I need to pay my mover."

Oh, God. What have you just done, Marion Flarey?

Too late, now.

"No problem," I said. "Friday works. Friday is perfect."

3

So I followed Vicki out to her car and signed the lease agreement. Bravely. Smiling as I signed. And then I was standing alone, again, on the street outside my Tower.

Thinking, okay.

Now what have I done?

Did I actually just hand someone a bad check?

And also, WHY was my phone still blowing up?

And I need a plan. All I need is a plan.

Yeah. All I need is to come up with $2250 by the end of the week.

I took a deep breath.

There was no way I could possibly come up with $2250 by the end of the week.

Unless…

Unless—wild card—you could do a story that ended with you holding $2250 by the end of the week… Put yourself in the story and…

NO.

I felt a little surge of nausea.

Just no.

Because it was bad enough to find myself in the middle of some crazy story when I wasn't even trying. And hadn't I sworn off of that? All of it? Hadn't I sworn that I was going to be normal, and not a freak, and that I'd never again believe in things that couldn't possibly be true?

No. I needed to find another way. I needed to get my hands on $2250 the way normal people do.

I needed to get a job. And not just any job. A really good-paying job working for a really kind person who wouldn't think twice about fronting me a couple weeks' worth of pay...

I steadied myself.

I thought of Teagan.

Teagan, who was working on a cruise ship, saving her money for med school.

You couldn't get more normal and rational than that.

I fished my phone out of my bag and took a quick pic of the apartment.

At least, now, Teagan would stop worrying about me. Stop urging me to move into the condo she split with the other cruise ship people, which was ridiculous and impossible although, yes, she was a sweetheart for suggesting it.

I walked a few more steps and framed another pic of my beautiful, stately, white-sided Tower.

And then I checked my texts. And ugh. Two from that jerk, that credit card collection person. And double ugh, fresh hot text from one of my two roommates. And it was a long one—she liked sending long ones—asking again if I was on schedule to move out, the landlady kept calling, the landlady needed to get the place re-painted.

Like I didn't know that already.

And *Marion, you promised to be out by now.*

Like I didn't know that already, too?

Ugh ugh ugh. The Tweedles. I'd found them via Craigslist. And they were very nice people. A couple of undergrads. And sure, to them I was the third body to help them cover the rent for a couple months. And although I'd tried to get along, I didn't get their jokes, I wasn't able to muster quite enough faux enthusiasm about their boyfriend dramas or their classmate dramas, I didn't go gaga enough over the fresh wads of designer clothes they disgorged from their pup tent-sized Lord & Taylor shopping bags about eighty times a week.

I wasn't normal enough for them, and they knew it, and I knew it.

But it had been a place to live.

A cheap place to live.

And I'd been very grateful to find it.

I sat down on the bus stop bench and took a deep breath.

You've got this, Marion Flarey.

all good, I texted TweedleRoommateDum. *just put dep on new place. be out by end of the week at the latest*

Smiley face.

Right. What's the emoji for how my stomach curdled after I hit send, sitting there on the bus stop bench, re-reading my text.

I mean, if—just suppose—suppose I failed to get my hands on first month last month security deposit, and therefore ended up without a new place to live? Then what?

I could squat, right? Mere Tweedles couldn't force me out, could they? If I really wanted to, I could demand my rights. There are laws protecting people like me, you know!

On the other hand, it's horrid to be stringing people along, even when they're Tweedles.

And yet, there I was.

Stringing stringing stringing.

I swiped the screen to delete the stomach-churning Tweedle text and at that very moment there it was, at long last, incoming from Tea:

what what?

Okay! Now this was more like it.

I grinned from ear to ear.

I sent her the pics of the apartment.

Caption: *what do you think????*

She texted right back.

OMG OMG

I knew she'd be psyched. That's Tea. Lives the most exotic exciting life you can imagine, working on a cruise ship, the entire planet is, like, her personal playground. And yet when her best friend lands a Tower she is as excited as a friend could possibly be.

I sighed. Happy sigh.

I went back to the message screen to see what else had come in.

And ARE YOU KIDDING ME.

No wonder my phone had buzzed ten thousand times while I was touring my new apartment!

That Candace!

Okay, not ten thousand times.

But—I counted—she'd sent seven texts.

SEVEN.

And how'd she even get my number? From Mom?

mayfly

Don't call me that!

Trying to tug at my heartstrings. Won't work!

you gotta help

surprise is missing

pls?

Surprise? Mom's cat? Hmmm…

pls, mayfly

my kid wont stop crying

OMG. Seriously.

Did she not get it?

I wanted nothing to do with her, her son, or anybody else in that cockamamie family.

pls answer

So I answered, all right.

GO AWAY.

All caps. Typed as hard as I could without bruising my fingertips against my poor phone's slightly shattered screen.

Like I was going to get into it with Candace.

Candace, my sister actually stepsister.

Also known as the you-know-what starts with a "b" who'd stolen my boyfriend.

4

I didn't go straight back to my soon-to-be-former apartment.

I needed some more packing boxes. So I took a little detour, walking a couple blocks out of my way to a crappy little shopping plaza that was my go-to spot to scrounge.

The front of the plaza was pretty awful. Cloudy plate glass windows under cracked, faded signs. Liquor and lotto tickets, tattoos, We Buy Gold. The back was worse. A parked delivery truck with dirty scratched paint, filthy litter that had been there so long it had turned into paper mache mush that was spread flat as vomit against the pale crumbling blacktop with its scraggly weeds poking through the cracks.

The last wisps of happy, found-an-apartment serendipity that I'd been carrying around with me for the last hour or so curled up and died.

This was Reality. Me, skulking around a crummy old shopping plaza, scavenging for free boxes.

"Stop it, Mayfly," I muttered to myself. "Now is no time to go wobbly. You can do this."

Mayfly. My old nickname, which I sometimes wonder fits a little too well. Because have you ever seen a mayfly in the air? They swoop up, then swoop down. Up, then down.

If that were a person it would for sure give her the stomach willies, swooping up and down like that.

Which may explain why my stomach felt like it did, an afternoon flying as high as could be, now dragging my belly on the ground looking for boxes.

Ugh.

A movement caught my eye.

I looked over just in time to see a fox trotting by on other side of the chain link fence at the back of the parking lot. And I wished for a moment that fairy tales were really true, in which case this would be a talking fox, and would now squeeze through that break in the fence and walk up to me. "Marion, I can take you to your perfect job! It pays great and offers great benefits and I hear there's a $2250 signing bonus! Just jump on my tail, Princess, and hold on."

Right. The fox didn't even turn his head.

Just trotted up the fence line and disappeared.

Well. Next best thing, hahaha. I found some decent boxes. Three, in fact. And two were the strong ones made with that extra thick corrugated cardboard. Which was good, because I need that kind of box for my books.

I schlepped them back to my place and let myself in.

Said a little thanks that as irritated as my ex-roommates were, at least they hadn't told the landlady to go ahead and change the locks.

• • • • •

The apartment was a half house. But it was barely nicer than that awful plaza, and it was on one of those awful roads that slice through cities everywhere, today, that are called roads but are more like highways, noisy and busy and thick with people driving too fast, who you'd never recognize again even if they passed you every day. Most of the nearby property had long since been zoned commercial, with the periodic exception of this or that shabby house, which had been converted to rental units because only renters would consent to living in such a spot.

So. Dingy on the outside. Dingy on the inside. Weird odors exuding from the walls and vents and baseboards, zero water pressure in the showers, crud beneath the stove that would keep you awake at night if you dared to peek at it.

But it was close to a college. The Rochester Institute of Technology. It was always rented. And it was soon to be re-painted, supposedly.

And poor people can't be choosers.

And as if the place needed to be even gloomier, the Tweedles had owned all the furniture and they'd taken it with them when they moved out. Understandably.

So now?

No couch, no chairs, no TV, no desks.

No beds, either. I'd had a futon, but I'd sold it. Cash to cover food. After the money from selling my laptop had run out.

All that was left was my clothes. A few pots and pans.

And books, of course. It wasn't every single book I owned—I'd left books in Tibbs when I went away to college—but there were quite a few. But I'd managed to accumulate another nice little library since I'd left home for good.

I'd moved everything downstairs, into what had been the living room, after I sold the futon. I guess I figured if I was going to sleep on the floor, it didn't matter what room I was sleeping in. And with everything downstairs it looked like I really was getting ready to move out. Effective in the event that one of the Tweedles made a surprise on-site visit to check my progress.

"You can figure this out, Marion," I muttered as I yanked a piece of packing tape off the roll and sealed a box. "It's almost over." I tore off another piece of tape. "You've seen the clearing in the forest," I said aloud. "You've seen the light shining from the windows of the prince's castle."

Ugh. I really shouldn't do that. The words sounded stupid and forced and sarcastic. Just words, my voice echo-y and thin and bouncing around in the shabby emptiness of that horrid, horrid half-house.

No. Stop it, Marion. I marked the box 'Clothes' and re-capped my Sharpie and checked my phone but Teagan had gone dark again.

Prolly her break was over and they'd pulled out of port and she was perched on her lifeguard chair while servers twirled past holding trays of champagne cocktails overhead, and now Teagan was flirting with rich gorgeous young bare-chested men and making dates for drinks, later, in secret because staff aren't supposed to fraternize with the guests.

I noticed the mucky feeling of trepidation about my real-life predicament had subsided. And that consequently my stomach began to nip with another sensation.

Hunger.

I went to the kitchen to fix dinner.

A gourmet meal, hahahahaha: potato chips au poivre.

Recipe: one bag kettle fried potato chips, a steal this week at the Dollar General. One small carton sour cream. Couple packets of pepper from the Panera condiment rack.

To serve: Open sour cream. Sprinkle with pepper. Scoop with chips.

I am sooooo hilarious, aren't I?

Nom nom nom nom nom…

Dinner over. Last box.

Books. Fairy tale books.

A few were textbooks from either my undergrad classes or my pitiful half-assed attempt at my master's, but most were volumes I'd picked up here and there over the years from secondhand bookstores and garage sales and flea markets.

There were about twenty boxes of books, altogether, stacked on the floor around me.

I layered the last few books into the last box, but I didn't tape it shut, and I kept one book back.

A Norton textbook. Not vintage but cool because it has a lot of fairy tales you may not have heard of.

The long literary kind.

I plugged in my phone and arranged one blanket on the floor to be my mattress and opened the book at random.

There was just enough light coming in from the streetlight outside the house...

I started to read.

Just what the doctor ordered. Instead of phone calls from irritating creditors and potato chip dinners and the rather horrifying prospect of a bad check coming due against a nearly empty bank account, I was in France. And there were fairies and ogres, and a young woman whose skin was so white she was known as Blanche...

I suppose Marie-Jeanne Lheritier, the author, meant us to imagine normal white person skin. Like the way a fair-complexioned person might look if she'd managed to stay out of the sun her whole life. But I pictured Blanche as even whiter. Like porcelain doll white. Like a ghost. So white she glowed.

The phone buzzed again.

I picked it up. On the outside chance it would be text from a stranger who had texted my number by accident and we'd strike up a conversation and he'd turn out to be cute and funny and single and my one true love...

Or—let's be practical here—maybe it was a callback from one of the places where I'd applied for a job and they realized I was such a perfect fit could I please start tomorrow morning?

Yeah, right.

It was Candace.

Again.

Seriously?

I didn't bother to read the text. I set the phone to Do Not Disturb and put it back on the floor.

Face down.

5

I woke up the next morning feeling like I'd felt every morning since I'd sold that damn futon. Like elves had snuck into the room in the night and beat every muscle and every bone in my body with their stinking elfin hammers, which were made of elf-iron and capable of doing considerably more damage than you might think, despite their elfin size.

I sat up and rubbed my shoulders to try to make the pain subside.

I went to the kitchen and poured a glass of water from the tap.

I got my bag and checked my wallet. Coupla tens, coupla fives, coupla ones... I could afford a cup of coffee. Splurge.

And today I'd find that job, right? You know. The job the magical fox mentioned, the one where they'd front me $2250 by Friday.

Is there any job on the planet, by the way, that pays $2250 in the first week, meaning within four days of you being hired, despite the fact that you are a master's program dropout and the highlight of your resume is your two-month stint as assistant manager, Buzz Me coffee shop? (That would be the coffee shop that went bankrupt, right around the end of aforementioned two-month stint.) (No, I do not bring bad luck. That is *not* my issue. Really.)

"Coffee first," I said as I stuck the money back into my purse. "Then job. Today's the day I find that job."

And I splashed water on my face and stuck my bangs back with a clip and put a little mascara on and stepped back to make sure I looked employable in a service-job sort of way and then there came this BANG BANG BANG on the front door so loud the mirror on the wall jiggled.

Oh CRAP.

I nearly jumped out of my skin.

Because someone banging on your front door that early in the morning, when you sort of owe various parties various amounts of money?

It could mean only one thing.

It had tracked me down. Reality had tracked me down.

I considered dropping on all fours and hiding.

BANG BANG BANG.

Ugh.

Cowardice gets you nowhere. Open any book of fairy tales if you don't believe me...

I squared my still-aching shoulders. I walked to the door. I pushed my eye up to the peep hole.

And: OMG.

It was...Winchell?

I stepped back and rubbed my eye and leaned forward and looked again.

Yes. It was Winchell, all right. I recognized his jowly face, jowlier because of how it was fish bowled by the fun land distortion of the peephole lens.

"Marion!" he called, banging on the door again. "You there?"

Ugh.

So, of all the things that are annoying about my family, maybe the most annoying—at least, the most annoying at that particular time in my life—is that they won't freaking take "no" for an answer.

Winchell, you see, is my stepdad. Candace's father.

I never really warmed to the guy.

And even if I had, I was in no mood to entertain him on the day after I'd handed a bad check to Vicki, when what I really needed to do was figure out how to get my hands on the $2250 I would need to deposit in my checking account by Friday to make the check not-bad.

I wondered if Vicki was the sort who would report me to the cops for kiting checks.

Meanwhile, Winchell must not have realized I was standing on the other side of the door because he banged on it again.

I re-considered my original plan. Considered dropping down on all fours and hiding until he gave up and went away.

But I didn't. I twisted the deadlock and opened the door.

Winchell stood there, blinking at me.

Like he almost didn't recognize me, which he maybe didn't. Seven years is a long time when you're in your twenties. It's like 49 adult years.

He looked the same, though. A little older. A little fatter. And still allergic to razors, apparently. His gray stubble looked like it was at least two or three days old.

"Mayfly," he said.

Ugh. Again, with the nickname.

I suppose I looked annoyed. I know I sounded annoyed. "Hey, Winchell. What're ya doing here?" My eyes narrowed. "And how'd you even find me?"

"We need your help," he said. "Your mom's cat. She's gone missing."

"What cat?" I said. Pretendingly. Because of course he was here because of the Cat. Candace had put him up to it.

"Surprise," he said.

"Ah," I said, still pretending. "She's still alive?"

Surprise, the three-legged cat. White, with big dark brown spots like a pinto pony. We'd gotten her when I was in maybe 5th grade, so she had to be 20 years old. At least.

WTG, Surprise. I guess.

"Yeah," Winchell was nodding sadly. "But she's missing. And Quill…"

He didn't finish his sentence. He saw my eyes flash.

Quill is Candace's boy. And as I've mentioned, I wanted nothing to do with Candace. Let alone her kid.

"Sorry to hear it," I said, my eyes flashing knives at him. "But it really doesn't have anything to do with me."

End of conversation. I took a step back and started closing the door.

"Mayfly."

Was that panic in his eyes?

"It *is* about you. You need to talk to Effie."

I froze.

Was he serious?

"Effie?" I said, still not believing he had actually said what he'd said.

But he'd said it. And now he was nodding. And my brain started to work again and all I could think now was holy fucking what? He actually came here to ask me that? Of all things?

"You always said she could grant wishes," he said in a tiny little voice, which is exactly what I needed to hear. Not.

"Wishes?" I said. "You must be kidding me." As if Effie was a magic gumball machine. As if I could just waltz over to her house and curtsy and she'd wave a wand and... I mean, good lord, the nerve of Winchell to even ask, the way he'd always said—all of them said—that everything I'd ever told them about Effie, about what Effie had told me, was all made up. That when I came home from visiting the old lady up the road, I was telling made-up stories.

Winchell was shifting his weight from one foot to the other. "Marion," he said in a wavery voice. "We don't know what else to do. Your mom's been there twice. And then yesterday Candace tried. Effie wouldn't even come to the door."

I stared. They'd actually gone up there? To Effie's?

Hah.

They were that desperate. And clueless.

Also, it occurred to me that I could learn a little lesson from Effie, with regard to answering the door to my family members.

And wrt granting wishes, too, for that matter.

"So you already have her answer," I pointed out. "She can't help you. So, I'm sorry, but you've come at a bad time. You need to figure this out yourselves."

But to his credit, he didn't comment. Just stood there, skimming the room with his eyes, taking in the boxes and the blankets on the floor and the packing tape. Without saying a word.

And a few minutes later I'd locked up and was climbing up into Winchell's beat up old truck, which probably wasn't the same truck he had seven years ago but might as well have been. It had the same old junk in the back, half-rotted boards and a rusty metal toolbox and some lengths of PVC pipe stained green with algae and what looked like a bag of brick chips but was probably dried up clay.

I buckled my seat belt and gave myself an autosuggestion that under no circumstances was I going to chitchat with Winchell during this drive, even if it meant sitting in total silence for two-plus hours.

We pulled out onto the awful road and went through a couple intersections, and then we were on the four-lane, heading east. And I slumped in my seat, looking out the window without seeing anything, the numbing sound of the truck engine in my ears and the numbing blur of the highway outside in my eyes.

And I must have dozed because Winchell barked, "Jesus, buddy," at some driver who'd cut him off and my eyes flew open and I saw that we'd left the flat broad Great Lakes flood plain that frames the New York State thruway.

We were heading south. The landscape was becoming choppier and hillier and more forested.

And then I realized something.

I was going back in time.

Not actual time. But backwards against my own personal timeline.

And my right foot jammed against the floor of the truck as if I was trying to jam an imaginary brake.

And then my whole body went ice-cold as another thought hit me: what if this is all Effie's doing?

What if the whole apartment thing—the whole Tower thing—was a story she was doing and now I'd let myself get caught up in it?

And I gripped my phone and looked down at the cracked screen and told myself that I was making myself crazy. And I needed to calm down. I needed to text Teagan, how was Teagan doing, how was her day?

This was a simple trip home. Twenty-four hours. I'd get to hug my mom which would be nice and mooch some wine from Winchell, which would be nice because wine hadn't exactly been in my budget recently. And I'd go see Effie and she'd be nothing more than a little old neighbor lady with some eccentric personal habits who had no idea what I was talking about.

What missing cat? How am I supposed to do anything about a missing cat?

And then I'd be back in Rochester and these people would go back to leaving me alone.

6

If you're ever in Tibbs (joke. you'll never be in Tibbs) and you find our road, and you look off to the side at just the right moment, you'll glimpse the top bit of the roof of the dome.

It's hard to see from the road because, first of all, the trees.

Tibbs has a lot of trees. The countryside around Tibbs is mostly forest, which now that I think about it may be one of the reasons I believed so much in fairy tales while I was a kid. Like something about living in the middle of a forest makes it seem like stories that take place in forests might actually be real. Even if they're not. And so many fairy tales take place in forests.

The dome is also hard to spot because it's high up on the side of a steep hill. A hill so steep, in fact, that the driveway doesn't go straight up, because if it went straight up you'd be screwed in the wintertime when it got icy, you'd have to park your car down at the bottom, next to the road. Where it would get buried the next time the snowplow passed.

So instead the driveway goes back and forth, a mini switchback.

It was a gravel drive, or you might call it a gravel drive, charitably. It's really plain old dirt, with gravel in spots where it had washed out and Winchell had shoveled in some rocks to fill the holes.

So back and forth went Winchell's truck, me leaning toward the windshield, scanning everything the way you do when you're back around a place that you knew really well but haven't seen in a long time. You know? Looking for what had changed.

Until, finally, we reached the top of the driveway where it opens into the yard. Which is not a yard like normal people have but more a clearing in the forest that Winchell had carved out when he'd bought the place umpteen years ago. And it also seemed to have shrunk, because the trees there had spent the last seven years pressing in closer, working slowly on their master plan to one day re-engulf the entire clearing, and the dome with it.

It's what forests do.

And off to the right: the dome. And over on the left, the camper.

The dome's roof, a round mound of asphalt shingles, looked darker than I remembered, I suppose because the shingles were now older, and had gotten darker and streakier and more stained from all the sap and dirt that rinses off the trees when it rains. But the window frames were white. Startlingly white.

"Looks like you did some painting," I remarked, knowing Winchell would take that as a compliment. And I'd reconciled myself to the experiment, I suppose, so I might as well keep the peace as long as I was going to be stuck in Tibbs for the night.

"You can fix anything with a can of paint and a good attitude," he said proudly as he pulled the handle of the driver's side door.

Right-o, dude.

Then I noticed the vehicles.

First: a big delivery truck parked next to the dome.

I wondered if it maybe had something to do with Mom's pottery stuff. Her art shows or whatever.

There was also a car I didn't recognize, parked in front of the camper.

A white hatchback thingy.

My eyes narrowed. "Whose car is that?" I said, suspiciously.

And suspiciously, Winchell didn't answer. On the contrary, he was scrambling out of the truck, sliding down from the driver's seat like a seal into the water off a slippery rock, and off he went, surprising speed for a fat old guy, up the little slope to the front door of the dome.

"Winchell?" I barked after him.

"Lana!" I heard him yell for Mom. "I'm back. I've got Marion!"

Okay, how dumb am I? All this big long sob story about Candace's boy, Quill, crying over a cat and it hadn't occurred to me that this was more complicated than "grandson visiting for an afternoon and started asking where Grandma's cat had gone."

She was there.

Candace.

She was staying there. The white hatchback was my stepsister's car.

And yes.

Yes, in case you're wondering?

I did feel, all at once, like I'd been seriously played…

• • • • •

I sat there a moment, seething.

Telling myself, first, that I was stuck there for 24 hours.

Then telling myself well, okay, I can do anything for 24 hours, right?

Deal with it, Marion Flarey.

I steeled myself and got out of the car and followed Winchell to the dome.

And Mom was there, which was okay. Out of all of them, I had actually missed my mom. And she came around the kitchen island, and came over, and I went to her, and she didn't look all that different. Maybe a few more grays at her temples. Maybe a bit more distant but she'd always been like that—she's an artist, I may have mentioned— she always looked a bit like half her mind was somewhere else.

She put her arms around me.

She felt small and thin. She's built like me.

So yeah, as annoyed as I'd been to be trapped like that by Winchell into coming to Tibbs, it was awfully good to see my mother again.

"Mayfly," she murmured. "So good to see you, honey."

"It's only for the night," I said, which was defensive on my part. Because if I started to get soggy, who knows where this would all end up.

I'd already agreed to too much.

"Maybe all your little chicks are finally back to re-feather your nest, eh, Lana?" Winchell said, watching us.

(I know. That made zero sense. Winchell.)

Meanwhile, Mom finished her haven't-seen-you-in-so-long hug and took a step back. "You're awfully thin, Marion. Where's your suitcase?"

"No, I'm not." And technically, I wasn't. Technically I was skinny fat, which is what happens when you've been surviving on cheap carbs. But at least I wasn't totally flat-chested like back in high school. "And I didn't bring a suitcase. Just a bag of stuff. It's still outside."

I looked around for Candace.

Where was Candace?

"We made up a bed for you," Mom said.

My mind went on full alert. And lookit that, Winchell now slipping away again, there he went up the stairs at the back of the dome, and poof, was now disappeared through the master bedroom door on the second-floor balcony. With the same, rather disturbing swiftness I'd witnessed a moment before when he exited his truck.

And then it hit me.

"Wait a minute," I said, glaring at the master bedroom door and then turning to Mom. "What do you mean, 'you made up a bed?'"

"In Candace's old room," Mom said, turning away to avoid my eye.

"Oh, no!" I said. "No."

"She and Quill—"

But I didn't stop to listen.

I was not going to stay in Candace's room. Candace's crummy old room in the dome. And double-no-way was I giving up MY spot to that boyfriend-thieving witch Candace.

Not even for one night.

I whirled and ran back out and ran to the truck to grab my stuff.

Okay, so.

The camper.

It wasn't much to look at, I know. A ramshackle old aluminum thing that was old already when Winchell bought it or for all I know stole it twenty-whatever years ago.

He'd needed a place to live in while he built the dome and then, when the dome was done, he'd left the camper there for storage and an extra couple guest beds.

But then came a time when the camper became my room. My own room. Because I'd been smart and crafty enough to claim it, to fight for it. And because it was only fair. I already had a ton of books, by then, and they didn't fit in the bedroom I shared with Candace in the dome, so I'd started storing them in the camper. So it was only fitting that I move into the camper and make the entire thing my space.

Teenage girls need their own rooms. Candace got her room and I got mine.

I was fourteen.

And so the camper became my bedroom, my library, my sanctuary, my space. The space I'd carved out because I didn't belong anywhere and I wasn't like anyone but at least it meant I could be alone for a few hours every day with my books, and when I was alone with my books it didn't matter as much whether I was normal or weird or anything in between.

I grabbed my bag out of the trunk and turned around.

The camper door flapped open.

Candace stepped out.

The camper's front steps were built out of cinder blocks. Uneven, with weeds growing up around them, timothy and motherwort and milkweed. Not exactly a palace staircase. But Candace knew how to make an entrance, with her splashy flowy floral print top and her bright red lipstick and that haircut, which I hadn't seen before, clipped super short, side part, sculpted waves. A vintage look that I had to admit was striking and also a look I could never have since my hair is the straightest on the planet and totally flyaway.

And anyway this was no time to be envious about that witch Candace's hair.

She stood on the top layer of cinder block.

I glared at her.

Here I'd been formulating my plan. How I'd drop off my things and then gird my loins and hike up to Effie's and get that over with, somehow. And then I'd hike back and deliver my report to the Weekes-Flareys.

And then I'd be done. I'd be free to shut myself away in my camper and read and down a glass or so of Winchell's wine, because it would be implied that the least he can do to repay this tremendous inconvenience and breakage of my resolve to live my own life was to supply me with wine. And hopefully these people had Wi-Fi so I could maybe get online and do a little job-hunting. Maybe turn this whole thing to my advantage, a mini-getaway to get organized so that when I was back in Rochester my job search would be crisp and efficient and ultimately fruitful so that I'd be able to replenish my empty bank account in time to make that check to Vicki good so I could claim my much-needed and very beautiful Tower. I mean, apartment.

And to be honest, I was also looking forward to sleeping in an actual bed, after how many nights on the floor.

But now, come to find out, my mini-getaway spot had been invaded?

Grrrr.

And as I said, Candace knew how to make an entrance. She was now descending the cinder block steps like a queen at a ball. I could feel her sizing me up.

Grrrr.

But something else? She knew. I could tell. She knew she'd effed up, moving into MY room. So I ignored the I'm-so-regal schtick and started striding toward the camper. And I didn't stop, and I didn't say "hi." I nodded and passed her and went up the cinder block steps.

And I was right about her knowing she'd effed up, because then I heard her behind me, following me in. And she didn't sound like a queen. She sounded like she knew darn well that she'd better stay on my good side.

"You can have the bedroom, Marion, it's fine," she was saying. Placating me. "We'll sleep on the day bed. I don't mind, Marion."

Huh.

"Dad texted that you were coming," she said. "I've been moving our stuff."

But by then my eyes had started to adjust.

And I saw my books.

"Oh my God, Candace."

My books! They were in boxes. She'd boxed up all my books. All the books I'd left here in the camper—in my space—when I left Tibbs for college. The books I'd collected when I was growing up, the ones that I was collecting as I fell in love with fairy tales. Because of their charm and the magic and the possibility that no matter how dire things appear, if you persevere, you'll actually come out okay, in the end. That even the little guy can come out okay, in the end.

They were my books.

Mine.

And so, okay. I hadn't been back here for a very long time.

But they were *my* books. My property. And why wouldn't I assume they'd leave my books alone? That they'd be exactly as I'd left them? Exactly how I'd arranged them? And I'd spent so much time getting them right, I'd needed to use every possible niche as a bookshelves: the cupboards over the couch/day bed, the space on the little table next to the wall, the space along the wall underneath the little table... And of course they'd all been in order, all organized by collector and age and binding.

I'd known where every single book was. I can still close my eyes and picture exactly where I'd left every single book.

And Candace had pulled them all down and packed them all away.

Worse than that.

Candace, the…person…who had slept with my boyfriend… Had *touched* them.

I stood there, looking around.

Trying not to lose my mind.

Thinking that this was it. I was now going to fall down on my knees and sob like the doomed princess who is not in a fairy tale, but in a real dungeon, and there is No Way Out.

Then then I saw *him*.

The boy.

Quill.

How had I missed seeing the boy?

He was right there. Sitting on one of the boxes. Staring at me.

I gasped.

He looked exactly like his father.

RB.

An exact duplicate of RB, when RB was that age…

7

Jayzus, I whispered to myself, staring at little-RB-from-my-past.

And for this impossibly long moment neither of us moved.

And then little-RB-from-my-past jumped up. "MOM!" he yelled.

He ran past me.

Ran past his mother and out the door.

Like he'd seen a monster.

And I'm not a monster. I don't think?

I heard the door behind me slam shut and then slam shut again as Candace left to go follow her kid.

I looked around again at my books.

All those boxes.

And I suddenly felt so freaking exhausted. Like how'm I gonna get through this?

And: even one day of this is too much...

Ugh.

I turned and went down the narrow hall past the tiny bathroom and into the tiny room at the far end of the camper.

I dropped my bags of clothes and toiletries onto the bed.

I felt just about sick enough to puke.

It was the sick you get when you've walked into a trap that you knew was a bad idea, but you did it anyway. When you realize that no, this is not going to be a mini getaway. It's going to be 24 hours of torture when you could have been back in Rochester busting your hump looking for a job. And instead you're in Tibbs. Literally the middle of nowhere.

And what was even worse? I also knew I'd been kidding myself. Because honestly, Marion? What if you weren't here? What if you were in Rochester instead of Tibbs?

Do you really think you're gonna land a magical job working for an outfit that miraculously wants you so badly they eagerly front a month's pay so that you can cover your two-plus-whatever-grand nut, land that apartment, and therefore instead of being homeless move into your so-called dream apartment? With its beautiful windows overlooking your new domain and its almost-new kitchen appliances and your Prince out there waiting for you to sally forth and claim him?

I fell backwards on my bed.

Time to just cry. Time to just melt into a little ball of sad sad sad Marion Flarey and cry cry cry...

My phone vibrated.

If that's Candace I'm gonna scream...

But it wasn't Candace. It was Teagan!

u okay?

OMG. My best friend. Beautiful Teagan, standing on a cruise ship deck in the sunshine with the fresh salty ocean breeze whipping her sun-bleached hair and dolphins cavorting below and gorgeous tanned topless men promenading past, flip flops snapping against the polished deck, slowing as they passed her to give her the up-and-down...

And yet she had sensed my agony and had taken the time to text me.

no! I texted back. *Tea it is awful*

And I texted and texted. How Winchell had shown up and asked me to come help them find their cat, and Candace had taken over my room and packed up all my books, and how I'd done such a dumb thing, coming here instead of staying in Rochester, I should have kept my focus on landing a job instead of letting myself get all pulled off course by these Weekes-Flarey people...

And Teagan, of course, was perfect. All *omg omg!!* and *are you seriously kidding me??!!!* and the emoji—you know the one—that's red-faced with righteous indignation.

I started to feel better. And then she settled down to giving me practical advice, which is exactly what she always does and exactly what you'd expect from a woman as together and rational and disciplined as she is.

so million$ q: can you make it thru 1 night?

I considered the question a moment before replying. And I knew the answer.

i think so

I watched the screen, waiting for her to text back. Hoping she had time before she had to get back on the job.

k. be strong, u can do it!

And a string of hearts...

I love my Teagan. She was the medicine I needed. The exact medicine.

Think about it rationally. Think about it rationally and everything will be fine.

My phone vibrated again.

so how're u gonna find the cat?

And I started another text to answer her question. A truthful text. About Effie. Because Teagan had known me a long time. She knew about Effie and the theories Effie had taught me about stories, about what Effie called storywerking, and all of that.

But being Teagan—a STEM person through and through—the Effie stuff was a little too out there. A little too much for a text. So after a minute I re-read what I'd typed, and then thought better of it and tap-tap-tapped the back button, deleting what I'd started.

u know. walk up & down the road & call kitty kitty kitty. it's been lost awhile. odds are bad.

Send.

I'd wait until the next time Teagan was in town. She had a vacation coming later this summer. And then I'd relate, over cocktails, a slightly amped-up version of what had really happened, and we'd have a nice laugh, we'd joke about Effie waving her wand to turn a tomato into a cat crate, and the crate would have to be home by midnight or it would turn into pizza sauce.

I rolled over and took my charger out of the bag and found a wall plug and plugged in my phone.

And I thought that maybe I should head to Effie's now, but I started to feel drowsy and next thing you know I was opening my eyes, and the light was slanting in through the screen above my head.

How long had I been asleep?

Also, how long since I'd slept in an actual bed?

I checked my phone.

It had an eighty percent charge, which is huge for that old thing.

I sat, listening for a moment.

Nothing but the twitter of some birds outside the window.

I slipped out of the camper and headed down the backy-forthy driveway to the road.

I was there to do one thing and one thing only. And I was going to get 'er done. I was going to face Effie.

· · · · ·

Effie's driveway, about a half mile up the road from the dome, didn't look like a driveway. Too narrow, too choked with weeds.

And yes, there was a mailbox planted next to it, but it was banged up and rusty and listing to one side from getting smacked by plows in the wintertime. It didn't look like Effie was even using it anymore, and maybe she wasn't.

So I stood there thinking how deserted it looked, and just because Mom and Candace had supposedly been there and talked to Effie, didn't mean she was home right now. And maybe I should just pretend I'd gone to see her. Just keep walking up the road and turn around in an hour or so and go back to the dome and tell them all: nope. Sorry. Effie can't help…

They'd never know the difference.

And they'd never believed in her anyway…

The sun felt hot on the top of my head.

And of course what would happen next is that the driveway would be guarded by monsters, and thinking of this reminded me about ticks, blood-sucking, disease-carrying little arachnids that don't even have real heads, don't have brains, instead of heads and brains they have this mouth organ that cuts through the victim's skin and buries itself into the victim's flesh and starts sucking blood and the tick's body begins to swell with blood until it is sated and falls off and crawls away and lays its eggs…

I sighed, and bent over, and tucked the bottom of my pant legs into my socks, and pushed my way through the weeds which were thickest right there by the road where they got the most sun. I started up the driveway, holding my bare arms overhead to keep them away from the blood-sucking monsters grinning at me from their hiding spots behind every stalk and blade.

· · · · ·

Yellow pollen puffed into the air.

Tangled weeds caught at my legs and ankles, tugging, trying to trip me.

A deerfly divebombed at my head.

The driveway curled back and forth and rose and fell.

A frog chirped in alarm and splashed into a little puddle that had collected in one of the ruts.

But then, finally, the trees on either side of the driveway became taller and in their shade the air was cooler and the driveway less weedy. And I rounded the last bend and there was Effie's barn, the huge double doors open, her car—a big old four-door sedan, brown originally but faded and gray with dust—parked just inside.

I walked a few more steps.

Her house. Sagging more than I'd remembered. The spine of the roof had a noticeable sag in it. And the enormous sugar maple standing sentinel by the porch was also older, its crown thin and scraggly, and a huge limb had fallen maybe a season or two ago and lay, half-covered by greenery, next to the front steps.

And the lawn, which wasn't really a lawn but more a clearing in the forest.

A weedy overgrown clearing scattered with junk, only to her it wasn't junk. She'd been collecting it since forever, old shoes and rusting buckets and rusting enamel cookpots and old wicker laundry baskets. Metal signs and pieces of wooden posts and hunks of cars and farm equipment. So picture all this junk, rotting and rusting, poking up through undulating tangled mats of greenery, most of it weeds (or what we think of as weeds—Effie doesn't believe in weeds) but also things she plants and tends. Vegetables, berry bushes, flowers.

I stopped for a minute, looking around.

She hadn't noticed I was there, right?

Not yet?

I could still turn back?

I sighed and began threading along the little footpath leading from the driveway to the house.

Butterflies looped from flower to flower. Dragonflies, the red ones and the huge blue green ones, zoomed up, then hovered, then zoomed off.

I climbed the steps of the front porch.

The storm door was open. She liked to keep everything open, it was the way the country folk in Tibbs did. Nobody uses A.C. They open the windows to the breezes instead.

I rapped my knuckles on the frame of the screen. "Effie?" I called. "Are you there? It's Marion."

I listened. And welp, she still had budgies. I could hear them chirping and calling from their cages in the living room.

I held my breath, trying to make out if any of them were talking.

No.

Just normal bird noises.

I knocked again.

Okay. She must be outside somewhere.

I turned around, and as I did a little brown bird, a wild bird, flew up and perched on the railing.

He tilted his head, fixing his shiny little eye on me.

And then he flew off.

Flew around toward the back of the house.

Going to Effie.

Oh gawd.

Why did my mind insist on doing that?

It was just a bird. A random, wild bird.

I really, really had to stop doing that.

I pushed the thought away and went down the steps and picked my way around the house in the direction of the bird-spy, following the footpath that twisted through the junk.

And I admit.

My stomach felt a little sick.

• • • • •

I found her near the huge bluish stone in her back yard, the stone with its big ringed crown of lichens that I used to love to sit on when I was a little girl, because it made me feel so tall, so above everything else.

She was bent over, poking at the ground with a trowel.

Then she must have caught sight of me or heard me or maybe the bird was perched in the nearby bushes and was warning her, because she stood up.

"Ah!" she said. "Marion. What a nice surprise."

"Hi, Effie."

Her hair was pure white. Her right eyelid drooped more than it used to. But her blue eyes were still sharp as needles.

Then I noticed her arm. Her left arm. It wasn't through the sleeve of her sweater, the left arm of her sweater was hanging limp. Her left arm was folded up under her sweater, against her body.

"Geez, Effie. What happened to your arm? Are you wearing a sling?"

"Just for now." She bent back down.

I watched for a minute.

She was digging new potatoes.

"Here," I said. "Let me do that."

I took the trowel and knelt where she'd been working, a spot between the rock and an old tire rim that she'd stuck upright into the ground, and scraped carefully around the base of the potato plant. And the smell of Tibbs dirt filled my nostrils. Wetness and stone dust and old wood and worms and dead leaves.

I handed a tiny new potato up to Effie, who brushed it off and dropped it into the pocket of her overalls.

"So," she said. "I suppose you are here to ask about the cat."

My stomach lurched.

I should have been ready for the question. Why was I not ready for the question?

"Well," I said.

I handed her another potato.

"You know the family. They think..."

"That I grant wishes," she finished the sentence, sounding decidedly amused. "And not only that, let me guess. They think I've granted you three wishes, and you've used two, and now you're here to cash out on the last one."

"Something like that," I muttered.

"That should be enough potatoes for the two of us," Effie said.

"I can't stay for dinner. They expect me to eat with them. Back at the dome."

"Sure, they do." Effie sounded amused, again, but for a different reason, now. She knew darn well that dinners in the dome had never been exactly Normal Rockwell-worthy. We never sat down at the same time to eat together, except for maybe Thanksgiving and Christmas. Instead, Mom and Winchell kept the place stocked with stuff like frozen dinners and cold cuts. When you got hungry you picked something out and fixed it—made a sandwich or heated something in the microwave—and found a seat in front of the television.

Or bent over a book of fairy tales, if you were Marion Flarey.

"I've got fresh snap peas, too," she said. "You can always eat again when you get back."

I stood up. The wheel rim next to the plants was wreathed with wild morning glories, also known as bindweed, a plant that normal gardeners rightly view with horror, because it's a vine that wraps itself around any plant it can reach and also spreads underground via roots that are impossible to dig up because if you pull them they break and so instead of one plant you end up with dozens. Yes, exactly like when the magician's apprentice tried to break up the enchanted broom and every piece turns into a full-size enchanted broom which sinks the little apprentice even deeper into the proverbial doodoo. So before you know it you have bindweed vines entwining everything in reach, a smothering green embrace, leading the gardener to the inevitable conclusion that only the Magician Himself has the power to rectify such a hellish situation.

Only, of course Effie isn't a normal gardener. Her bindweed stayed, politely, where it belonged on its wheel rim trellis. Blooming with its flowers which are, admittedly, pretty. Bewitching, even. Pale little trumpets, white with a blush of pink in their deepest parts.

Silent trumpets. Signifying nothing.

I followed Effie toward the house.

• • • • •

We went in the back door, into her kitchen. It had frozen in time in the 1930s. Freestanding porcelain sink and ruffled curtains and the open shelves on the walls that were painted a chalky green color.

Her budgies had heard us and were going totally crazy whistling and chirping, and the noise made my stomach lurch again. Because of the pretending I'd done as a little girl, when Effie's budgies were talking birds that revealed secrets and told the future and gave clues that would help me realize my dreams.

I reminded myself of the truth. They were plain old budgies like you see in the back of every big box pet supply chain.

"Go on. Say hi to the birds," Effie said as she dropped the potatoes in a colander in the sink.

The cages were the same. Two of them, enormous standalone cages set on curved, cast metal legs, the dark wire of their walls coming together at their peaks into elegant domes topped by fleur-de-lis finials.

And inside them, birds flitting from perch to perch. Three in one of the cages: a white, a blue with a yellow face, and a green. And the second cage had a green, too, which gave me another stomach twinge because when I was a little, Effie and I had agreed that the greens were the prettiest, with their yellow breasts and the black stripes on their heads. And the greens' colors are also closest to the birds' original feathering, meaning they look the most like the ones that are still wild.

Effie had joined me. "These are my girls," she said, dipping a bit of seed out of a covered metal bucket near the first cage.

I went over to her and opened the door to the cage so she could refill the birds' dish. Then she dipped another scoop of seed and I turned to the second cage, where the two boy birds were sitting on a swinging perch suspended from the top of the cage, the blue facing one way, the green facing me.

"I love you," the green bird said.

I fell back a step, feeling my breath suck in.

"Once upon a time," the bird said, cocking his head at me from where he stood on the swing.

"Billy Beg?" I whispered.

Named after the character in the story Billy Beg and His Bull—you probably know the story—the king's son who escapes his murderous step-mother and then, with the help of his magical bull, slays the giants and the dragons and wins the love of the princess.

The green was still looking at me. "Once upon a time," he repeated.

He should have been dead. Shouldn't that bird have been long dead? Or not? How long do budgies live, anyway?

I didn't dare look at Effie, at those sharp blue eyes. "Thumbelina talks now, too," she said.

I turned to the other cage where the blue now hopped toward me, her tiny claws gripping the wires of the cage, studying me with her bright little eye.

"What does she say?" I managed to speak the words.

My voice sounded funny.

"She says plenty." Effie dropped the scoop back into the tin of seed. "When she wants to."

"Pretty bird," I said to Thumbelina.

She didn't answer.

I followed Effie to the kitchen. Telling myself silently to just get through this. Just get through this like it was a perfectly normal visit to an old neighbor lady, and pretty soon it would be over, and I could get back to my real life. And the potatoes cooked quickly, being so young, so it wasn't long before we were sitting down to eat.

"So. What story are you weaving for yourself these days?" Effie asked after we'd scooped potatoes and peas onto our plates.

Ugh. Of course she'd phrase her question that way. Steady, Marion.

I cut a little potato in half with the edge of my fork. "Well, uh, I love living in Rochester?" I said, and damnit if my voice inflected upwards so it sounded like I was asking a question instead of answering one. I drew a breath. "There's so much to, like, do there. And I meet people…"

"That's not much of a story. Do you plan to finish your master's degree?"

Ugh. So apparently someone—Mom?—had been keeping Effie updated on my life. Which meant this little grilling could go anywhere. "Uh, I'm not sure about the master's anymore, at this point," I said.

"You don't seem very sure about anything."

She was smiling. But her eyes were sharp enough to leave teeth marks. Metaphorically speaking.

And I had no answer. I pushed my potatoes around on my plate. "I've done my best," I said, and there was more gloominess in my voice than I would have liked.

"Oh, don't worry, Marion," Effie said. "I have no interest in re-hashing the past." She paused. "But there is that business about the cat."

"It's not a big deal." I pushed a potato around on my plate. "It's fine with me if we just drop it."

"Oh, we don't need to drop it. I'll help you with Surprise. But not tonight. You'll have to come back another day."

What?

"That's not possible." I stiffened a bit in my chair. "I'm only in town for the night."

"I'm sure," Effie said in a tone of voice that made me wonder what, exactly, she was sure about. She leaned over the table and poured some tea into my cup. "And hopefully the cat will come back on her own. They do, sometimes."

· · · · ·

It was dusk, already, when I started back to the dome. Which was a little odd to me. I hadn't been there that long, had I?

Although I guess I had been there awhile, because I'd helped Effie clear the table and wash and dry the dishes, and I'd carried the potato peelings out to her compost pile and helped her cover her bird cages.

I wondered how she'd hurt her arm.

I tucked my pants back into my socks and started down the driveway.

Fireflies blinked in the air. An owl hooted.

I reached the road.

I heard the faint sound of a jet plane and looked up to see its tiny lights winking against the pale blue ceiling of the sky that was starting, already, to show its first faint stars.

Well, I'd tried.

The Weekes-Flarey clan was just going to have to accept the fact that their cat was gone and—just like Effie had said—there wasn't any magical wand that was going to go poof and bring her back.

My job was done. I was going back to the dome to collect my

payment in the form of drinking a nice quantity of Winchell's wine, and oh by the way, use his Wi-Fi to start planning tomorrow's job search back in Roch.

8

So, the dome. The back half is bedrooms. Three on the first floor and above them a balcony and the master bedroom. And the front half is a big open space with kitchen on one side and family room on the other.

And in the family room there's a television. A big flat screen. Mounted on a frame (Winchell's handiwork, stained 2x4s mounted on huge pegs) because—just like in my hopefully-soon-to-be-tower/apartment—the walls of the dome are curved, so a flat screen won't mount flush like it would in a normal house.

Facing the television, arranged in a kind of arc, there's a couch and Winchell's easy chair and a couple other chairs and a bunch of floor cushions.

And, that night, the entire family was sitting there, watching television. Except Mom who was sitting there reading a book.

But of course when they heard the front door, they turned their heads in unison and looked at me, and Winchell held up the clicker and muted the TV.

"How'd it go?" Mom asked.

Great. "I don't know why you think Effie can do anything," I grumbled. Because of course the Weekes-Flarey clan would now give me the third degree. Like I hadn't warned them that their plan was doomed to fail.

"Well, did you tell her what's happened?" Candace, now, piling on. "What did she say, exactly?"

And I found myself on the brink, in that moment, of a major vent. Because didn't I have enough problems in my life without this, too? And did they have any idea how difficult Effie could be? How complicated it was?

Meanwhile Candace was continuing to press me. "You're the one who always told us that Effie—" she started to say, but then broke off, glancing at her son.

And she didn't need to finish. I knew what she meant. That Effie had magical powers. And if she thought we were going to be besties during my brief and soon-to-be-concluded sojourn in Tibbs, New York, that was not the way to go about it. "That's just great, coming from you," I said darkly. "And by the way, who gave you permission to box up all my books?"

"You moved out forever ago," she said. "How long were you planning to leave the camper stuffed with all your crap?"

"You might have asked, first."

"Yeah, because I can count on you to always answer my texts."

"Girls," Mom said.

Just like old times.

And I opened my mouth to really let Candace have it, once and for all, when from the corner of my eye, I noticed Quill get up from where he'd been sitting on a cushion on the floor.

He crawled into Winchell's lap and slumped forward, hiding his head, and his shoulders started to shake.

Crying.

So look what they'd done. They'd actually built me up, in the kid's eyes. They'd actually let that poor kid think I was some sort of fairy godmother myself, that I was going to sweep in there in a burst of sparkles and tinkling noises and drop the cat into the little boy's lap.

And I'm not a monster, despite the way Quill had run away from me in apparent terror earlier that day. On the contrary, seeing him all broken up like that kind of plucked at the space inside my chest where I guess you'd expect to find my cold, hard heart.

But at the same time, it's not like I owed anything to the kid. Candace and RB's kid.

"Dad," I said, trying not to notice Quill's shoulders. "Is there any wine?"

"I'll get it," Mom answered. She stood up from the couch and stopped to stroke Quill's head a couple times as she passed Winchell's chair, murmuring, "Don't worry, honey. I'm sure Surprise will turn up." In other words, promising the impossible happy ending in the hopes that it would smooth out all those prickles in the air.

I followed Mom into the kitchen part of the dome, where she crouched in front of one of the cabinets in the kitchen, pawed around a moment, then stood up with a bottle of wine.

"Zinfandel okay?" she asked me.

"Thanks." I took the bottle. "I'll be in the camper if anyone needs me. Oh, and what's the Wi-Fi password, please?"

· · · · ·

Winchell was the first one to knock at the camper door.

"Marion?"

No Mayfly this time. Must be serious.

The camper rocked slightly and sank from his weight as he stepped inside.

I was sitting at the little teeny kitchen table. My plastic tumbler was half empty. So was the bottle of Zin.

And I'd kind of abandoned the idea of getting started on my next day's job search. It turned out my phone was completely dead, for starters. So I had to recharge it. And while it recharged, I opened one of my boxes of books and started looking through it, my mind wandering down an increasingly gloomy path. Because I so desperately wished that I was the charmed child who goes out into the world and finds the golden bird and brings it back, but apparently, I was not. Apparently, I was the not-charmed child who goes out into the world and fails miserably and comes crawling back home disgraced, filthy-faced, clothes in tatters. Or worse yet ends up turned into a stone statue and has to wait, in total humiliation, for one of the other siblings to wander by and break the enchantment.

I wondered if Candace had a job. And how much it paid and was it salaried. She gave off a salaried person vibe, with her nice clothes and chic haircut.

Yeah. Envious of Candace. Not a good place for ol' Marion Flarey's head.

So when Winchell knocked, I was sitting at the little table near the couch-slash-daybed, fairy tale book opened up in front of me. But I wasn't really reading.

"Wine?" I said, holding up the bottle.

Winchell took another plastic tumbler from the cupboard, blew into it to purify it of dust and dead bugs, poured himself a couple fingers' worth of the Zin, tugged the waistband of his sweatpants and settled heavily onto the daybed.

"A contented heart begins with a contented family," he said.

Yeah, Winchell. Love those little platitudes you coin. As if they count as real communication.

"I did my best," I said.

He didn't answer.

And I could have just left it there. But I'd downed a half bottle of wine. And frankly, the man deserved to have the blame plunked squarely down on his pudgy shoulders, right? "What'm I supposed to do?" I said. "I told you it wasn't going to work. But you didn't listen to me. You kidnapped me and dragged me here, and then you—you built me all up like I was going to save the day."

I realized, as those last words slipped out, that I was still also upset about the kid.

Of all things, I was feeling guilty about the kid.

Winchell, meanwhile, took another sip from his glass and tried a new angle. "Effie doesn't have any family. You're the closest thing she's got. Maybe if you stayed a couple days. Spent some time with her."

I braced myself. I should have guessed that was coming. "No," I said, scowling. "Absolutely not. I *have* to get back to Rochester. And we had a deal. One day and you drive me back. Remember?"

He sighed and kind of slumped a little bit, looking around the room. "What is it, Mayfly? What do you have to do back there that's so important?"

"I'm between jobs, if you must know!" I said, exasperated. "I'm looking for work. And thanks to you—"

I broke off, because if I kept going, I'd reveal even more. Such as, for example, I was possibly about to be homeless.

And that was none of Winchell's business.

"I see," Winchell said when he realized I was done talking.

He tipped back the glass to finish the wine.

He looked thoughtfully at his empty glass.

"Work is to life what money is to happiness."

Huh?

I had no idea what that even meant.

"Night," I said, and began flipping through my book like I was looking for something in the pages.

· · · · ·

After Winchell left, I unpacked a few more of the boxes.

It was weird, seeing those books after so many years. I felt like I was conducting an archeological expedition, almost.

The deepest layer was the books I'd collected starting when I was a kid. The picture books, bought with my allowance or given to me as gifts. Then, as I grew up and became a teenager and got my driver's license, I'd started cruising the garage sales and flea markets. Hunting for volumes published in the 19th and early 20th Centuries.

Those second-hand books were my favorites. Musty-smelling and heavy. Pages brittle with age, they crackled when I turned them.

They don't publish books like that anymore.

And wow, I'd missed them.

And you know what? I decided not to leave them in Tibbs anymore. At least, not all of them. I'd pick out my favorites and take them back to Rochester with me.

Because on the one hand I might end up homeless, and even if I did somehow manage to get that apartment, the last thing I needed was more boxes of books to schlep around. Me, without a car. But on the other hand, they were my books. And somehow along the way they'd become part of my identity. And I hated the idea of leaving them here for Candace to mess with again. Touch them, or worse. I could see her doing something truly awful, like pack them off to the Goodwill or something. Like they were worthless, which wasn't true.

Not to me, anyway.

I got up and went to the screen door. The air wafting in was cool and smelled sweet, there must have been some bedstraw growing near the camper somewhere, giving off that sweetish smell of rural Upstate in the summertime.

A horned owl hooted again.

I wondered if it was the same one I'd heard earlier.

And a big beetle began thudding against the screen, trying to fly to the light, the screen thrumming faintly every time his heavy body hit.

Then came that summer-sound of the dome's screen door banging shut, followed by Candace's voice.

She was talking to Quill. "We'll get you another cat. A kitten. What color kitten would you like?"

I'd been piling books on the day bed as I went through the boxes, so now I scrambled over and started scooping them up, because if Candace walked in and saw I'd buried their bed in my books she'd probably lose it.

And I was tired of fighting. I didn't look up as they came in.

"Go brush your teeth," I heard Candace say to the boy, and then I heard him pull the little plastic stepstool out from under the bathroom sink and the clank of the pipes under the camper as he turned the water on.

I could feel Candace standing over me, waiting for something.

"I'm sorry I touched your books," she said, finally.

"Whatever."

"Garth's cheating on me. That's why I'm here. I left him. It's been a month."

Ah. "Sorry to hear it," I said.

Garth was her husband. I'd never hung out with the guy, myself. He was three years older which was like a different generation when we were in high school. But I'd always figured he was a decent person. He'd enlisted after graduation and served, I think, two terms in Iraq, and hey, he'd married Candy while she was pregnant with another man's kid, right? Agreed to raise him like his own son? There are worse men in this world. Although, if he'd cheated…

The pipes clanked again and again I heard the sound of plastic stepstool scraping over linoleum.

I wondered how much Quill knew. About Garth. About RB.

Probably everything. Kids always know everything. Kids are like the simpletons in the fairy tales who seem dumb because they wander around in their own little worlds, but in fact, they see a lot of things. In their innocence and non-judginess they see all the things the rest of us overlook.

I crouched and began putting the books from my leave-in-Tibbs pile back into one of the boxes.

Then I stood and scooped the take-with-me pile into my arms to carry them to the bedroom.

When Candace, watching me, suddenly smiled. A rather startling shift in her entire demeanor. "Oh," she said. "Speaking of men."

I felt a quick flash of…something. Alarm, probably.

I braced myself.

Her grin took on a sly cast. "Fletcher's in town."

What WHAT? The books I was holding slipped and I jerked my arms to keep them from sliding to the floor.

"And you should see him." Candace's tongue ran over her lips and her eyes flashed with amused devilment.

Fletcher.

So. Remember I mentioned there had been three Princes?

Fletcher was the first. The first Prince.

Or he would have been. If I believed in that sort of thing, anymore.
Breathe, Marion. Play it cool...

I stepped back to the table and set the books down. Because when they'd started to slide, they'd become impossible to grip and I needed to re-straighten them into a proper stack again. While meanwhile Candace was still talking. "And that's not all," she was saying. "I hear he's leaving his wife." Because she knew damn well that even hearing Fletcher's name would throw me for a little loop. And because that was Candace. She loved to stir up the drama.

But I managed to recover my cool, and so all I said was "oh." In a cool voice. While at the same time I picked up one of the volumes—an annotated Hans Christian Anderson—like I was re-considering whether to take this one or leave it one in Tibbs after all. And inside I was thinking *okay. His wife? I didn't know he was married...*

But of course he was married. Guys like Fletcher—rich, gorgeous, smart, and did I mention gorgeous?—don't just float around staying single.

"You should look him up," Candace was saying, now, in an advicey voice.

"Um, no." I slid the Anderson volume back into one of the boxes on the floor. "That's not going to happen. I have no desire to reconne—to see Fletcher," I said.

Nip this baby in the bud.

But of course she didn't take the hint. "You would if you knew what was good for you. He's effin' dee-licious. The girls at work are drooling. You could catch him on the rebound, Mayfly!"

And I almost did it. I almost opened my mouth to ask her for more details. Because Candace is the sort of person who attracts gossip like little black dresses attract lint, and probably three quarters of the time what she had "heard" was dead wrong but dang, I'll admit. I was... curious.

What red-blooded twenty-something (I'm still twenty-something damnit!) wouldn't be?

Had Candace seen him? Herself, in person? And who had he married? And was he really split up with his wife?

And did his family still own the stone house?

But then the toilet flushed, and Quill trotted down the little hallway and climbed up onto the day bed, filling the room with the peppermint smell of his toothpaste.

The interruption brought me back to my senses. Thank you, my charming mini prince.

"Well. Good for Fletcher," I said with a quick, could-care-less little shrug. "But I'm heading back to Rochester tomorrow. Ol' Fletch will have to wait 'til some other century to re-connect."

I'd finished re-adjusting the stack of take-with-me books.

Quill's face was a bit blotchy.

He'd been crying again.

Not my problem.

On the other hand, you've never seen a sadder looking little face. Sad like kids look sad, when they think the hurt is really truly never ever going to end.

And I should have kept out of it. But no. "Hey," I said, making like I was talking to Candace although I really was talking to her son. "I'm surprised you didn't keep any of my books out. To read to Quill."

No reaction from the kid.

"You like fairy tales, Quill?" I said, giving him a quick friendly-aunt smile.

"Marion…I don't know…" Candace muttered.

Figures that she'd try to step in. "They're just stories, Candace. There's nothing wrong with fairy tales. And reading to kids is good for them."

Candace was frowning. "Well. Maybe one. It's late."

She didn't sound very happy, and it wasn't hard to guess why. She saw reading fairy tales as the gateway drug. First you get hooked on fairy tales, then you start disappearing for hours at a time and when you reappear you're babbling on, you have all these wild stories about a little old lady that lives up the road and her talking birds and sometimes the house is different inside and other times it's not there at all, all that's there is an old foundation and rotting beams and a fallen chimney and bits of broken glassware glistening here and there in the weeds and saplings where the rooms used to be.

I'd had a wild imagination.

But I knew better, now. I knew that fairy tales are literature. Intellectual stimulation. Entertaining diversions. Oh, and also objects of folk art, meant to be studied rationally and discussed by scholars in peer-reviewed journals.

"So?" I asked. "Quill, you in?"

The boy was looking back and forth, first at me, then his mom.

"Say thank you," said Candace.

"Thank you."

It was only the second time I'd heard him speak.

His voice was really small.

And ugh. Because the kid was for sure traumatized anyway, what with being uprooted from his house and who knows what kind of fights Candace and Garth were having, and now moved into the camper. Followed by the whole cat thing.

But even worse, I had the sudden icky feeling that he'd picked up on my vibe as well. With his little kid antennae. You know, all my old junk about RB—about RB and Candace.

And it wasn't his fault. It wasn't his fault that his little face was like a seven-year-old RB and I couldn't see it without wanting to... I dunno. Scream. Punch something. Punch his mom.

Punch his dad...

I looked at the stack of books I'd pulled to take to my bedroom.

My hunch was that Quill might do better with a story that wasn't all prettied up and dumbed down. And you can't do better than Grimm.

I held up a book. A thick book.

Its gilt-edged pages gleamed and flashed, and Quill's eyes changed a bit as he saw it.

Curiosity.

So maybe he'd stopped thinking about that cat for one second, at least?

"Come on, Quill," I said. "We can go into my bedroom and read while your mom makes the bed."

. . . . .

"This was our bedroom, before tonight," Quill said as he climbed onto the bed.

"Uh huh." I propped the pillows against the camper wall—the room was so small the mattress filled it almost completely. So the wall was the headboard. "But when I was growing up, it was my bedroom. Your mom's bedroom was in the dome."

"Uncle Ace's bedroom is still there."

Interesting. My half-brother. Mom and Winchell's love child. Who'd also left Tibbs, and as far as I knew had also cut off all contact. Notice a pattern, there?

"Grandpa turned mom's room into a jacuzzi," Quill added.

"Grandpa has a jacuzzi?"

"Yeah. Grandma says he loves it more than he loves his Doritos."

I laughed. And the kid must have thought it was funny, too. He cracked a faint smile. And I was struck again by that same odd feeling that had hit me when Winchell was standing on my stoop that morning, back in Roch. That my stepdad was a grandpa.

And Mom was a grandma.

"What kind of stories do you like?" I asked, more or less to change the subject.

"Pirates."

Figures. "There aren't any pirate stories in this book. But let me find one that will be close." I scanned the table of contents. "Here's a good one. The Brave Little Tailor. Hey, hear the owl? He's been hooting all night."

Quill nodded and we listened for a moment. Then he crawled over next to me and his little body snuggled into my side.

60

What a peculiar feeling that was. He was so small. It felt more like having an animal up against me than a human. A rabbit. Or something bigger than a rabbit. I dunno, a lamb or something.

He was so small. Small for his age, I guess.

But then, RB had been small for his age, too. And he'd ended up playing football.

"You know what a tailor is, right?" I asked as I opened the book.

"Someone who sews things."

"Yep. Good one." I paused a second. "But you know, back when this story was written down, you didn't buy your clothes in a store. You either sewed them yourself, or if you were rich you had a tailor sew things for you."

"Are you rich?"

Okay. Weird question. But I guess kids ask weird questions. "No. Are you?"

"No. An' Mom says we'll be really, *really* poor now that she's getting a divorce."

I had a sudden impulse to ask the kid what he thought about the whole divorce thing, but I thought better of it.

And in any case, Candace could probably hear everything we were saying.

"Well, let's hope that doesn't happen," I said instead. "It might not. Okay, this is kind of a long story…"

I started reading. And it went over pretty well, I thought. And what's not to like, the way the little tailor won his princess? Plus this was the actual Grimm Brothers version, so the giants he tricked ended up in a pool of their own blood. Nice and gory but not too gory.

Then after the giants had been duly dispatched, we got to the place where the little tailor, in another feat of valor, traps a wild boar in a chapel after it rushes at him with a foaming mouth and gnashing teeth.

"What's a boar?" Quill interrupted me.

"A wild pig. Only they are really big and mean. Hang on." I reached for my phone and tapped it and brought up a photo of a boar. "Lookit the size of those tusks. Eek."

"Your screen is broken. Can a boar kill you?"

"Yes, I'm aware my screen is cracked. Not broken, just cracked. And yes, a boar can kill you."

"What I mean is, can a boar kill a grown man?"

"Yep."

"What's 'gnash'?" he said.

"It means the boar is clacking and grinding his teeth together, 'cuz he's so ferocious. Like this." I bared my teeth and moved them against each other. "It doesn't sound as ferocious when I do it." I pointed at the photo again. "Scaaary."

He nodded.

"You find boars a lot, in fairy tales," I said. "Back in the olden days, hunting boar was a way for people to show how brave they were."

"Like the tailor."

Of course, boars also played a part in other sorts of fairy tales. Like in Beauty and the Beast, you've probably noticed the Beast is often depicted as having a boar's head. But there are darker stories as well, the tales where princes, enchanted to look like boars, fall in love with ladies and force them to marry with horrifying results. But also of course, I didn't go there, with Quill. With Quill, I kept it all on the safest of levels.

Candace must have finished getting the bed ready. She was standing in the doorway. "Almost done?"

"Almost."

I finished reading the story.

"Thank you, Aunt Marion." Quill slid off the bed and pushed by his mother standing in the doorway.

"We have that one on video," Candace said.

It took me a moment to realize what she was talking about. "Oh, geez," I said. "The Disney thing? With Mickey Mouse?"

"It's a nice cartoon," Candace said, defensively.

"Sure," I said. And yeah, bad me, unable to resist a bit of sarcasm. "That's exactly right. Nice. So. Hoped he liked the story. 'Night."

I shut the book and set it aside. And I told myself to calm down. Because so what if we've done what we've done to fairy tales? Taken these marvelous stories with their roots in ancient mythologies, rich with clues to metaphysical truths and re-wrought as literature by some of the most fascinating literary figures of the 17th and 18th Centuries, and had utterly infantilized them, drained them of their blood and their life and turned them into plush toys and candy?

It's what happens.

People through the ages are always re-interpreting stories. And if we've collectively decided to jettison the blood and guts of the old fairy tales in favor of kiddie cartoons, and if collectively we find the new versions more diverting than the original stories, what business is that of mine?

And my job in Tibbs was done. In fact, more than done. I'd gone above and beyond, because I'd not only gone to see Effie, I'd read a bedtime story to the boy which was pretty nice of me and probably meant he'd fall right asleep right away instead of crying more about the cat.

Done.

I was gonna be gone tomorrow. Outta there. Back to Roch.

Candace, however, hadn't taken the hint. She was still standing in the doorway. "You know," she said, "you really ought to look up Fletcher before you leave town."

Wow, brazen, wasn't she?

Like I'd fall for her little tricks.

"Forget it, Candace," I said, keeping my voice low so Quill, hopefully, wouldn't hear. "I tried to get the cat back and it didn't work. You're gonna have to figure that one out on your own."

I'd done my part.

I needed to take care of myself. I needed to get back to Rochester and get that job and get my apartment and get on with my life.

9

I slept in the next morning. Not super late but it was after nine when I finally let myself start to move.

I heard voices through the window. Voices coming from the dome.

I was all hot and sweaty. My parents' lot faces east so there's no shade on the camper until the afternoon, and I hadn't lowered the bedroom blinds, so it was an oven in there, the sun blaring in, throwing its big skewy rectangle of golden heat across my bed.

I pushed the covers off.

And I love wine, but it had been ages since I'd had two glasses—wine hadn't been in the Marion Flarey budget for a looong time—and between that and the heat, my eye socket bones were throbbing. Boom, boom, boom, in time with my heartbeat.

I got up, groaning. I splashed some water on my face and a little on my hair to keep the wispy bits back.

I found a couple ibuprofen in the medicine cabinet and swallowed them. I changed my shirt.

And I went to fetch Winchell.

But guess what?

"Sorry, hon. He's gone out," Mom answered when got to the dome and asked where Dad was.

She was feeding pancakes to Quill. The boy was sawing off hunks and jabbing them with his fork, but he was also watching my face.

Which made me suspect they'd been talking about me. He was watching me for my reaction.

I didn't disappoint. "Whaddya mean, he's out?" I wailed. "He's supposed to drive me back to Rochester!"

"He had a delivery this morning. It's okay. He'll be back in a couple hours."

My stomach dropped. "A couple hours! I have to get back, Mom. I have a lot to do!"

"He didn't want to wake you. I'll make more coffee. You want coffee?"

I groaned. Coffee? No. I didn't want coffee. I wanted to get back to Rochester and find a job and rescue my life from the disaster it was about to become.

I groaned and flopped heaving in a chair next to Quill.

He'd put his fork down.

"Eat your pancakes," I said.

He reached for the squeeze bottle of fake syrup and drizzled a squiggle of caramel-colored fluid across his plate.

I sighed. Why had I agreed to come back to Tibbs, again?

"Can't you afford real maple syrup?" I said to Mom.

She was filling the drip pot with water from the tap and either didn't hear or decided to ignore my question, and I made a mental note. As soon as I got my next job, I was gonna buy a bottle of real maple syrup and mail it to the kid. I was not going to sit by and let him hit puberty without tasting the real thing. We live in maple syrup country, for crying out loud.

The coffee pot started hissing and popping.

"Where's Candace?" I said. Maybe she could drive me back to Rochester?

"At work," Mom answered.

So much for that idea.

Quill's legs were swinging as he chewed. "Wanna see the jacuzzi?" he asked.

"Don't talk with your mouth full," I answered.

Mom handed me a mug of coffee and then pulled out one of the other chairs and sat down at the table. Which immediately put me on guard. This was, for sure, gonna be a "now let's talk a bit" moment.

And I didn't want to talk.

"So, Marion," she said. "How is Effie doing?"

I blew across the top of my coffee. "She seems fine. Like always."

"She misses you."

Ugh. No guilt trips, please! "She seems fine," I repeated.

I had that creepy feeling you get when someone isn't really saying what is on her mind. I had the creepy feeling that my mom was trying to tell me that she missed me.

But she didn't quite dare to say it.

And I sure as heck wasn't going to ask.

"We check in on her from time to time," she was saying as I swallowed a mouthful of coffee and avoided eye contact. "She always asks about you. She won't tell us what happened to her arm."

I felt a twinge of guilt. Because, you know. Little old lady pushing ninety living alone, and what had happened to her arm? Had she fallen? Had she seen a doctor?

But no. No. Do not go there, Marion Flarey. I have my life. I've put this all behind me. My kooky family, my past, all this crazy baggage…

"Will you be stopping back in to see her again before you go?" Mom asked.

Ugh.

I stood up. "I doubt I'll have time," I said. "I'm taking some of my books back with me. I have to go pack."

No way was I going to agree to go back to Effie's.

• • • • •

Quill must have inhaled the rest of his pancakes whole, because not two minutes passed before he clattered into the camper, looking for me. And then he shadowed me for the next hour and a half, talking non-stop, his face getting more and more flushed because the higher the sun got, the more the camper heated up.

So I guess we were friends, now.

I learned that Grandpa had a job trucking vegetables—that explained the delivery truck I'd seen parked by the dome—and I learned that Candace worked at the school but wasn't a teacher, she worked in the office. So it was a salaried job, just like I'd guessed. And Quill was pretty sure his front tooth was loose, and he had a friend named Tira, but she was just a friend, not a girlfriend.

"Why are you looking at every single book like that?" he said after we'd exhausted the subject of just-a-friend Tira.

I sliced through the packing tape of another of the boxes. "I'm taking some back to Rochester with me."

"Will you read me another story, Aunt Marion?"

"Maybe. If there's time."

"Mom said you used to read stories to her when you were both little."

"I guess."

"She said she could read, too, but you liked to read fairy tales out loud."

"Right." I held up a finger to shush him and cocked my head, listening. "Sounds like Grandpa's back," I said, looking at Quill for confirmation.

He nodded. "That's his veggie truck. He lets me ride with him, sometimes."

The driver's side door was open when we got there but Winchell hadn't gotten out yet. He was looking at some papers on a clipboard. But when he noticed us, he set the clipboard down.

"Morning, kids," he said.

"When can we head out?" I eyed him as he climbed down from the truck.

I was on guard for him to try to play some trick.

"I brought something for you."

Here it comes.

He leaned back over the seat of the truck, then turned back around and next thing you know, he was handing me a rose.

A little rose, not open yet. Pink.

And I was like, huh? That's weird.

"You always said roses were your favorite," Winchell said.

Um. Okay. This was confusing. Because I did not remember ever having a favorite flower, let alone expressing my floral preferences to my stepfather.

But if you say so, Winchell.

"Thanks," I said out loud. "So can we get going?"

"There's something else, Marion."

Hooh boy...

"You said you need a job, right?" He smiled widely. "Guess what. I found you a job."

10

Okay.

So.

No.

No way on God's green earth was I going to let Winchell set me up in some sort of stupid middle-o'-nowhere job and trap me here in middle-o'-nowhere Tibbs, chasing after the perpetual missing cat. I'd rather be the girl stuck fast to Simpleton's golden goose while he runs about the countryside.

Not. Gonna. Happen.

"You said you needed a job, right?" he repeated, probably because he could tell instantly that I wasn't exactly pleased to hear his pronouncement. And then, without letting me answer—because you can be damn sure he knew that if he let me answer he wasn't going to like what I had to say—he added, "It's a new kombucha brewery and tasting room south of town. They converted an abandoned barn. They need someone to pour and look after customers. It pays $17 an hour. Plus you'd get tips."

Wait. *What?*

I must have misheard that, right? Seventeen what what what?

"They're living wage guys from downstate." And he grinned again, that hustler grin he flashes when he figures he's got the upper hand on someone.

But to be honest, I was in so much shock I was forgetting to be annoyed.

To be honest, that seventeen-what-what-what thing had hit me like a cup of ice water in the face.

Seventeen fucking dollars an hour?

So pause a second and those of you who have enjoyed so-called career success go pour yourself another glass of Cristal and tell your private chef what dressing you want drizzled on your baby arugula.

For the rest of us: holy crap, that's a lot of money. That's, like, better than barista money. Better than Wegmans cashier money. Better than...

And then I thought, OMG.

Plus tips?

I'm no human calculator, mind you. But for some reason the numbers began clicking together in my head. Take home, after taxes would have to be close to $500 above the table, plus whatever I could swing in tips. And I could mooch food and stuff from my parents, so my living expenses would be zero.

I could put all the money toward the apartment.

Which meant... OMG. If Vicki would just cut me a bit of slack, I could have the $2250 to her within... Could I swing it in three weeks? Before the end of the month?

Was that even possible?

I realized Winchell was watching my face. Reading me like a book. (Note to self. Practice poker face. In front of mirror. Nightly.)

And no!

No.

I could not let this happen.

Because what was I thinking? It wasn't going to work. Because first of all, as amazing as that figure was, it wasn't enough. I also had my student loans, and unless I let those payments lapse...

Even more pressing was the timing.

Vicki wasn't going to wait three weeks for her money. She needed it in three days. She needed it to pay her mover in three days. Which meant I needed a job that was going to pay a lot more. In a much shorter time frame.

And I wasn't going to find that sort of job in beensy little backwater Tibbs.

Winchell was still studying my face. "So this is what you need, right?" he said. "You said you needed a job. It's a good job."

Argh.

"I can't, Winchell," I said. Ugh. Pleading, now. "You don't understand. I have…responsibilities. Things to do. I'm in the middle of moving…"

"You can borrow my truck and go get your stuff and bring it here," he said.

And no, no, no. Dumb idea, even if there was room for my stuff, which there was not. The camper was already too cram jammed.

But I didn't even care about that. It didn't even matter.

Because I realized in that very moment that I was never going to get that apartment.

Damn you, math. Damn you, cold hard nasty numbers. Damn you, reality, that is never a fairy tale. That was never going to give way and work out and give me my beautiful Tower in the Park Avenue District where all the cool people are.

I was going to slink back to Rochester and text Vicki that I'd changed my mind, and go to the laundromat and find one of those homemade printed sheets with the little tabs at the bottom saying "roommate wanted" and get back into a cheapcheapcheap shared apartment with someone who hopefully wasn't a serial killer. And who would hopefully let me move in that day because otherwise I was going to have to pile all my worldly possessions on the street and cover them with plastic bags to keep the rain off, because of course it was going to start pouring that minute and not stop for forty days and forty nights…

Reality.

That's what I was going to do.

Reality.

I blinked and wiped my eyes.

"Hey," Winchell said.

I looked up and immediately took a step back, because he was starting over toward me, and I didn't want him doing, you know. Father stuff. Putting his arm around me, or whatever.

I don't need any sympathy from my family.

"I'm fine," I said, rubbing the back of my sleeve, hard, across my face. "Just, please, can you please take me back to Rochester?"

"Marion, if it would help? I could give you a little loan."

OMG.

No way.

Was that Winchell talking?

Winchell? The guy who put the pinch into penny pincher?

It couldn't be true.

It was a trap.

It had to be.

He was tossing that "loan" word out there to knock me off-balance so that I'd get confused and agree to something that I most certainly did not want to do…

No way was Winchell going to loan me any money.

And gah! That Quill. Oh go away, Quill! Stop staring at me… Stop waiting to see what I was going to say…

Because damnit, those eyes…

RB's eyes…

Hazel.

Hazel eyes. Like mine.

I focused on Winchell to keep myself from looking at Quill. "We don't have a lot of money, Marion," he said. "You know that. But if it would help—you know. Get you out of your trouble."

Trouble. Get me out of my trouble.

He probably thought I was trying to pay off a loan shark or a drug dealer or something.

An image of my beautiful Tower flashed in front of my eyes. Which is what I get for letting stories start to build themselves in my head. Because as soon as you let them in, they take on a life of their own.

"Uh, how…" I coughed slightly. "How much…of a loan?"

"A thousand dollars?" he asked. "Would that do it?"

Oh. My. Gawd.

No way. No way would he offer such a sum.

Maybe to Candace. His blood daughter. But not to me.

Also, if I took the money, I'd be one foot deeper into the Weekes-Flarey family quicksand. A place I definitely did not want to be.

But.

The Tower.

My Tower.

And wait a minute. Was it possible that I'd been wrong, thinking that a short little stay in Tibbs was the wrong direction?

Maybe this was one of those times when something you think is a detour is actually The Right Path?

"A loan," Winchell said. "You have to pay me back. But it's interest-free. And you could take your time paying it back. Six months, say."

"Lemme check on something," I muttered, and turned on my heel and went to the camper to find my phone.

hey vicki, I texted. *it's marion*

Good, she had an iPhone! Because my phone was telling me my text was delivered…

I waited.

She texted back.

hey

I took a deep breath and started typing. *i'm working on the money and it's going great. i'm wondering tho, can i maybe venmo it to you instead of u cashing the check. in chunks as i get it.*

I waited again, watching the screen.

Ooh! Little circles rippling, rippling… She was typing back.

Oh gawd. Please Vicki, say yes.

Damn it. Little circles stopped rippling. Text bubble disappeared.

$1000 today, I texted. *$625 next week, $625 week after.*

It's money in the hand, Vicki. Be my best friend, Vicki…

The text bubble reappeared.

I waited.

Seemed like it was gonna be a long text, but when it came through it was two words.

1000 today?

YESSSSS.

I texted back as fast as I could.

yep. 2day. gimme an hour, two tops. we have a deal?

Waiting, waiting, waiting...

ok

YESSSSS.

beautiful! thank you SO much. tear up the check & i'll get the $ to you in a jiff

I found Winchell in the dome, putting a mug of cold coffee into the microwave.

"I need the money in cash," I said. "Today."

Mom was washing dishes at the sink. She turned around when she heard me speak and shot Winchell a funny look. Like maybe he hadn't discussed this little plan with her.

"Dad found me a job," I explained to her. "I'm gonna stick around for a few weeks."

I glanced around the room.

No sign of Quill.

"Just one thing. Don't think this means I get Surprise back." I lowered my voice. "You—all of you—gotta stop telling Quill I can get Surprise back. She could be..."

I didn't finish my sentence. Didn't say the word "dead." But they knew what I meant. A lot can happen to an outdoors cat in the country. Owls, hawks. Coyotes. And cars, of course, even on a country road like ours.

"We understand, honey," Mom said. "We're just grateful that you tried." But I noticed that although she was talking to me, her eyes kept darting over toward Winchell.

She probably couldn't wait for me to get out of there so she could find out what the heck he'd done.

I felt a pang of guilt.

A thousand bucks was a lot of money to them. No doubt.

But I pushed the guilt aside.

I mean, what choice did I have?

"There's something else, you guys." I paused. "Actually two things. I only brought one set of clean clothes. So Mom, I'll need to borrow a shirt, please. And second, I need to get my stuff from Rochester. And what am I supposed to do with it? There's no room in the camper. Candace will flip out."

"Of course I can lend you some clothes," Mom said. "And you can put your things in the dome, for now. There's room. We'll figure it out."

We?

I sighed and looked around. And guess what. I don't care what Mom thought, there was no place for my stuff in the dome, either. It wasn't a particularly large structure to start with, and Mom and Dad had lived there for decades, which meant they'd been doing what people do. Filling their home with junk. Furniture and books and knickknacks and gadgets that worked and gadgets that were broken but they intended to fix. And plants. And mementos. And interspersed throughout, the clay pots and bowls and sculptures that Mom had made over years and decided to keep rather than sell.

And Candace's room was apparently now Dad's jacuzzi spa, no way could I store books in a room he filled periodically with steam, and maybe Ace's room would work, although if I knew my dad, that was probably full of crap as well.

"I may need to stack stuff there," I said, pointing to the space on the floor behind the couch.

"Of course, honey," Mom said.

My stuff should be safe there. I'd leave it all it its boxes. And because it would all be in boxes, in a few weeks when it was time to move back out, I could just load everything up and boom. Outta there.

Insert gif of me rubbing my hands together, job well done.

Winchell was standing by the sink, peeling the paper from an oatmeal muffin.

"So we're gonna head out to the bank now, right?" I said to him. Because I needed to make sure he didn't forget the loan thing. Or change his mind.

"Sure." Winchell took a bite of muffin, and a chunk of muffin stuff fell from where he was biting but he caught it, deftly, against his shirt. "Bank," he mumbled. "Then we'll swing by that kombucha place."

I wondered how he'd found this so-called job.

Gah. My stomach.

Too late to back out, now.

I tucked a lock of hair behind my ears. "Well, if that's the plan, I need to take a quick shower."

· · · · ·

I started feeling a bit more relaxed once I was cleaned up.

I wiped the bathroom mirror to make a semi-clear spot in the fog, and leaned forward and daubed my lashes with a bit of mascara.

I clipped my bangs into their barrette.

This could work. As long as I kept my focus, it could work. Of course it might be a bit of a challenge to keep my family at arm's length—and seriously, for my own mental health I would have to keep my family at arm's length—but maybe I could come up with a plan, like maybe I'd sort and re-shelve all my fairy tale books and hey! I could maybe query some publications with some ideas for articles on fairy tales. Maybe research-type stuff. The kind of thing I'd be doing now anyway if I was still working on my master's. The kind of thing where you are indulging in your love for fairy tales but it's respectable and can maybe lead to an actual paying job, because you aren't letting the other bits ooze in, the bits that normal people interpret as superstition or worse.

That would keep me busy. I'd have an excuse. I could work on that kind of thing, alone, in the camper, at night when I got home.

I pictured myself, fiercely defending my alone time, a big Do Not Disturb sign on the camper door… Okay, maybe on my bedroom door, as I couldn't really ban Candace from the camper. Unless I set some ground rules, like maybe I'd demand a certain block of time to have the camper to myself to get my writing done...

That, and some ground rules about Effie. No more begging me to ask favors from Effie.

This could work.

I dropped my phone into my bag and squared my shoulders and left the camper and started across the yard toward the dome to get Winchell.

I heard the sound of a vehicle down at the base of the hill, on the road. Which usually meant there was a car driving by, but this time the engine geared down and started getting louder.

Someone was coming up the driveway.

I paused.

I saw the top of a black pick-up truck wind back and forth up the switchback.

Then it made the final turn and came fully into view.

And in my heart, I knew who it was.

Who it had to be.

And I froze.

I should have run back into the camper, but I froze.

And the truck stopped, and a man stepped out, and for a split second I told myself it wasn't him.

Because he'd grown a beard.

But who was I kidding?

It was him, all right.

It was RB.

11

RB.

What do you need to know about RB?

His real name is Royal.

Yeah, I know. That, coming from a fairy tale person? Tempted to eye roll, there. But I'm telling the truth. And of course it doesn't mean anything.

Royal Brinley Brown.

And so you're straight on this?

Fletcher was my first Prince.

RB, on the other hand... I'd known RB my whole life.

And if I'm being perfectly serious, my whole life I'd had this funny feeling about him, which you'd maybe understand. Like, you know someone really well, and in a way, you trust that the person gets you.

That kind of connection happens between people, sometimes, when you grow up in a small town.

And then—this was after Fletcher's mom made him move away and smashed my heart like so much teenage roadkill and Effie despite being my so-called fairy godmother basically told me to live with it and I'd managed to patch my heart back together—RB and I started dating. Which technically makes him my second Prince.

But then, well... I dunno.

Everything went wrong.

And then Candace got mixed up in it.

And argh. I can admit this, right? In a way, it was partly my fault. Like: a very tiny fraction of it was my fault. But I was in college, and RB had graduated already because he was two years ahead of me. So he was back in Tibbs, and you know? Things are hard, when it's like that. A long-distance relationship. We were having arguments. I don't remember what about. But I had the whole college thing still going on, while RB was back home dealing with his dad's business.

It was…hard.

And then I find out he was dating freaking Candace.

I know, I know. Technically, RB and I weren't together any more at that point.

But that's no excuse. She had no business dating him.

Sisters don't do that.

Not real sisters.

And then, to make matters worse, doesn't she end up pregnant and of course she keeps the baby, which I fully support of course, but really? Really?

How am I supposed to deal with all that?

With any of that?

• • • • •

So RB was walking over toward the camper.

And of course he saw me. He had probably seen me from his truck halfway up the driveway, knowing RB.

I did a quick scan of him as he approached. Using my head only, above the neck only, because no way was I gonna let RB have any of that other kind of power over me, if you catch my drift and I bet you do.

Although I liked the beard. It was a full beard and it gave him an old-timey, romantic gentleman look like he'd time-traveled from the 1800s or something. And he seemed to be a bit taller than I remembered. I guess some guys do put on a few more inches in their early twenties, right? And like he probably worked out, because his shoulders were broad, or maybe his work kept his muscles looking like that. And that his legs were the same, slightly bowed, which gave a kind of cowboy look when he walked…

"Marion," he said.

Right. And there you go. The one person who maybe should be calling me Mayfly. And he called me Marion.

Not that I wanted him to be, you know. Personal with me.

Far from it.

Also, he had an expression in his eyes like he'd just learned he's got terminal cancer and had two weeks left to live.

"RB," I answered, tit for tat.

"Been a long time."

No kidding. And could ya find a more clichéd cliché?

"What brings you to the dome?" I said, all prim. On the outside. Because on the inside I was…I guess "turbulent" would be a good word. My guts were churning. Because as bad as it was to find myself yanked back into the kooky bosom of my kooky family, this?

This?

Even worse.

"I'm here to pick up Quill."

"Ah."

To pick up Quill. If you think those words zapped me, you'd be right. Even though yeah, picking up Quill meant he was part of his son's life, which is an admirable thing, not gonna argue with that.

I just really, really did not like being reminded of the whole stepsister + my boyfriend = kid thing.

And right on cue I heard the sproingy noise of camper screen door as Quill pushed it open and then the door clattered shut and he darted past, saying "hi" as he ran, and then, without stopping, ran to the dome.

"Your mom is getting him a snack," RB said, as if I'd asked a question.

"Right." Me, trying not to squirm or look uncomfortable while also thinking in spite of myself, crap. What's RB's relationship with Candace? At the moment? Given that she was on some sort of hiatus from the ol' husband? Was it possible that Candace and RB were…

You know.

Dating?

Was RB swooping in now that Candace had walked out on her husband? To renew their relationship, blah blah blah?

Or worse yet! Maybe RB was the reason Candace had left Garth? Maybe it wasn't Garth cheating, like Candace had claimed?

Ugh.

You can see how this would be too much for me, right?

I mean, I love dramarama as much as the next person. But...

But I'd had enough.

"I'll, uh, I'm on my way to the dome myself," I muttered.

Gawd I sounded like an idiot.

I snuck a peek at RB's truck as I passed.

Bunch of tools in the bed. He'd taken over his dad's plumbing business after he graduated. So by the looks of it was still at it.

I noticed, also, the fishing gear. Rods. Tackle box. A little trapezoid-shaped cardboard carton, white and fresh with a metal wire handle, like you see in the city for Chinese takeout. Only inside this box would be nightcrawlers, not Chinese food: a big ball of nightcrawlers in the bottom with a layer of moistened wood shavings on top, or maybe shredded newspaper.

One of the rods was short—kiddie size—and the line had a neon yellow bobber clipped to it.

RB was here to take his boy fishing.

Cute.

Also, by the way, a smart move if you're hoping to endear yourself to your child's mother.

I went inside, just in time to nearly collide with the fruit of RB and Candace's loins as he dashed in the other direction, Ziplock bag of animal crackers in one hand and Ziplock bag of apple slices in the other.

And Mom had a shade of a smile on her face.

Also, have I mentioned how weird it is that my mother is now a grandmother?

I stood inside the dome door and spied on RB and the boy through the screen.

RB's got one of those big four-door trucks, so he held the door while Quill climbed in, and then he crawled partway in himself to help the kid with his seatbelt.

I expected RB to get into the truck and drive off that point, but— oh crap—instead he started back up the slope toward the dome.

I jumped back from the door.

Gawd please not let him realize I was standing there!

I scooted over to the sink. Pretended I needed to wash my hands, and also tempted to splash water on my face. To try to cool it off.

I listened for the door to open.

It didn't.

I glanced over.

He was standing on the steps.

"Hey, Marion?" he called in through the screen.

Oh gawd.

I was trapped.

"What?" I said.

"Quill forgot his water."

Water? Where'd Mom disappeared to? But quick scan and there it was, twelve-ounce plastic bottle of spring water on the counter next to the fridge.

The screen made it hard to read RB's face. It was dirty, the way screens get from the seed fluff that is always blowing around, especially the poplar fluff that can get so bad in early summer. And the sun on the dirty screen made it kind of glarey.

"Here," I said, opening the door and handing over the water bottle.

"Thanks." He turned to leave. "Good to see you, Mayfly."

Mayfly.

The word kind of echoed around in my head.

"Ready, Marion?" Winchell. He'd emerged from somewhere.

"Yeah, sure," I muttered.

I followed my stepdad to his truck.

RB's truck was gone.

And okay, it was one thing to see Candace and her kid, the mini-RB. It was another to realize that part of this package I'd signed up for—my plan to temporarily shack up in Tibbs while I accumulated a little cash—would also mean this. That sooner or later, I'd run into RB.

That as long as I was in Tibbs, my past was going to keep jumping out from its hidey holes to haunt me.

I needed to be better prepared. That was my only option. I'd need to be an absolute rock. And not just any rock. An unmovable, uncrackable hunk of solid granite. An unmovable, uncrackable hunk of solid granite for a few short weeks, and then I could escape and put a good two hundred miles or so between me and these crazy people who I did not want back in my life.

"Okay, kid," Winchell said as he started the truck. "Bank first, because when your finances are in order, your world sleeps, and when your world sleeps, it dreams only sweet dreams."

I gripped the straps of my handbag and bared my teeth in what hopefully passed for a friendly love-your-pearls-of-wisdom-Dad smile.

While inside I was thinking: unmovable, uncrackable hunk of solid granite.

Get your money from Winchell, land this stupid but incredibly high-paying job, get Vicki paid, and get the hell out.

"I'll need to borrow your truck first thing tomorrow," I said. "To drive to Rochester and get my stuff."

"Sure thing," Winchell answered.

12

I found myself stealing looks at Winchell as we drove into town.

A little voice inside was warning me to be careful. Wary. Because part of me still didn't quite believe that Winchell was actually going to fork over the money.

He was always so tight. Even when he was supposedly making tons and we were all going to be rich. Me and Candace were like ten or eleven when that all started, and the way Winchell talked to Mom you'd have thought we'd soon be dressing ourselves in Vera Wang and vacationing in the French Riviera and installing a pair of ten-foot tall marble lions at the foot of our driveway to intimidate any plebs who dared to visit.

So naturally, given all the talk about unimaginable riches, Candy and I began petitioning him for, you know. All the things. Like, Candace spent the week leading up to her eleventh birthday dropping obvious hints about how all the other kids had Razor scooters.

Didn't work, she got a Bratz doll and socks.

Socks. Ha.

And then the time we teamed up to present a well-reasoned argument for why we should get allowances. Also didn't work.

I asked, another time, why we never went out to restaurants for dinner. I must have tried the "mom shouldn't have to cook every night" angle because remember Winchell snorted that doling out frozen TV dinners doesn't count as cooking, and he and Mom weren't the kind of people who liked eating out, they liked to spend their evenings quietly, they didn't need to be seen.

Yeah. "Seen." In Tibbs.

And don't even ask me about the whole cell phone battle. That came a bit later. I was well into my full-blown glory of teenage hormone-fueled craziness, and by then, all that stood between me and being separated forever from my sweetheart was a cute little phone and sure it was over a hundred dollars plus a monthly contract but didn't Dad want me to be happy?

I got so far as to pack a suitcase after that blow-up. I was going to run away forever from my evil skinflint stepdad. Until I stopped to consider that it was a 40-mile walk to the nearest Big City and even though it was only September, the temperature was in the 30s.

Stymied, again.

So much for teaching Winchell a lesson.

Although in a way, he did get a lesson, because that company he was working for? It folded and he lost everything.

It was an MLM btw. Multi-level marketing company. Tells you about all you need to know about Winchell.

Also: that disaster happened my senior year of high school, which scuttled my hopes of getting my parent's help paying for college. Which explains why now I was dealing with all that stupid student debt.

And as far as I knew, he'd never found another gig that was anything like the one he lost. So in theory, he had more reason to be miserly today than he had back then, in the days of the cell phone battle.

Certainly my mom wasn't making fuck-you money. I mean, she sells pottery. On Etsy.

It probably covered the TV dinners.

So don't blame me for wondering if Winchell was planning some sort of bait and switch.

I was ready for it.

Like, watch him try to kite a check like I'd done to Vicki.

And sure enough, when we pulled into the bank parking lot, he shot me a bit of a side eye as he turned off his truck engine.

"So, how much did you say you needed, Marion?" he asked.

Like he didn't know.

"You said you could do a thousand," I said, feeling my jaw tense because this was so like Winchell, watch him ask now if I could do with less.

And there it was. "You sure?" he said.

"Winch—" I stopped myself. "Dad. If you can't afford it, I understand, I really do. But let's be honest with each other about it, okay? Let's turn around right now."

Calling his bluff.

"Oh, we can afford it, Marion. It's just a loan." He nodded, making the loose skin under his chin waggle. "But I would like to discuss when you will pay it back. You know. Being up front is always the best idea in these situations."

Argh.

What did I tell you?

"Whatever you think is fair," I said.

"Oh, and one other thing."

He was blinking now. Which put me even more on edge.

"Okay. What is the other thing," I said.

"You'll try to talk to Effie again, right?"

"Uh, Dad?" I said. "Did you not hear me, last night? She can't help us. There's no point! And honestly, I can NOT believe you would bring this up again after you offered to help me out, and, you know what? Forget this. Just take me back to the dome. Just take me back to Rochester."

"No, Mayfly! I'm sorry." And yeah, he got it, finally. He saw he'd pushed me too far. "Never mind on that. I'll get you the loan right now. I won't mention Effie again."

Right. And also, you know what? He had another thing coming if he thought I was going to give in. Ever.

I followed him into the bank.

I stood near the plastic-looking couch by the entrance while he walked up to the teller.

A minute later I graciously accepted the stack of bills from his hand and hustled to the ATM in the foyer, and I deposited that cash so fast you'd have thought I was scared it would poof, disappear. Hah.

And then I Venmo'd the thousand straight to Vicki.

And I followed Winchell back out to his truck, trying not to notice how the happy feeling of being able to send that big a chunk of money to Vicki was quickly giving way to a sinking feeling in the pit of my stomach, because when you take a loan from someone, you're caught.

I'd just need to find a way to pay it back, like, really really soon.

And what if this job he'd found turned out to be a false lead? What if it didn't pay what he'd said it paid? Or if we got there and I found out they'd hired someone else already and the position was no longer available?

It's not like I could trust Winchell to have all the details exactly straight…

• • • • •

"So, anyway," I said casually when Winchell and I were back in the truck. "How'd you find out about this job?"

Trying to assuage my nervousness, which was mounting by the minute.

"I know people," he said.

"What people?"

And he told me the story. How he'd bought that delivery truck four or five years ago, and it was a great deal because ever since he'd been able to bring in a little money trucking vegetables from local farms to restaurants and, sometimes, to farmers' markets.

So that explained how he and Mom had survived after the feds arrested the CEO of that bogus MLM company.

Anyway, thanks to the trucking business, Winchell had gotten to know all the locally sourced food purveyor types.

I mentally filled in some of the dots he omitted. Because after all he's Winchell, and now his only source of income involves trying to make himself useful to growers and buyers. So you could bet he was spending a good part of his time jawing with them, looking for angles. And, turns out, some guy from downstate was starting this kombucha brewery, and he was trying to source some local strawberries to flavor one of their brews, and by complete coincidence Winchell ran into him this very morning at one of the farms Winchell works for.

And he learned about the job.

"I told him you were perfect for it," Winchell said.

Right. I was thinking something along the same lines when Winchell first mentioned this Dream Job of a Lifetime, the $17 per hour thing that meant I'd actually have a chance at getting my Dream Apartment of a Lifetime. Of course I was perfect for this job. After all. I've had kombucha. All kinds of kombucha. The regular kind and the hard kind, that has alcohol in it and can get you buzzed. And I like it. The kombucha part and the getting buzzed part.

Plus I'd done a little bartending and I'd waited tables and I know how to change the tape in a cash register. How hard could the job be?

"I told him you could run the place," Winchell said as he steered his truck through Tibbs' four corners and we started up the hill.

"Run the place?" I said. What the heck did that mean?

And suddenly it occurred to me that maybe I might be slightly underqualified for this Dream Job of a Lifetime.

I felt a little sick to my stomach again.

Because Reality. Because Effie might claim that Reality is actually a story, and there are ways to play the story with your mind that can change how it comes out. But I knew better, and besides, how could I do a story about this job when I had no freaking idea what it would even entail, and also I now had a funny feeling that Winchell had oversold me. Like, did this brewery guy know I was a nerd with a worthless English degree, and an introvert, and more than a bit strange, and that my employment history was a spotty list of short-lived stints at a very large variety of service jobs?

Or had Winchell pitched me as budding Upper Management material?

But I didn't say anything of this out loud. I was stuck, and I knew it.

Just swallow all that nervous fluttering that is starting in your guts, Marion, because, you know.

The Tower.

And the thousand bucks I just took from Winchell, which meant I was even deeper in debt than I'd been 24 hours ago.

Argh!

I watched the trees blur by.

The truck slowed.

We pulled into a big potholey parking lot next to an enormous barn.

I leaned forward to read the sign. Booch4U. Big wooden sign, brand new, mounted on 4x4s held in place by bright white cement footers.

Okay. So far, not so bad.

I turned my head to look at the barn.

Unlike the sign and the cement footers, the barn was ancient. The exterior walls were weathered almost bare except for a little blush of red up near the eaves, and the gray metal roof was streaked with rust.

"This is it," Winchell said. "Cool place, huh?"

I didn't answer. I was thinking that I sure as hell hoped the place wasn't open at that particular moment, because there were only two other cars in the parking lot, and if those were the only customers, the "lotsa tips" part of my fiscal calculus was basically doomed.

Death by math error.

We went in. Me in front because the last thing I wanted was to look like a little kid being led into the place by her daddy.

Barnboard walls with framed prints of farm animals. Rusty old implements suspended from the ceiling on chains that also looked rusty but hopefully weren't, because it would be bad if that pitchfork or that hand cultivator with the spoked wheel and the tines came crashing down on a customer's head.

And then my eyes had adjusted, and I saw two guys standing at the far end of the room by a row of three huge stainless-steel kettles or tanks or whatever they were. One guy tall, stubbly beard, good hair. So that had to be the manager or owner or whoever he was—my maybe new boss—he was talking to a kid.

Wait, a kid? I was really old enough to think the second guy was a kid? Oh, crap!

But that's how he struck me. Young enough to be in high school, still. Chin-length, dirty blond hair, a surfer type despite the fact that Tibbs is at least 200 miles from anything resembling an ocean.

They'd broke off talking when they saw us. The older one nodded and came toward us, while the kid picked up a hose and started climbing a step ladder near one of the tanks.

"Upton, here's Marion who I told you about," Winchell said.

Like he was delivering me. Delivering the goods.

"Right," Upton said, yanking my hand into a he-man businessman handshake, eyes flicking from Winchell to me and back again in a way that suggested that maybe I wasn't exactly measuring up to Winchell's description. "Thanks for stopping by. You ever work in a tasting room before, Mary?"

"Marion," I said, and my face instantly got all hot because maybe the first thing you say to your possibly-new-boss shouldn't be to correct him about your name. "And, uh, no, I've never worked at a brewery, I'm afraid." Oh gawd I was blowing this. "But I do have a ton of experience in service, uh, most recently, uh, I was a barista. At a very popular coffee shop in, uh, Rochester—" And I broke off, suddenly gripped by a serious case of brain freeze because I'd just referenced a job at a place that went bankrupt due to a still-unsolved embezzlement scandal, and yes I'd been employee of the month but when your stint was only three months long that doesn't look so great on the resume, now does it?

"Right," Upton said again.

And then there was an awkward pause during which I got the distinct feeling that Upton was avoiding looking at me while he did some sort of calculation in his head, giving the distinct impression that he was hoping maybe if he didn't look at me I'd disappear, and Winchell meanwhile was oblivious to Upton's obvious ambivalence about the prospect of hiring me. Winchell was beaming like he'd just brokered an end to a global war.

"Do you have any questions about the job?" Upton was clearly buying time while the calculations in his head completed. He hitched one hip up, moved backward a bit and half-sat on one of the stools at the bar.

"Uh, I guess." I glanced at Winchell and then hurriedly looked back at Upton because the way my stepdad was grinning was the last thing I needed to see at that particular moment. "My dad said you needed someone to, uh, pour and generally keep an eye on the place."

"Right," Upton said for the third time, one corner of his mouth turned down.

"I'm, uh, a very hard worker," I said, feeling the color in my cheeks deepen because what the heck had Winchell gotten me into? This guy didn't want anything to do with me.

"We've only been open for six weeks, now," Upton said. "Business is slow at times. Be prepared to be bored."

Ugh. So my impression of the parking lot had been correct. As was my impression of the likelihood of extra money from tips. "I have some social media experience," I said. "I could help, uh, create buzz."

I waited for Upton to say "right" again but he just sat there. But at least he was looking directly at me, now.

"Well," he said, "I guess we'll give it a try. I've got a conference call in fifteen minutes. I assume you can start right now."

"Oh!" I looked back at Winchell. Who had not mentioned that this job's start date might be right now. "Uh, Dad, can you pick me up after… I'm sorry, Upton, what time do you, I mean we, close?"

"Last call's at eight o'clock weeknights and Sundays," Upton said. "Nine on Friday and Saturday."

"But I'll have to stay later than eight," I said, for Winchell's sake but also so Upton would be impressed hopefully with my initiative and stand-up-and-take-charge attitude. "To clean up and everything."

My phone buzzed from inside my handbag and forced myself to ignore it. Focus, Marion.

"Okay," Upton said, pulling his own phone out of his pocket. "Let's do a quick run-through and get you started."

"Great," Winchell said. "Call me when you're ready for me to pick you up, Mayfly."

"I assume you can make change," Upton said. "Do you know how to use Apple Pay?"

I didn't. And I considered pretending that I did, because how hard could it be, right? But then I quickly fast forwarded in my mind to a not-too-distant-future scene in which Marion Flarey was struggling to figure out how to run a customer's credit card and having to ask the customer for help, or worse, having to interrupt Upton during his critically important conference call to admit that I'd told a little white lie earlier and had no idea how to work the Apple Pay interface and did he mind giving me a hand...

"It's been a while," I said lamely. "Maybe you could give me a little refresher."

The corner of his mouth dropped again. "Right."

We went around to the business side of the bar and I put my handbag in a cupboard under a shelf of glassware, and he started talking fast, too fast, running through the basics.

How to enter a sale, and the most important thing was to take peoples' cards right away if they wanted to start a tab and actually the most important thing was to print a new receipt every time anyone ordered another pour—got that, Mary?—don't ever try to remember what they'd ordered in your head, because that's how bars lose money. Bartenders forget what they've served to people, especially when it gets busy, and people are dishonest as fuck, they won't tell you, they'll just drink for free.

And he told me I could give out free splashes but not free pours and watch for people who take advantage of free splashes.

And then he looked at his phone again and said he had to go and please re-do the chalkboard. Josh would tell me what flavors were on, and if I was smart, I'd list them on the board in the same order as the taps. Ask Josh if I had any questions.

And then I was alone in the bar.

Asking myself what the hell had I gotten into.

I could hear Upton's voice behind his closed office door as his conference call started.

I heard a clanking noise in the back where Josh was doing something with the brewing tanks.

And again: what exactly the hell had I gotten myself into?

Because whatever Winchell had told Upton about me, when he sold Upton on me taking this this job, be honest, Marion, it was only a matter of time before Upton realized that I had no idea what I was doing and fired me.

My phone buzzed again from its hidey hole in the cupboard.

And I considered ignoring it, again, but it could be Teagan, and I really hated to miss her when she had a break and was able to text, and plus I really really needed some encouraging words from my BFF at that particular moment.

So I slid the cupboard door open and fished around in my bag for my cell.

It wasn't Tea.

It was Vicki.

And, uh oh…

i have someone else who wants the apt.

OMG.

I swear, my heart nearly stopped beating. And my head started doing that crazy thing heads do, sometimes, like I wasn't even reading the words logically, I wasn't seeing the actual words, I was sure in that instant that she meant she had changed her mind, she was giving my Tower to someone else.

I was just about ready to call her. In full frantic, losing-my-mind mode. Beg her, beg beg BEG her to not do it, not give my Tower away…

A bubble started bubbling on my screen. She was texting something else.

Deep breath, Marion.

I re-read her text as I waited.

And maybe I shouldn't be panicking. Maybe all she means is she has a backup in case I fall through?

And sure enough:

so pls just lmk if anything changes & i will return the $, k?

OMG. Yes, k! Double yes, k! k!

I texted back.

absolutely!!! but nothing will change! will get next $625 to you v v soon

I took another deep breath to calm myself, scolding myself for jumping to wrong conclusions there for a second, hahahahaha Marion don't do that, you prolly just took seven years off your life.

And wasn't it nice that I actually had a job and that text I'd just sent was the actual truth?

Most likely?

Assuming I could fake things long enough to actually get the hang of it. Without getting fired in the meantime?

13

Newsflash: it's exhausting to be on your first day at a job where you are new, and you're pretending you know what the heck you're doing, so you walk around with a smile pasted on your face trying your best to project calm confidence while on the inside you are continually on the brink of a total psychotic breakdown.

So. Very. Exhausting.

And wouldn't you know it, barely fifteen minutes after Upton disappeared into his office, customers started coming in.

Starting with two boomer couples. All, "Wow, honey, look at this place," and, "I didn't even know it was here," and, "I've never had hard kombucha before, have you?" Walking toward the bar, eyes fixed on the chalkboard.

"What'll you have?" I said, noticing as I spoke that the words that sounded completely ridiculous, like something out of a movie.

I wiped the bar nervously.

They scanned the flavors, murmuring to each other, and then finally one took a step closer. "Can I get a sample?"

"Yeah, sure, yeah," I said and picked up a glass from the shelf under the bar. And then the others asked for samples. And nobody cared for the first flavor they tried, so they all asked for a second, and I wondered exactly how many splashes Upton would think was too many.

But finally they each found one they liked. And they ended up drinking a pint each, and then two of them had a second.

And they tipped okay, and I printed a receipt every time they ordered so I didn't accidentally give away any drinks.

So far, so good. Upton even came out after his call and he eyeballed the receipt in the glass on the table where the couples were sitting, which meant I was following the rules and my job was safe for now.

Then he disappeared again and for the first time I started to relax a little bit.

The space was huge, with the original plank floors and wooden picnic tables for seating. They'd put down some artificial turf on one side to make a space for games, corn hole set painted black and white in a Holstein cow pattern, and a big Jenga set made of 2x4s, and they had board games, too. Which, I figured, meant that maybe it was supposed to be a family-friendly place, especially considering that there were some non-alcoholic kombuchas for sale as well as the adult beverage kind.

There was a big kitchen off to the side, but they weren't using it. They weren't serving any food other than bagged chips and jerky. But then some people showed up, as it got near dinnertime, carrying boxed pizzas. Which turns out came from that pizza joint in downtown Tibbs, miraculously still in business after all this time. So they ordered booch and then ate their pizza at the picnic tables.

And then a few more people came in. More boomers, plus some date-night couples, and just as I was starting to panic a little about making sure I could keep up with everything, Josh strolled up from the back and helped me wait on people. So that was nice.

And it turned out Josh was the brewer. And I also revised my estimate of his age. He was definitely not a high schooler. But he couldn't have been much more than 22, 23, so I wondered if he'd ever met my brother Ace. But I didn't get a chance to ask, because then Josh found out I hadn't tasted any of the product—I wasn't sure I was allowed to—but he said, "dang, you have to know what we're selling." And turns out, that kombucha was good. Really good. Josh knew what he was doing as a brewer, and he started telling me how he came up with the flavors and I also made mental notes as he pitched choices to the customers. For example, we had five different flavors of the alcoholic ones on tap that first day: raspberry, ginger and lime, blueberry vanilla, salted caramel, and one with Mosaic hops, and I noticed how Josh played that hops-flavored option to the guys. "It's bone dry," he said. "If you like beer…"

And of course the men all went for it.

And time sped up a bit, then, too, because I was dancing dancing dancing as fast as I could, pouring samples, praising Josh's extraordinary palette to the customers, re-chalking the board when the salted caramel keg kicked, bummer, it was the top seller before it ran out.

Then Josh had to leave and I was on my own again, and a few more people came in, and then a boomer lady with two long salt-and-pepper braids told me the lady's restroom was out of paper towels, which I was pretty sure were stored in the back, so I went to look for them, couldn't find any extra paper towels anywhere, getting more and more nervous because where were they? And should I ask Upton? And finally I gave up and decided to ask him and he wasn't in the office and OMG how long had I been looking, I dashed to the front of the bar again and oh CRAP.

Even more new customers had come in, and Upton was serving them. And he shot me a look that made it clear I'd done something very much in violation of the rules.

"Where were you?" he muttered as I came back behind the bar.

"Looking for paper towels?"

He didn't answer—ominously—but was already turning to the next couple in line and asking to see their IDs. While I stood there feeling stupid.

"Glasses need washing, Mary," he said as he stepped past me to pour the next set of pints.

Ugh. And apparently my rules violation was an egregious one, because he never left me alone again, that entire shift. Instead he kept tending bar until close, while I kind of hovered, helping out as much as I could but mostly feeling superfluous and very, very stupid and useless and stupid and OMG Upton wouldn't fire me over this, would he? Because I went to the back to look for paper towels?

But finally the last customer dropped a couple bills on the counter—Upton pocketed them—and it was eight p.m. and time to close.

"I couldn't find the paper towels," I said.

"Right," said Upton. "They're on the shelf next to the storeroom door."

I went back and of course I still couldn't find them, until I realized that what I was looking for was not clear plastic-wrapped two-packs of paper towels like you buy in the supermarket but a large unopened corrugated cardboard box. Marked 'Paper Towels' on the outside. Doh.

"Found them," I said.

Upton handed me a mop and reappeared a little later to ask me if my dad was on his way.

"Yeah," I said. "I can wait for him outside if you need to leave."

"Right." He was avoiding my eye. "So, uh, you know, I wanted to go over something else with you."

"Sure."

"This is basically probation at this point. Standard thing when we make new hires. Two weeks."

I swallowed. "Of course."

I wondered if two weeks' worth of salary and tips would be enough to pay Vicki the rest of what I owed her.

I knew the answer to that question: no.

Upton disappeared again, and I finished mopping and then stood near the plate glass window at the front of the tasting room, waiting for Winchell and thinking about how here I was, undertaking what might be an impossible task because was I really suited to manage a whole tasting room operation, like that, when I couldn't even find the freaking paper towels? And I thought about how in a certain type of fairy tale the hero-slash-heroine is given an impossible task, and so maybe this wasn't unprecedented and maybe that's the spirit, Marion Flarey. Maybe I should just think of my situation that way, like I was the princess in *The Seven Swans*.

And then I stopped myself because really, Marion? That's how you think you're gonna save yourself?

And Upton was kind of a jerk, really. But he was a jerk that I needed right now, and he wasn't a jerk with magical powers as far as I knew. And sure he had that angular masculine jaw that generally looks good on a guy, but that stubbled facial hair? A bit dated, don't you think? I mean, grow a beard, guy. A real beard. Grow a beard like RB's.

And considering that I'd be in Tibbs for at least a couple more weeks and needed as many excuses as possible to avoid the Weekes-Flareys, wouldn't it be nice if some guy a little like Upton but a lot, lot nicer wandered into Booch4U once in a while? Because as I may have mentioned once or twice or fifteen times, my life had been missing a particular element, a.k.a. "the Prince," for longer, now, than I cared to admit...

And you know, my mother might be able to lend me something more on the feminine side for work tomorrow, and maybe I should order some new hair products and borrow Candace's curling iron to try to do something with my plain straight bob-like-any-other-bob hair...

Headlights lit up the two-by-fours holding up the sign out front and the dark shape of a vehicle pulled into the lot.

Not Winchell.

It parked right in front of the brewery. One of those compact SUVs. BMW logo on the grill. And although I couldn't see the driver—there was a glare on the windshield from the tasting room lights, still on behind me—it was a woman. I could tell by how she kind of sat up and craned her neck to check her makeup in the visor mirror. And then I could see she was retouching her lipstick.

And she was obviously waiting for someone because she didn't get out of her car.

And Josh had already left.

Which meant that rather-cute-Upton had a girlfriend.

Figures. Even Upton had a mate.

Gah.

But also none of my business.

· · · · ·

So I pretended to look at my phone on the way home, thinking, meanwhile, that I couldn't wait to escape to the camper and find a story to read, maybe an Impossible Task story to boost my morale, but when we got to the top of the driveway my heart sank.

The lights in the camper were still on.

"Quill was hoping you'd read him another story," Candace said as I came through the door.

She didn't look very happy about that. In fact, she looked downright grouchy. I suppose because she realized that Quill had decided, after one night, that fairy tales are extremely cool, which they are, of course. So it probably half-killed her, asking me to read one to him, while in the back of her mind she was probably nervous as shit that we'd finish the story and a minute later I'd whisk him away to Effie's on my magic broomstick and expose him to lord knows what kind of crazy shit.

Which, as you can imagine, didn't exactly make me enthusiastic about playing the read-a-fairy-tale good aunt role. I mean: fine, Candace. Your son wants a story? You read him one. Read him a story about baseball or rescue animals or Abraham Lincoln. Something safe and normal and Good For Boys.

Quill, on the other hand, was sitting on the edge of their bed, thumping his heels and looking at me. Expectantly.

That kid.

Gawd I was tired. Worn out.

Not in any shape to read stories to little kids.

"I dunno," I said. "I'm pretty tired."

I stepped over to the sink, hopeful that my dodge would work, and as I twisted the faucet handle I noticed a heavenly smell and for a split second I thought it smelled too sweet, almost unreal, and then a second later I realized what it was.

The rose that Winchell had given me.

Apparently, someone—Candace, must be—had stuck it in a little bud vase, and the vase was now sitting on the narrow strip of counter between the camper's tiny sink and the wall.

The stem on the rose wasn't very long. It was one of the climber type roses, not a store-bought rose. And the bud had started to open up a little bit.

I leaned over and inhaled the scent.

Good on you, modern rose, for smelling like a rose despite decades of breeding designed to make you all showy and show-offy instead of attractive to pollinating insects.

I wondered if Josh had ever thought about a rose-flavored kombucha.

I drank my glass of water and turned around.

That volume of Brothers Grimm stories was on the day bed next to the boy.

"Okay. One story," I said.

Quill jumped down and grabbed the book and darted past me toward my bedroom.

14

I got settled and took the book and leafed through it for a minute or so.

I noticed again that peculiar feeling of having a little bunny-rabbit body snuggled up next to mine.

I noticed also a bit of a silent alarm ringing somewhere in the back of my head, because what I really needed was to re-group, not involve myself with Candace and RB's kid.

But too late for that.

"Here's the one we're gonna read," I said. "It's called *The Six Swans*."

And yes, I'd picked it because of the Impossible Task angle. And quick summary in case you haven't read any fairy tales recently, *The Six Swans* is the one where the king's sons are turned into swans by their wicked stepmother. They're rescued, eventually, by their outrageously brave sister, who reverses the spell in part by sewing six shirts out of asters.

Asters are daisy-like flowers. So I don't know how you'd sew shirts out of asters. Does it mean from the petals? It has to be the petals, but how do you sew shirts out of flower petals?

But that's the point, I guess. It's part of what gives fairy tales that otherworldliness. Written fairy tales, I mean, not the cartoon kind, in the cartoon kind, they can make it otherworldly with special effects.

Paint eyes, nose and mouth on a candlestick and make it talk and voila. Another world.

But in the written stories, the otherworldliness creeps in, almost as an aside. Some heroine has to complete an impossible task. And you move past it when you're reading because of course it's arbitrary, it's a device. It's whimsical. Sew a shirt out of aster petals, how hilarious!

On the other hand it's also a bit of a signal. It's saying that real heroes, real heroines somehow do the impossible.

And in The Six Swans, it's even more impossible than sewing shirts out of aster petals, because our heroine also has to keep completely quiet the entire time.

Six years with no talking, no laughing. Worse yet, six years, and she can't tell anyone what she's doing or why. Why she's sewing shirts from aster petals and why she won't speak.

Which might be harder than sewing the shirts, to be honest. Because seriously, can you imagine? Keeping that big a thing inside you for six years?

Her brothers even tell her it's impossible.

Impossible.

And yet she gives it a go. The ol' college try. It might be impossible, she thinks to herself, but you just watch.

Good luck filling her shoes...

And she mostly succeeds, except owing to another evil queen she fails to finish the last sleeve of the last shirt, so one of the youngest brother's arms fails to transform back. It remains a swan wing. A bizarre twist, and so much for the idea that fairy tales are always these happily-ever-after things because not so fast, partner. Sometimes they add more than a little pinch of bitterness to linger in the sweet. And the story also, by the way, maybe has another lesson in there somewhere, something about the power of holding words back versus letting them spill out all the time, although I didn't really want to think about it at that moment because I really, really needed to get some sleep.

Fortunately, the story was short.

Unfortunately, Quill kept interrupting with questions.

Starting as soon as I began reading the first line. "Once there was a king who was hunting in a vast forest—"

"Why do fairy tales always happen in forests?" he said.

"They don't. Sometimes they happen in villages or palaces," I said. "So anyway, the king was hunting, and he began chasing a deer so intently that his men couldn't follow him. Then evening came, and the king realized he was lost."

"Why do people always get lost in fairy tales?"

I sighed.

"I have no idea," I said. Thinking to myself, how do you know this much about fairy tales and also, c'mon kid. Just listen to the story.

"But you're supposed to know," he said.

"Know what?"

He didn't look at me. He was looking at the page. His voice was small and solemn. "Why the king got lost."

"How'm I supposed to know that?"

"You're the fairy tale lady."

Huh? "First of all," I said, "I'm not a lady. Ladies are old."

"Daddy says you're the fairy tale lady."

I stared down at him. At the top of his little head, with the short little hairs whorled around a muddled pair of cowlicks at the top.

"My biological father," he added, and now he tipped his head up to look at me, making sure I knew he meant RB, not Garth.

Such serious eyes, that kid.

"I'm not the fairy tale lady," I said. "I studied fairy tales in college. There's a difference."

"I'm not going to college." He looked back down at the book.

"You have to go to college," I said in my most reasonable and adult voice. "How else will you figure out why people get lost in fairy tales?"

"So you do know why," he answered.

Ugh. Major backfire there, Marion Flarey.

Okay, then. We'll introduce little Quill to the concept of literary devices. "Because it advances the story," I said. "It's how the story gets the hero out of his comfort zone so something can go wrong, or so the hero can have an adventure. Or the heroine," I added quickly. "It can be a girl, too."

He sat still for a moment, considering my answer, then shook his head. "If that were true, the king could have used a map to leave his comfort zone."

Holy shit.

"Good grief," I said out loud. "What are you, seven going on thirty-five?"

"No."

"I was being ironic," I muttered.

"So, are you going to tell me?" The short little hairs on the top of his head were glistening in the lamplight.

I sighed. Try again, Marion. "Okay. How about this? Fairy tales are about a stable situation that gets disrupted, which creates problems a hero, or a heroine, need to solve. But we humans don't like problems. We like it when everything is calm and stays exactly the same all the time. The same routine all the time, and everything always predictable. Got it?"

He nodded.

"So this king? He's…a king. He has everything. He has a kingdom, he's rich, he's got servants who wait on him and do all his chores for him, he's got kids. It's not like he's running around trying to mess up his life. Right?"

He nodded again.

"So getting lost, it's…it's a metaphor—"

"What's a metaphor?" Quill said, solemnly.

Ugh. "A metaphor…it stands for something. Like a sign."

No good, Marion. Start over. "Never mind what a metaphor is," I said. "What I'm trying to say is, getting lost is a mistake that the king makes. The mistake messes up his life, which he would never do on purpose because he's got everything he needs. So now what happens in the story is—because he got lost—he meets a witch, who tells him she'll help him get out of the forest and not starve to death, but in exchange he has to marry the witch's daughter, who is also a witch. See? If he hadn't gotten lost, he wouldn't be stuck marrying a witch, which ends up causing other problems, which the hero will have to solve eventually by being very, very brave. Okay?"

His little head bobbed in a nod. "Yes."

"Getting lost…it turns things upside down. It forces the king to make a bargain he wouldn't otherwise make."

He looked up. His eyes looked enormous. "Is that why Surprise got lost?"

I felt a quick pulse of alarm.

This was dangerous ground.

Because it's one thing to deal with fairy tales on the level of metaphor and symbolism and literary devices. But blurring the line between fairy tales and real life?

Dangerous ground.

"Well," I said. "It's, uh…"

I hesitated.

Because I knew what I should be doing. I should be telling the boy that the reason Surprise got lost was because in life—real life—bad things just happen, sometimes. And it's awful and painful but it's real and trying to assign meaning or detect the "why" is a waste of time.

A complete waste of time.

But I hesitated. Because I felt, suddenly, that I couldn't say those words. If I said those words, I'd somehow be lying.

To a child.

I cleared my throat. I tried to quickly gather my thoughts. To figure out how to discuss this thing that is so much a part of me without saying something that might sound kooky or scary. "Well, Quill." I cleared my throat again. "You see, it's, uh…it's complicated."

"Hey! Whatcha guys talking about?"

Candace!

I hadn't heard her coming. But there she was, standing in the doorway like she had the night before, only tonight the hall light was on, so she was backlit, and I couldn't see her expression.

But I didn't need to. I'd heard her tone. Bright and jumpy.

She'd been listening. She'd been listening and she hadn't liked what she'd heard, and she'd pounced.

"We're, uh…you know. Reading a story!" My voice sounded every bit as false as hers. "And uh, we're not very far along, yet. But, you know."

"Sure. Got it. Marion, can I speak to you for a minute?"

Oooooh boy.

I followed her down the hallway.

"What was that all about?" she hissed when we'd reached the other end of the camper.

"It was nothing, Candace. I was explaining about symbolism."

"Keep your voice down, please." Her eyes were on the hallway instead of me. "Just please stick to the story, Marion. He's not old enough to—I don't want you talking to him about—you know."

I didn't know whether to laugh or scowl. "Oh, come on. I know better than to talk about Effie or any of that, if that's what you're worried about. Although to be honest, it's a little ironic to hear this from you when not forty-eight hours ago you were begging me to come to Tibbs to—"

She cut me off. "Stop it, Marion."

"It's a bit hypocritical though, wouldn't you say?"

"Shh!"

"No, you 'shh.' Seriously, Candace. One minute you're acting like you believe I have an actual fairy godmother, the next minute—"

"Jesus!" Cut me off again. "Do you think we would have asked you for help if we thought there was any other way?"

Our eyes locked.

And damn it.

She was a mom. What I saw in my stepsister's eyes was that she was a mom, and she wanted to do something for her kid whose heart had been broken because he loved a cat.

These people. The Weekes-Flarey's. The kid had somehow changed everything about them, or something.

I dropped my eyes.

"You're wrong," I said in a low voice. "There's nothing I can do. Effie's not a fairy godmother. She's a funny old lady who made up a bunch of stories and told me a bunch of things she shouldn't have told me."

"Oh? Then explain the What's Her Face."

I stiffened.

The doll. The What's Her Face doll. They'd come out when we were kids. You could customize them, drawing their faces and change their wigs.

I'd wanted one for my eleventh birthday.

Badly.

And—like an idiot—I'd told Candace my fairy godmother would make my wish come true.

"Mom and Dad did that," I muttered. "You know it was them who did it."

"That's not what they said. They told us they had no idea where that doll came from."

The box in the wrapping paper. Sitting on the kitchen counter that morning, and nobody knew who'd left it there.

"It was Dad's idea of a joke," I muttered.

"Right. And how about your chickenpox? How did it go away overnight like that? I was still scratching myself like crazy for weeks. I have scars still, Marion."

"Mine weren't as bad as yours."

"That's not what you said at the time, Marion. You said Effie could make it go away."

"I was a little kid. I said a lot of things. That doesn't make them true."

We fell silent for a moment.

I was looking at the floor.

I could hear her breathing.

And then: "Go back to Effie," she whispered. "Talk to her. Be nice to her."

"Oh. My God," I spat. "What are you talking about? I *was* nice to her."

"You've never been nice, Marion. You hate Tibbs, you hate us, and…"

What?

I felt a surge of temper. "You haven't given me a lot to be nice about, Candace," I hissed, venturing dangerously close to Topics That We Should Probably Not Broach. Like how a certain stepsister had slept with my boyfriend and gotten preggers by him and oh yeah also I'm still waiting for an apology? "And now, if you don't mind, I'm gonna go finish the story that I'm reading to your son, because it's late, and I need to get to bed, because I need to get to get my stuff from Rochester tomorrow morning, which means I need to be up at…" I paused and did some quick clock math. "Oh God. Candace, I need to be up at, like, 5:30 if I'm going to get to there and back before work."

And that shut her up. Finally.

I went back to the bedroom and finished reading the story.

Only now, Quill didn't ask any more questions.

· · · · ·

Considering how exhausted I was, once the story was done and Quill was gone, I should have collapsed immediately into a near-coma-like sleep. The second I shut off the light.

But instead there I was. On my side, on my back, on my other side.

A mosquito bite on the back of my right arm suddenly activated and began to itch, which reminded me about the chicken pox, and I didn't want to think about that, it hadn't happened like Candace said. We'd remembered it wrong, we'd mixed it all up…

The pillows felt thinner than they'd been the night before.

My neck began to kink.

I sat up. I re-plumped the pillows. I lay back down.

I heard a noise which I thought at first might be a wild beast but hahahahaha no. It was someone snoring.

I lifted my head, ow ow my neck, to listen through the screen.

The snoring was coming from the dome.

Winchell!

I could actually hear Winchell snoring from there, in my bed.

And then I started to worry, irrationally, about my stuff, because it occurred to me the Tweedles hadn't texted me recently which was possibly ominous, and I considered texting them to let them know I had a place for sure and would have my stuff out tomorrow.

And would Winchell remember that I needed to use his truck in the morning? Only maybe it didn't matter whether he remembered, because he has his delivery truck, he could use his delivery truck if he needed a vehicle, right?

And where did Candace get off, pushing me about Effie like that?

And what crazy universe had I stumbled into where Candace— the person who used to laugh in my face for saying Effie was my fairy godmother, who would call me a liar and that she was going to tell Mom and Dad that I was making things up—had now done a complete 180 and was insisting Effie had magical powers?

And where I was now arguing the other side?

And don't even get me started about Effie. How if she'd just helped me with one teensy weensy little wish my whole life would have turned out differently. I'd be HEA instead of SOL.

Damn it.

I straightened the covers and plumped my pillow again and laid back down, thinking O, Delightful Metaphorical Prince, how much longer must I wait for you?

• • • • •

One a.m.

Because you know what? It wasn't all in my imagination, that those things had happened. The present appearing that nobody knew where it had come from, and the chickenpox welts gone overnight, and the other things, too. Billy Beg talking to me—long conversations, not mimicking words and phrases the way budgies do in real life—and the time the light inside Effie's house turned all funny, all different colors like a rainbow.

Effie was strange.

Strange things had happened, sometimes, around her.

And no, I didn't understand any of it. And I didn't really relish the idea of revisiting it, either. Of revisiting my childhood. Or, even worse, revisiting that time after childhood, the time between childhood and adolescence when something shifted, and suddenly I found myself truly on the outside, on the other side of a something that I couldn't see or touch but was as immovable and absolute and opaque as the thickest of stone walls.

And was I ever going to get to sleep?

And how could I possibly drive to Rochester and back and then go in to work on less than four hours of sleep?

I needed to postpone. I needed to get more sleep if I was going to cope with the new job and that Upton guy. I needed to re-set my alarm and in the morning I'd text the Tweedles and tell them I absolutely promised to get my stuff the day after tomorrow.

And okay. Effie hadn't said she would *not* help me about the cat.

What she'd said was, "come back another day."

And I didn't really want to.

But I supposed it wouldn't kill me to try.

15

Tibbs is high elevation. Even in the middle of summer you wake up and it's foggy in the morning. Chilly and foggy.

So when I stepped out of the camper the next morning, it was like I'd walked into a pale cloud. Only where the sun slanted through the cloud I could see it wasn't a cloud but a fairy mist of tiny water droplets, tiny as dust dancing in the air, whirling and eddying and then suddenly flying sideways in a little puff of a breeze and then settling and whirling again. And the fog was condensing on the tree leaves and they were dripping.

I could hear it dripping, quiet taps that were like rainfall only not quite. Softer than rainfall.

Candace was up already, standing by the coffee pot with a carton of flavored non-dairy creamer. "I thought you were driving to Rochester this morning."

And how is that your business, Candace?

"I've postponed," I said aloud.

I poured myself a mug of coffee and glanced reflexively at my phone. Too early to text the Tweedles. One did not wake the Tweedles from their beauty sleep if one knew what was good for one.

I settled on one of the stools at the kitchen island and flicked at my phone again and started scanning r/folktales on Reddit until I became aware that Candace was still standing there, looking at me.

And yes, I was annoyed. Human nature being what it was. She'd begged me to go back to Effie's, and I'd said no, and then I'd changed my mind, so it was like I'd lost an argument with her and I didn't like how it made me feel.

"Is Winchell up?" I said politely. "I need to make sure he doesn't forget I'll need a ride to work."

"I can drive you if you want," Candace said. "It's not far out of my way. I'm leaving in about an hour."

Right. "Don't you have to be there at nine?" I said. Because I really did not want to be stuck in a car with her for even one second let alone the twenty minutes it would take to get from here to the brewery.

"Not during summer break," she said to me and then, to her son, "Grandma will be right down," and then sure enough the master bedroom door opened and Mom appeared, and I called up to her to remind her that she was going to lend me a clean shirt. Because fortunately we're the same build—small-boned—and double-fortunately, her taste in clothes isn't awful, for a mom. I mean, some of it is pretty retro-hippy which I can do without, but she also owns a fair number of low-key cotton tee shirts. Earth tones. I can live with earth tones.

And the jeans I'd worn would do for another day or two.

And then as I was folding up the shirts I'd picked, Mom suddenly dropped a hand on my arm.

"Honey," she said, "I just want you to know how nice it is, having you here, and seeing how well you and Candace get along."

I swear, my mother has no idea what is going on. Zero idea.

· · · · ·

The fog was starting to lift as I walked up the road and the birds were going crazy, flitting in and out of the trees. Hunting for breakfast. Hunting for bugs.

"Hullo, bird," I said to a little yellow and black bird, some sort of warbler, that landed in a nannyberry bush at the end of the driveway. "Which way to the magic fountain, little bird?"

The bird flitted back into the underbrush and disappeared.

Because there is no magic fountain, and saying the words does not bring back the world you lost when you lost your childhood.

I tucked my pant legs into my socks.

And then I said, "Damn it."

I'd left my phone back in the camper. And what if the Tweedles had turned over a new leaf and were rising with the sun, now, and this very moment they were at the half-house hauling all my stuff to the curb?

Ugh. Stop it, Marion Flarey. Because this was not the correct frame of mind for my morning's quest. I needed to stop worrying about myself and focus on little Quill.

• • • • •

Effie's front door was open when I got there, so I rapped the frame of the screen with my knuckles, and a minute later she appeared in the doorway to her kitchen and waved me in.

"Ah, Marion. Just in time for tea," she said.

I followed her through the front hallway, which was lined with shelves full of all the crazy knickknacks she'd collected, or maybe her parents had. They looked old enough to be things her parents had collected. And then, in the kitchen, Effie went to the sink and started picking through a pile of fresh leaves on the counter.

With her good hand.

"You never told me what you did to your arm," I said. "Have you had someone look at it?"

"That depends," she said, dropping a handful of leaves into her small pink teapot.

Which was not, as you now understand, the response a normal person would make. I felt a little flash of irritation. "Well you really should have a doctor look at it," I muttered, but just loud enough so that I knew she'd probably hear me.

"In that case, no. I haven't had anyone look at it."

The kettle on the stove had started to whistle and she stepped over and picked it up.

"Nobody's looked at it, and I'm going to be a stubborn old woman and refuse to go to a doctor, so don't even bother arguing. It's a sprain and will heal up just fine."

"You don't know that." Me, still muttering.

She let out a quick little laugh. "No aaaarguing!" she said in a singsong voice as she poured the hot water over the tea leaves.

I clamped my mouth shut and stood up and took two teacups from the shelf and set them on the table. It was one of those antique enameled tables, white with black legs, and a floral pattern in the middle, a nosegay of pink roses tied with a pink ribbon. When I was a kid, I thought it was the most beautiful table in the universe.

Effie sat down across from me and poured our tea, which smelled green like grass when it's freshly cut, only mixed with something slightly minty. "I guess this means you're staying in Tibbs, eh, Marion?"

"I'll be here for a couple of weeks, it turns out." I dribbled a little honey from the honey jar into my tea. "My plans have changed slightly."

Effie's blue eyes glinted. "Isn't that a nice surprise," she said, and something about the way she said the word "surprise" made me think she was needling me a bit about the cat, which made my heart rate pick up and I had to remind myself to stay calm.

Don't eff this up, Marion.

"I got a job, which was unexpected," I said. "I'm going to work here for a while to save up some money. I'm saving for an apartment I found back home."

Without exactly planning to I emphasized the word "home" which I suppose made it clear that "home" was not Tibbs.

"Speaking of surprises," she said (emphasizing the word "surprise" again, I was sure of it, this time!) "how is Royal?"

I was lifting the teacup to my lips as she spoke and although I should have been more careful because it was still boiling hot, but instead of taking a little sip I took a quick gulp.

Ow ow ow ow.

"RB?" I managed to squeak a moment later in a squeaky post-burned-mouth-accident voice.

"That boy of his is adorable."

I fanned my scalded tongue with my hand. "Yeah, Quill. He's a very cute kid." Ow ow ow.

"Whatever happened between you and Royal, anyway?" she said. "It must have been a spectacular break-up, to drive him into the arms of Candace. You must have really broken his heart."

Oh, dear. Please let's change the subject.

"Well, Effie. Whatever went on between them is none of my business, is it?" I blew the surface of my tea, watching the tiny little ripples form and spread out over the surface of the liquid, and yeah, my mind went someplace it shouldn't have. Because if Effie had helped me when I'd asked her—if she'd actually been a fairy godmother like she was supposed to be when I'd needed her help with Fletcher—none of the other stuff would have happened. I would have never dated RB and we would never have broken up and maybe he would have gone with Candace, but it wouldn't have mattered to me and who knows? Maybe they would have been able to work things out, and Quill would have been raised in a happy home with his biological father cuddled up with Candace on the couch every night...

So you see how you tug at one string of the story and the whole saga unravels.

I pushed all that stuff out of my mind because if I didn't, I was going to get totally off track, again. "So," I said, setting down my teacup and forcing myself to look at Effie, to face her square on. "Speaking of Quill." And something flashed over the old lady's face. She expected this. She expected what was coming next.

But that was no reason to waver. "I'd like your help, please," I said. Honestly and humbly and courageously. "Not for my sake, at all, but for the boy's. He loves that cat. He is heartbroken. I—we—would be very grateful if you would help us get the cat back."

"Surprise. The three-legged cat," Effie said, taking a sip of her tea. "Disappeared suddenly. And now you think I can just go like this"— she waved her good hand in the air—"and the cat will materialize in front of our eyes?"

Oh, crap. "No," I said in a small voice. "I never said that."

"Look at me, Marion."

Her eyes were so sharp. Not icy. Just sharp. Even the eye with the red, droopy lid: sharp. Bitingly sharp.

My face felt hot.

"Fine. I'll help you." Her expression turned thoughtful for a second and then she smiled. "But first? You have to bring me something."

Oh no. Please. No. "Bring you something?"

"Bring me…. let's see. The Pot with the Golden Star."

I groaned. "Really? Effie. That's…that's so random."

"Pardon? What's that mean? Random?"

"It's what the kids say, today," I muttered. "It means, uh… unexpected, I guess."

I was thinking to myself unexpected, and also devoid of meaning.

But I didn't say the harsh part out loud.

"Well." Effie's smile had returned. She was clearly very pleased with herself. "I think this will work out very nicely."

I wasn't so sure. "Please, Effie," I said. "Can't we just—"

"The Pot with the Golden Star," she interrupted. "What's done is done. More tea?"

"Effie. Can't it be Candace? Have her do the pot thing, instead of me? It's her son who is crying about the cat."

She shook her head. "Too late."

I felt my brow knit. "How about if I fail. Then can Candace…?"

"Well. Possibly. But I wouldn't go there at this particular point in the story, if I were you."

She drained the last of her tea.

She had a clock on her kitchen wall. One of those starburst clocks that were popular fifty years ago. And I'd been glancing at it during our conversation.

I had to get to the dome.

And then I was wading down the weed-choked driveway, and then I was on the road, and I broke into a trot because I had that awful feeling again that I'd been at Effie's for too long and I was going to be late for work, and that was most certainly a violation of my probation, and I still needed to text the Tweedles and what if my stuff was now sitting in the curb and what if it had started to rain back in Rochester and my books were ruined?

And how was I supposed to deal with that whole fetch me the pot thing?

And also: Effie was insane.

I realized that, now. I realized that I'd known it for some time. She was crazy. And maybe it didn't seem like it when I was in her house, talking to her. Maybe when I was with her, she seemed okay. Familiar and okay.

But the more space I put between her and me, the clearer it became.

It had been a huge mistake to go see her this morning, to put myself back in her clutches again like I had.

I needed to pull back from all of this nonsense and just focus on my job and saving enough for first-month-last-month-security deposit.

When was I going to learn?

16

Of course when I got back to the camper, I couldn't find my phone. Of course. I thought I'd left it in the camper but it wasn't there, so I went to the dome, practically colliding head-on with Candace as she barreled out the door to leave for work—no, Candace, I said I didn't need a ride from you, I'm not ready to leave yet, I'll get a ride from Dad—no phone in the dome, so back to the camper and then finally just before I reached the point of running around and screaming and throwing things I thought to check the bathroom and there it was. On the back of the sink.

I must have set it there when I combed my hair before I left for Effie's. Only now the screen was splattered with water droplets and white flecks of toothpaste, so must be Quill had brushed his teeth after breakfast, and then I wiped the screen and I wasn't careful enough and some of the toothpaste worked its way into the cracks, so now instead of translucent cracks noticeable at most angles in most light, they were bright white cracks clearly visible at all angles in all light.

This was shaping up to be a fabulous day.

Also I saw then that I had a text from Teagan, but it was an hour old, meaning too late to text her back and catch her live, probably.

I sent her a row of emojis. Hearts and flowers.

And was that the front door of the dome that I heard? Because oh, crap, I didn't want to miss Winchell and it would be just like him to forget I needed a ride to work...

I ran out the door.

His truck was still there.

My heart was pounding.

Calm down, Marion.

I found Winchell puttering in the kitchen and reminded him that I needed to get to work, and then I asked him when I could borrow the truck to get my stuff and he said not tomorrow but the day after.

Phew phew.

I texted the Tweedles. *be back to get my stuff day after tomorrow,* and I got a pretty quick *k* back from Tweedle Dum. So phew.

My stuff was not sitting on the curb, I was going to be able to get my stuff and wrap up the Tweedle saga successfully.

I reminded Winchell again that I really really needed to get to work, and finally he finished whatever he was doing—it looked like he'd been gluing a handle back onto a coffee mug—did he really need to do a fix-it job at this particular minute?

And then finally we were in the truck and on our way.

"So, Mayfly," he said which made me immediately brace myself with an oh no what now? feeling. "Mom says you went to see Effie again this morning?"

"Oh. My. God." How had she known?

She must have seen me leave and made a lucky guess. And hadn't Winchell promised he'd never pester me about Effie again?

"Just quit it," I said. "All of you. Quit it. Effie cannot bring back your cat."

No way was I going to tell him or Mom or Candace or anyone what Effie had said about that Pot with the Golden Star thing.

Not that they'd understand, even if I told them every sordid detail.

And I swiped my phone and pretended, for the rest of the drive, that I didn't mind the bright white cracks and that I was engrossed in my subreddit. While in reality I was saying over and over to myself, like a mantra: just go to work, do your job, earn the money for the Tower. One day at a time. Three, four weeks total. Just go to work, do your job, earn your money for the Tower…

. . . . .

The brewery wasn't open for business yet when we got there, and the front door was locked. So I walked around to the back of the barn.

The back door was a heavy steel thing, painted white but the paint all scratched and the scratches all leaking rust. And I opened it and then stood, holding it, for one last moment. Running through, in my mind, all the things I needed to pay attention to now. Re-do the chalkboard, check the TP and paper towels in the rest rooms before we opened to avoid a repeat of yesterday's disaster, unlock the front door, don't forget the lights on the sign…

I heard voices.

People talking.

And then I let go of the door and it clunked shut and…

Silence.

The voices were coming from the brewing area.

I was pretty sure one of them was Upton's. I was pretty sure another of the voices was Josh.

But I was also pretty sure there was a third voice.

Which I didn't recognize. Or did I?

Because something about it made me freak out a little bit. Even though I couldn't hear it well enough to make out the words. It was like the resonance of the voice was enough to send a little zing through my body, a little spidey sense zing that told me *here we go, Marion Flarey, now you're into it even deeper than before.*

And I should have turned around right then.

I should have dashed back around the building and run down the road waving and yelling for Winchell to turn around and come back.

But I didn't.

I just stood there, frozen in place like poor Joringel when the witch cast a spell on him so he couldn't move a muscle while she turned his beloved into a nightingale and stuffed her into the wicker basket.

And someone came around the corner.

And it didn't matter that I hadn't seen him in, like, fifteen years.

How could I not know who it was?

Even after all those years?

It was my high school dreamboat boyfriend.

My first Prince.

It was Fletcher Beal.

·　·　·　·　·

So, grown-up Fletcher Beal was freaking gorgeous.

It didn't take me long to notice.

Meaning that: it took me about as long to notice Fletcher Beal was freaking gorgeous as it takes a lightning bolt to shatter a poor lone tree minding her business in the middle of a field in a rainstorm.

He was even more gorgeous than teenage Fletcher Beal. Even more gorgeous than teenage Fletcher Beal was that night, oh-so-long ago, when he took my hand and led me onto the gym floor and put his arms around me and pressed me close...

Because Fletcher was the "it" boy of my high school. The boy who should have been with someone popular and socially adept, not Marion Flarey. The boy with the perfect body, broad shoulders, muscled without being too big, slender waist so that his jeans always slid kinda low on his hips making your eyes follow down and your mind "go there" even when you were only fifteen and not really ready to go there for real. And that hair, light brown with natural highlights and just a little bit of wave in it so that it curls around his ears when it gets long.

And—oh gawd—those fall-into-my-arms-right-now, crazy-kissable cupid-bow lips.

The boy who—I know this will sound like a fairy tale, hahaha, but it's actually true—was a straight A student but still super cool, and a terrific athlete, the star of every team he ever joined. And whose family was rich.

Or at least, rich compared to the rest of us people living in Tibbs.

The boy who'd taken me to my first high school dance.

And wouldn't you know it?

He looked even better today than on that night we'd danced across the gym floor under those crepe paper streamers.

"Marion," he said, stepping toward me. "I thought it might be... I can't believe it. It's...you."

"Fletcher?" I gasped, grabbing the shelf next to me because my knees were literally wobbling.

And then I thought, Marion! What are you doing?

Get ahold of yourself.

It—everything that happened—was fifteen years ago.

Fifteen years!

And he's *married.*

Right? Married? Isn't that what Candace had said?

My eyes, like they had a mind of their own, went immediately to his left hand and *shit shit shit* he was wearing a ring.

And then my extremely disobedient and naughty eyes flew back up to look at his face and OMG, he was locking his eyes onto mine, he was doing that thing he always used to do that made me feel like I was the center of the universe and why is everything spinning around me?

"I could hug you," he said.

"Uh, uh," I gulped and fell backwards, pushing my right hand out toward him as I did, so what would happen next would be not a hug but a super-professional handshake, because no!

No hug!

And it worked, I guess, because yeah, he took my hand only no! My plan was actually a fail because his handshake—how is it even possible?—*felt* like a hug, his big warm strong hand clasping mine, how can a guy make a handshake feel like he's taken you into his arms?

"What're you doing here?" I said, the words coming out a little like I was choking.

Or out of breath. Because I kinda was.

He laughed. Eyes, still on mine, but dancing now. "This is my place," he said. "Didn't anyone tell you? I own it."

WHAT?

I stared.

And then the gears in my brain re-started and squeaked into motion and a moment later OMG.

That Winchell!

That Candace!

They'd known!

They HAD to have known!

They HAD to have known all along that Fletcher—that he—that if I started working here I would...

"My company invests in start-ups, and we think hard kombucha is going to be the next big thing, and of course I will always have a spot in my heart for..." he paused, and I stopped breathing and then he continued. "For, uh, Tibbs. Hey, are you okay?"

"Um, sure, of course," I muttered. "I'm fine. So, um, you're living in Tibbs, now?"

"No. No. I come in every couple of weeks and stay a few days," he answered.

My head was still fizzing into mush, I was trying to focus on his words while also picturing the ass-kicking I was going to deliver to Winchell and Candace when I got home.

And Mom! Had Mom known?

"I'm staying in our old place. The stone house. You remember the stone house?"

Oh, gawd.

The stone house.

Like I could forget it. And not only because, as the crow flies, the stone house is not more than a couple miles from the dome. The fact was everyone around knew the stone house. Even people who lived in other parts of the county, not in Tibbs. It was legendary. So huge and old-looking and castle-like. So unlike the modest houses the rest of us lived in.

And by the way? The fact that there was nothing between the dome and the stone house except forest was something I once felt had to be a magical sign revealing that Fletcher and I were supposed to be together. Because why else would his mother buy that house, of all houses, after she'd left Fletcher's dad? Which meant this impossibly gorgeous boy had ended up in Tibbs, ended up practically a neighbor, a thing that would otherwise have been extremely improbable?

Wealthy people from Long Island don't just stick a pin in a map and decide to move to Tibbs.

But the stone house was part of Fletcher's mom's divorce strategy. An excellent way to ensconce her son far, far away from his father while the lawyers did their lawyery thing.

In fact, it was something we'd had in common, Fletch and me. Our crazy broken-up families.

And then she'd done the unthinkable.

A wicked, wicked thing.

It was summer. I was going into 10th grade, he was going into 11th.

He'd taken me to the spring dance.

I was in love. Like in the movie, I was in love truly madly deeply.

And his mom remarried.

Isn't that how these things always take an awful turn?

Young prince and young princess fall in love.

Wicked parent remarries…and boom.

Two young lovers learn they're to be parted forever.

Fletcher's mom decided to ship him off to prep school.

Prep school.

I'd never even heard of prep school. What the fuck is a prep school?

I thought I was going to die that summer. And this was before Facebook. It was before the iPhone. And as I've mentioned, Winchell refused to spring for cell phones for us kids, even if he was supposedly making a fortune at the time on that stupid multi-level marketing supplement scheme. What'd ya need a cell phone for, he'd say, if you need to call home borrow one from one of your friends.

So when Fletcher's mom moved him away, he might as well have been turned into a swan. Or sunk down into the earth to live with the gnomes, like the girls who plucked the blood-red apple from the tree.

He might as well have been shut into a wooden box and tossed into the sea to float off to a distant land.

I was in love. Horribly, passionately, painfully in love.

I thought I was going to die.

And yeah. I asked Effie to bring him back. Asked my so-called fairy godmother to bring him back.

And her answer? A shrug and a, "No, Marion. I can't do that."

Well interestingly enough, maybe my fairy godmother couldn't bring him back.

But...

And was this even possible?

Life had.

Life had brought him back. Because here he was, standing in front of me.

As gorgeous as ever. More gorgeous than ever. The traces of baby fat completely gone, the slender wiry teenage muscles now transformed into gorgeous man muscles, the wispy face hair transformed into an elegantly trimmed beard...

Gorgeous.

And married.

And my boss.

And he was looking at me like the wandering prince gazed on the face of the sleeping princess, the beautiful Brier Rose, right before he kissed her.

And no. NO.

I couldn't let it happen.

Whatever this was...whatever dastardly scheme Candace and Winchell or Fate herself was trying to pull off here?

I could not let it happen. I could not let the trap spring closed.

I don't remember what I said next.

Something stupid, I'm sure, something about how a keg needed changing or I'd promised Upton to do an inventory of our glassware or what was that noise? Was there a customer at the door?

Something ridiculous, I'm sure.

But the key thing is: I escaped.

I squeezed by him somehow and left him standing there and scrambled to the front of the building.

And I didn't look over my shoulder to see if he'd followed. On the contrary, I pulled the stepladder out from its nook near the restrooms and dragged it over to the bar and started scrubbing the blackboard so hard I'm surprised it was still black when I was done.

And then I re-lettered it with the day's kombucha menu, in colored chalk, and you should have seen my artistry with those letters, it was second only to Michelangelo's work on the ceiling of the Sistine Chapel.

Only sadly it didn't take me quite as long.

So then I had to come up with task after task that required me to keep my attention fastened like glue to something, anything but the space around me, for fear that I'd look up and Fletcher would be standing there and our eyes would meet and...

Then finally it was time to open and I unlocked the doors, and thank goodness, a few minutes later, people started straggling in. And I served them, and chatted them up, and was extremely careful to focus on our wonderful customers with one hundred ten percent of my attention one hundred ten percent of the time.

And I only let my resolve waver once.

I peeked over my shoulder past the brewing kettles toward the door to the office and oh gawd, there he was.

Disappearing around the corner by the rest rooms.

So see? I was right.

He was watching me.

He's married.

Keep telling yourself that, Marion Flarey.

Tell yourself a million zillion times so that its carved indelibly into the noodles of your brain.

He's married and he's not my lost prince. He's not. He's not. I can NOT let my brain go there. I handed a customer a tulip glass filled with a fizzy pour of coffee-chocolate-flavored kombucha.

And I saw a car moving across the parking lot, a beautiful old Audi, moving across the parking lot and turning onto the road and driving away.

You know the kind of car. Expensive but not new, so not pretentious, and yet also vintage-y enough to be meltingly cool. And so of course I knew it was Fletcher's car. One hundred percent something Fletcher would drive...

And he was leaving the brewery.

He was gone.

I was safe. For now, at least.

And also, Candace was going to pay for this. Candace was going to hear from me, and she was going to learn a lesson she would not soon forget.

17

Things got really quiet at the brewery after our early-evening rush. And Upton actually left, so he must have been starting to trust me a little, and Josh wasn't brewing that day, so I was all alone.

So as things wound down I cleaned up and texted Winchell, and then I locked the front door and flipped the sign over so the Closed side would face out, and then left through the back door and walked around and leaned against the base of the big sign in the parking lot, waiting for Winchell, and thinking about how I was going to get my revenge for everyone keeping it a secret from me that Fletcher owned the brewery.

I felt a little nauseous and unbuttoned my jeans to give my belly a little more space, which seemed to help a bit.

How could they not tell me Fletcher owned the brewery?

It was still a little light out, because the sun doesn't set until 8:30 at night, in the summer, in Tibbs. The road blacktop was still warm enough that I could smell its bitter, oily smell and the air felt heavy and damp after being inside, in the air conditioning, and a mosquito found me and managed to bite the back of my leg before I noticed and swatted her. Which meant, great, another itch to bother me when I was trying to sleep, tonight.

Then finally, after what was a lot longer than it should have taken for Winchell to get from the dome to the brewery, which means he probably didn't leave right away but farted around for a while, first, I heard his truck and then he pulled up next to me and I opened the passenger door.

"Dad!" I said. "Why didn't you tell me Fletcher Beal owns the brewery?" And just like that my eyes were suddenly wet.

"Fletcher?" he answered.

Are you kidding me.

I blinked, hard. "Fletcher Beal," I said. "He took me to... We used to date."

"Never heard of the guy," Winchell said. "I thought Upton Munster was the owner. Didn't you date RB?"

Oh. My. God.

I threw my hands into the air, metaphorically speaking, and climbed into the car. "No, Upton Munster is not the owner," I said. "He's the manager. Fletcher Be—oh, never mind!"

Because obviously this was a fruitless conversation. Because not only had Winchell completely mixed up who owned the brewery, he'd completely mixed up Fletcher Beal with Royal Brinley Brown.

I looked out the passenger window the whole drive back and when he asked me something about how my day had gone, I said, "Hmm? Oh fine," and he got the message, I suppose, because after that he left me alone.

And then we got to the dome, and to my chagrin, Candace's car wasn't there. My revenge was going to have to wait.

I went to the camper and plugged in my phone and changed the water in the bud vase.

The rose had opened a bit more.

And where the heck had Winchell gotten the idea that roses were my favorite flower? And doesn't that show you how he basically never paid any attention to me and had no idea that I'd once dated Fletcher Beal until Fletcher's mom broke us up and ruined my life and it was a wonder I'd survived?

Then I went back to the dome because after weeks of surviving on bagged chips, those Weekes-Flarey TV dinners weren't tasting so bad.

Mom was in the kitchen, putting dishes away. Yeah, they don't have a dishwasher. Crazy, huh? They do all their dishes by hand. But that's what I was saying about Winchell being tight. Although since they don't do big family meals, and we're in theory supposed to clean up whatever dishes we use, and half the time we're eating frozen dinners, it's not like there are ever towering stacks of dishes that all need to be done at once.

I put an Oriental chicken and rice dinner in the microwave.

"So guess what, Mom," I said, watching her pull plates out of the rinse water and stick them into the rack. "I ran into someone at work, today."

"Oh?" she said, absently, because Winchell isn't the only one who is off in his own little world half the time, although in Mom's case at least she has an excuse, being an artist.

"Someone I knew in high school," I said.

She wiped her hands dry on the towel hanging on the knob below the sink and gave me a blank look. "Who was that, dear?"

"You remember Fletcher Beal? The guy who took me to that dance?"

"The spring dance?" she said. "Didn't RB take you?"

Holy.

Holy…holy what?

I couldn't even find the words.

"RB?" I said, my voice already halfway to a shout. "Why does everyone think… Oh my God. RB?"

And I'm sorry, but all I could think of was that here I'd been tricked into this encounter with my Lost Prince and instead of having even the slightest hint of empathy my step-dad and now my mother had gone immediately to… RB?

And so sorry, but I did something a bit childish. I said, "RB?" again while doing the "make me gag" motion with my hand, pretending to stick my fingers down my throat.

And at that very second a movement caught the corner of my eye and crap crap crap.

Quill.

Standing there.

He'd seen everything. He'd materialized out of thin air just in time to see everything. And there he was, standing there a few feet away, face upturned, big eyes watching my every move, he'd seen the fingers down my throat and my tongue and the grimace and he'd heard the gagging noise, and how was he to know why hearing his father's name made me react like that?

Guilt flushed through my body, heating up my face, and my mouth started to form the words *I'm sorry* but too late, he'd turned away, and how could I apologize for that? How do you apologize to a little kid for having shown him that the thought of his father makes you want to puke?

I turned my head to look back at Mom.

Her forehead was puckered.

"Uh, well," I said in a voice that sounded kind of choked up because I was really, really feeling pretty crappy at that particular moment, "I didn't go to the dance with, uh, RB. I went with a guy named Fletcher Beal. Remember? Moved here when I was in 7th grade? Lived in the stone house?"

"Fletcher Beal," Mom repeated vaguely.

She was looking at Quill, not me.

Also, she had no idea who I was even talking about.

I gave up. What was the point?

I looked at Quill now, too. "Uh, hey, Quill?" I tried to sound cheerful, like I hadn't just made gagging noises about his father who had just spent a wonderful day with him, fishing and bonding and stuff. "Wanna go pick out a story to read?"

He didn't look over at me.

He shook his head.

Ugh.

The ickiness in my stomach hardened and it occurred to me that perhaps my first punishment was that I really was going to puke.

"Grandma," Quill said. "Can I color?"

"Sure, honey."

I stood, utterly and justifiably sidelined, watching Mom lay some paper out on the table and fetch a box of oil pastels because of course, with her being an artist, she doesn't give her grandson the five dollar pack of kiddie crayons, she gives him the forty dollar box of pastels.

He slid pastels out of the box and picked one up and ran some green and then brown across the paper, and a crude T-Rex took shape.

His fingers were now stained green and brown and there were green and brown smudgy fingerprints on the table around the paper.

"Hey, that's pretty good, Quill," I said in a weak voice, hovering near him while trying not to seem like I was hovering.

He didn't answer me.

He was adding big yellow triangle teeth to the T-Rex's mouth.

And I stood there thinking: I need to clean up my act. I need to become something like 10,000 times a better human being, because yes maybe the thought of RB made me want to retch but somehow being honest about that in front of RB's son was wrong. Very wrong.

From now on, without exception, I was going to say only nice things about RB in front of his boy.

"My oath to you," I whispered, watching Quill choose a cerulean blue and slash it back and forth across the top of the paper to do the sky.

Oath.

I'd said the word "oath."

See, this is what happens when you're raised on a diet of fairy tales. Even whispering that word, that night, made a little chill go up my back and a little twist turn around in my belly. Because you've learned to believe that oath is a power word, like a promise only not sunny and sweet like a promise...*oath* has a darkish feeling to it, like wow be careful because it will come back on you with some kinda bad luck if you break it...

And even when you're old enough to know better, the feeling is still there. Rising up and haunting you when you least expect it.

· · · · ·

So I spent the next hour or so in a kind of limbo, picking at my meal and hanging in the dome trying to figure out how to tell if a seven-year-old boy was still mad at me or not. The door to Candace's old bedroom opened and out walked Winchell in a billow of steam, towel wrapped around his waist, skin above the waist as pink and plumped up as you can imagine it being after he'd had a nice long soak in the jacuzzi, and I reminded him I needed to borrow his truck in the morning and he said he'd leave the keys on the counter for me.

And then I heard a car pull in and who doesn't show up, finally, but Candace.

"I bought you wine," she said, holding out a paper bag with the top twisted tight around the bottle inside.

I glanced in the direction of Quill, who had stopped coloring and was now playing with that kiddie game system on the couch, and instead of taking the bottle I grabbed Candace by the arm and pulled her toward me. "Candace," I said in a low voice. "Why didn't you tell me Fletcher owns the brewery?"

"You didn't ask," she said in a completely normal voice. She waved the bottle at me. "Take it. It's a Cabernet. You like Cabernet, right?"

"That was a dirty trick, Candace," I said, still guarding my decibel level. "You knew, didn't you."

"How is that a dirty trick? He's gorgeous. And he's getting a divorce. And you're single, right?"

"He's wearing a ring!" I hissed.

The self-satisfied look on her face faded a bit, but of course she didn't back down. "What I *heard*," she said, "is that he was getting a divorce. Marla told me. She heard it from her brother-in-law who helped Upton install those sconces. The ones in the barn." She set the wine-bottle-shaped bag on the counter.

"Sounds reliable," I said. "And by the way, whether he's getting a divorce is beside the point. You should've told me he owned the place. I would have at least been able to *prepare* myself."

She shrugged and opened the freezer to pick out her dinner.

I glanced discretely at the bottle.

I went over and pulled the bottle out of the bag.

A California Cab, and not a bad brand.

She must have spent at least twenty bucks on it.

Twenty-dollar bottles of wine hadn't been in my budget for months.

Well. She probably had a guilty conscience for not telling me the whole truth about Fletcher being in Tibbs. So that's what she gets.

Winchell came down the stairs now, hair still wet and slicked back but fully covered, thank goodness. Gray track suit, his normal evening attire.

The microwave beeped.

And Candace got her dinner—chicken alfredo, by the smell of it—and plunked down on the sofa. "What's on?" she said to Winchell. And then, "Quill, honey," she said. "It's almost bedtime. You need to put the game away and go brush your teeth. And what's that on your hands? Mom, what's Quill got all over his hands?"

"He was drawing with Mom's pastels," I said. And then I took advantage of my opening. "You want me to get him cleaned up and tuck him in, so you can eat your dinner?"

She craned her neck around to look at me. "You mind?" she said.

I shook my head. "How about it, Quill?" I called over to the boy. "We can read a story. We have time, right, Candace?"

And I waited, hopeful, letting my offer dangle there in the air.

"Quill?" I said, trying not to sound like I was begging.

"I want Mommy to tuck me in tonight," he said.

Ouch.

Ow ow ow ow ouch.

And that's how I ended up reading by myself in the camper, shut into my bedroom because I didn't think I'd be able to stand it when they came in, listening as Quill brushed his teeth and then Candace raised her voice a bit because he took too long to change into his pajamas.

Being a good aunt was harder than I thought it was going to be.

My own fault, of course.

My own, damn fault.

I plugged in my phone.

I considered how early I needed to get up to get to Rochester and back in time for work. Because I'd been thinking I could squeeze it in if I got up at 5:30 but was that realistic?

I re-did the math.

And okay, new plan:

4:00. Wake, quick shower, dress. Jeans (mine), tee shirt (Mom's—so that freshly shaved and deodorized armpits would stay that way).

4:15. Slip into dome. Brew coffee. Retrieve keys to Winchell's truck.

4:25. Armed with coffee in travel mug, set out for Rochester. Break speed limits but by only 7-9 mph max to avoid getting speeding ticket.

6:45. Arrive at old apartment. Lug boxes from apartment to bed of Winchell's truck with caffeine-fueled swiftness and efficiency.

7:00. Text the Tweedles that apartment is finally vacated and keys are by the sink.

7:05. Set out on return trip.

9:15. Arrive at dome. Lug boxes from bed of Winchell's truck into dome living room by drawing on remaining stores of caffeine, with assist from Candace and/or Winchell if possible.

9:30. Unpack the box with the Jim Beam label marked Clothes and retrieve jeans and nice blouse, the button down with the stripes.

9:35. With Mom's tee shirt swapped for nice blouse, leave for work with five minutes to spare.

I set my alarm.

And okay. Time to calm down and get some sleep.

And then just get to Rochester and get my books.

I'd try and figure out how to make friends with Quill again some other day.

18

I was dreaming, a very nice dream involving caterpillars that turned, when they matured, into actual cats instead of butterflies.

Cats with wings.

And then the alarm went off and the lovely buttercats were gone and I was awake, and the first thing that crossed my mind was that something was wrong, now, about my job, that stabbing panicky feeling you get when something awful had happened, and then I remembered.

Fletcher.

Fletcher Beal owned the brewery.

Ugh.

I gave myself a little talking to. Telling myself that despite appearances, nothing had really changed. Job: intact, so far. Loan from Winchell: accepted. Vicki: waiting patiently for next installment against first month last month security deposit.

I was going to be fine. Sure, things had been a bit off the rails lately, but this was not the time for self-pity, I wasn't the only Millennial in this ridiculous listing boat, with my worthless degree, my pile of debt, and still no idea what I'm going to be when I grow up. I wasn't the only Millennial who set out in the forest like a king, only instead of hunting a deer, hunting a career, and looking up one day and thinking oh crap. I'm lost. Because all my life, I'd loved fairy tales, and every time I spoke to the guidance counselor at the high school and she asked me what my interests were, all I could think of was fairy tales. I mean, what kind of answer was that? What is a guidance counselor supposed to do with that? So of course she tells me to get a liberal arts degree or an English degree—that's what I ended up doing—and then what? Well, how about a master's?

And so okay, a master's, only now I'm racking up even more debt, and I'm looking at my course load and my debt and trying to figure out what my thesis will be and: boom.

Boom. I'm lost.

Because being an expert in fairy tales? News flash. Being an expert in fairy tales pays shit. It pays nothing. The best I could expect was maybe an adjunct professorship somewhere, assuming I could even get a job at all. And then the whole thing with RB and Candace, and yes there was also the other guy, the third Prince, only that was more like a crush than an actual boyfriend although I always had the feeling that RB somehow knew about it. So no wonder he and I were a disaster, our communication skills weren't exactly first rate.

So I quit school. I dropped out. Saved myself the cost of finishing my master's, got myself away from my then-crush (his name was Piotr, not that it matters). (And he was a professor, too, so you can see how it was impossible.) (Not that it matters.)

And about all I knew was that I'd had enough of boys—men, I guess, by then—and I'd had enough of racking up the student loan debt.

I mean, don't get me wrong. Fairy tales are beautiful. They are beautiful, and some of them are so beautifully written. True literature. If all you've read is Brothers Grimm or Perrault or Hans Christian Anderson, pick up something by Giambattista Basile sometime and prepare to be blown away. Prepare to laugh your ass off. Or Marie-Catherine d'Aulnoy, who was positively freaking brilliant, and had an incredible life—she had to flee Paris at one point because her husband, who she'd tried to get killed, was hoping to get his revenge—and she became a secret agent for France, and took bunches of lovers, and ended up back in Paris hosting one of the most glamorous literary salons in 18th Century Europe.

Where she spun elaborately gorgeous fairy tales, and also wrote them out and published them.

I'd been thinking about doing my thesis on Marie-Catherine d'Aulnoy.

But becoming the world's authority on Marie-Catherine d'Aulnoy does not pay the bills. An obsession with fairy tales does not pay the bills.

On the contrary. In fact, forget what I just said about Basile and d'Aulnoy. If you're an actual grown-up, put the fairy tales away. Pack them in a box, tape it shut, drive to the nearest bridge and toss the box over the railing. It will free up space in your tiny apartment and also make it easier if you get so far behind in your rent that you have to skip out in the middle of the night.

Not that I've ever done that.

Hah.

Just, whatever you do, don't wake up one day and find yourself twenty-nine years old, i.e. technically an adult, and still in the back of your mind letting yourself wonder what they're really about. Fairy tales.

Because I tell you. They are nothing.

They're about nothing.

And I had a job, which had seemed reasonable 24 hours ago, but now apparently meant that I would be running into not one, but two of my ex-boyfriends in this godforsaken little town.

I grabbed the second pillow and pulled it over my head.

I did not want to get out of bed. I did not want to drive to Rochester and back...

I threw the pillow aside and sat up.

Just get through it. Three more weeks and I'd have the money I needed for my beautiful tower and I could quit, and leave Tibbs, and I'd never have to come back.

Just like before. Just like I had it before.

And Fletcher hadn't been at the brewery my first day. And he'd said he wasn't living full-time in Tibbs. So he wouldn't be around much, right? In fact he was probably gone already. He was probably back where he'd come from, back downstate, minding his burgeoning portfolio of highly lucrative start-ups while being gazed upon adoringly by his tall, exquisitely beautiful wife with the face and figure that looked like they'd been purchased but were entirely God-given natural.

He surely wouldn't be at the brewery every day.

Right?

I checked my phone.

Ugh. It was already 4:16. I was behind schedule.

I'd skip the shower. I'd go with a fresh application of deodorant and a clean shirt and be on my way.

• • • • •

A few minutes later I tiptoed quietly down the little hall from my bedroom to the other end of the camper.

And oddly, the camper's screen door wasn't latched.

Candace must have gotten a bit sloppy last night. She'd forgotten to pull the door all the way closed.

And remind me later to speak to her, because how many other nights had she done that? And maybe that's why I kept finding new mosquito bites?

And then for some reason I took another look at the daybed.

And there was the back of Candace's head. She was sleeping on her side, I could hear her snoring slightly.

But where was Quill?

He wasn't there.

Quill wasn't in the bed.

• • • • •

I checked the dome. Whispering his name but kind of loudly, "Quill!" so that it kind of hissed.

He wasn't in the dome.

I went back out the door and ran around to the little shed that Mom uses for her clay works studio behind the dome.

He wasn't in the shed.

And I thought, oh my God. He's gone into the woods. All that talk the other night about fairy tales and getting lost in the forest? He's decided to go get lost in a forest, Candace was right, reading fairy tales was a really really bad idea and what if he had tripped and hurt himself or climbed a tree and fallen or run into a pack of coyotes?

And my chest felt tight with panic and I ran around to the front of the dome, thinking that I'd wake my parents first, not Candace— Candace was going to lose it, Candace was going to lose her mind— when suddenly I had another thought.

Effie's.

Would the boy go up to Effie's?

I whirled and started down the driveway.

Had to stop to catch my breath when I reached the road because man oh man, I was not in very good shape at all, it turns out.

I began to jog up the road.

It was foggy again and only barely getting light out. All I could see was maybe twenty or thirty yards of pavement in front of me and the dark trees on either side of the road.

"Quill?" I called out into the thick, pale fog. "Quill?"

I stopped to catch my breath again.

I started jogging again.

And even though the air was cool I was starting to sweat, and oh my God there was no way I was going to make it to Rochester and back this morning...

And then I saw him. Dark little boy-shaped form standing in the fog next to her mailbox, preparing himself to plunge into the weeds that guarded the end of Effie's driveway.

"Quill!" I yelped, and then I broke into a spring, and a moment later I was kneeling next to him, holding him in my arms.

"Quill, it's okay. It's okay. It'll be okay."
Wiping his tears.
Not really understanding what would be okay or why.
Only knowing that those were the words I had to say.

19

I texted the Tweedles and negotiated one more, final, one-day extension on getting my stuff out of the half-house.

They were not happy about it. I got the *jesus marion really* and the *omg* and the *we r so sick & tired of this*, but I told them I had a family emergency and in the end they said fine and I promised that absolutely without fail I'd be there tomorrow morning.

It was a little after six.

The microwave beeped and I took the mug out—hot chocolate— and took it over to Quill and sat with him on the couch.

"I was thinking about a fairy tale last night," I said cautiously as he sipped his cocoa. "It's called *Jorinda and Joringel*. Aren't those funny names?"

He shrugged. "I have a funny name," he said.

"I don't think Quill is funny," I said.

"Not my first name." He gave me the side-eye. Meaning, of course, dummy, Quill is a perfectly fine, non-funny name. "I meant my middle name."

Yowsa. I was trying. I really was. But it seemed like I kept stepping in it, with this kid. "Ah," I said. "And, uh...what's your middle name?" Thinking as I said it, geez, Marion. How is it that you don't know your nephew's middle name?

"It's Atlas," he said.

"Atlas," I repeated softly. Thinking to myself *Quill Atlas Brown*.

It wasn't Candace who'd come up with that one.

No way.

It had to be RB, picking a name like that.

Quill took another sip of cocoa. He now had a cocoa-colored moustache.

"You know who Atlas is, right?" I said.

He nodded. "Daddy told me. Atlas holds up the world. He stands like this." Quill handed me his mug and stood up and bent forward and held his arms out behind him with the palms up.

"That's right." He sat back on the couch and I handed back the mug. "Careful not to tip that, it's still pretty full. Your dad's a smart man. Did you have fun with him yesterday? When you went fishing?"

"Sure," he said.

"It was nice of him, to skip work so he could spend time with you like that."

See? I was reformed. I was now carefully pointing out what a great person RB was. "Did you catch anything?"

"No. Yes. Sunnies. But we didn't keep them."

He meant sunfish.

"They're kinda small to keep."

"Daddy says you can eat them."

"Trout are better. You should ask him to teach you how to fish for trout."

"Daddy says if you got lost in the woods you would eat sunnies to survive."

"He's one hundred percent correct," I said, once again saying very nice things to the boy about his dad. "Your father is an expert woodsman, you know."

Quill nodded. "He's taking me again tomorrow." He looked up at me. "Fishing."

"Is he, really? Wow. That's great." I tried to think of something else to say. I mean, what I wanted to say was along the lines of "and he loves you very much," but it might have sounded forced, and I was on thin enough ice with little Quill, I didn't want to risk pulling junk like that. So I decided to go back to the subject of names. A safer subject. "Anyway," I said. "I don't think Atlas is a funny name, at all. It's a great name. It means your parents know you'll grow up to be powerful and strong."

"I'm little."

Ah hah! Another chance to put in a word for RB. "That doesn't mean anything, Quill. Your dad was small when he was your age, too, and look at him now." I smiled. "In fact, he was so little that I once nearly squashed him."

He looked over. Big eyes. "You did?"

I nodded. "Uh huh. It's how I met him, in fact. I fell on him."

Big eyes.

"Shall I tell you the story?" Teasing him, a bit. Of course he'd want to hear the story.

"Yes, please."

Damn. Could the kid be any sweeter?

"It was on the playground," I said. "Me and my girlfriends were taking turns pushing each other on the swing. And I guess we were getting careless because my friend Sandy pushed me too hard, and the swing seat twisted funny and somehow I let go and yikes. Down I went."

I paused suddenly. Funny, how memories can come back to you like that. So vivid. So that for a split second it was like it had just happened. The crazy sickening feeling as I let go with one hand and suddenly the seat below me wasn't under me anymore, and I guess I must have panicked and tried to jump off or something. I don't remember exactly, only I think I fell backward.

And then, instead of hitting the ground like I expected and probably richly deserved, I hit a boy. "I fell right on your father," I said. "Right on top of him."

And suddenly I burst out laughing. It struck me as so funny, all of a sudden. The way, sometimes, a thing that's funny hits you harder when you've been too tense, too anxious, too tight. It hits you and suddenly you release and omg, the laugh feels so good.

And Quill caught it.

He started laughing, too.

But then I got serious again. "We shouldn't laugh!" I said. "It hurt him. I was bigger than him! It broke his collarbone. Have you ever noticed the bump on his collarbone?"

Eyes all big again. "Right here," he said, touching himself to the side of his neck, on the right side. "There's a lump."

I nodded. "Yep. Sometimes if you break a bone it gets a lump where it heals back up."

"He lets me touch it."

I nodded. "It just feels like a hard lump." And the thought jumped up into my head *I've touched it, too*, and I felt myself kind of stiffen because the thought was too close and too real, and of course I knew better than to say it out loud but even thinking it was too much.

And what was I doing here, anyway? Letting my head go back in time like that, letting myself tell RB's son stories from my past like that?

This was wrong. It was all wrong...

I gave myself a little shake. "Hey, Quill, I got kind of sweaty running up the road to find you, so I need to take a shower. Can I leave you here for a few minutes? Will you be okay?"

He nodded.

"No more running away, right? If you want to go see Effie we have to check with your mom, and you and I will go together, or maybe your mom will even go, too. Okay?"

"Aunt Marion?"

I felt my body tighten.

I knew what was coming.

"Effie can get Surprise back for us. Right?"

Ugh.

"I think so, honey." I swallowed. "But you...you need to be patient, okay? Just wait a little while longer."

He nodded.

And I left him and slipped back into the camper to shower and change into a clean shirt.

And I did my best to avoid thinking about work, avoid thinking about whether Fletcher would be there, and it was good that Quill and I were friends again but seriously. I just needed to make good tips today because seriously, I just needed to get the money together and get the hell out of Tibbs...

20

So the whole ride to work I sat there thinking *please don't let Fletcher be there today. Please don't let Fletcher be there today.*

I might as well have asked Effie to materialize a cat. Because the answer to my prayers was no.

He was there. All day.

Worse yet, he didn't seem to be there to, you know, do any work. He seemed to be just hanging around. Hanging around and giving me the distinct impression that he wanted to talk to me but couldn't quite bring himself to walk up and say so.

Which is just as well, because I didn't want him to.

And then my luck ran out, because a delivery truck stopped out front and the driver wheeled in a stack of paper supplies and I signed for it and took the invoice to the office and dropped it in the box on the desk and rounded the corner and GAH!

We practically collided. We came so close to colliding I could feel the force-field between us... No, not a force-field, because a force-field would be a repellent and whatever it was between us, it was definitely not a repellent.

"Marion," he said in that voice that was so familiar and so sexy that if I wasn't careful my knees were going to start shaking. "I need to ask you something."

"It's not a good time," I said, ducking past him. "The ginger-lime kicked. I need to change the keg."

"I'll change the keg." Oh, God, he was following me? "Marion. Let me take you to dinner."

No no no no no. I froze in my tracks. "Dinner? I can't! I have to work tonight, Fletcher."

"I've talked to Upton. He said he can close tonight."

OMG.

I forgot the keg. Reversed course, dodged around Fletcher again and headed to the front of the building. Got to the tasting room and bent over the sink to wet the bar rag, began furiously wiping down the bar, despite that it was obviously already perfectly clean. While he stood at the far end, he'd followed me.

He stood, watching me.

Like he had no plans to take "no" for an answer.

So I switched tactics and started throwing out excuses. "I can't give up my shift, Fletcher. I need the money."

"Marion," he said, and now he was coming down the bar, now he was so close I swear I could feel the warmth of his body, I could smell him. His cologne or body spray. Or maybe it was just him. I wouldn't be surprised if Fletcher was born with a scent like that, musk and balsam and spice.

Really, Marion. Get a grip.

"Our dinner tonight," he was saying. "It's a business dinner. You'll be on the clock. It won't reduce your hours."

Breathe, Marion. Breathe. "Thank you but no, Fletcher, you see, I also have to be up super early tomorrow. I have to drive to Rochester and do some things. I'm busy. I can't—"

He turned away from me. "Upton!" he called out.

Oh, no.

Upton appeared from the direction of the office. "Yeah, Fletch?"

"Marion is going to need tomorrow morning off, too. She'll be coming in at noon." He looked at me. "Is noon good?" And then, without waiting for my answer, he turned back to Upton. "You can cover for her until noon, right?"

OMG.

Upton's face didn't change. Perfectly poker-faced. "Sure," he said. "That's fine."

And he went back into the office while I stood in shock. "What are you doing?" I squeaked when I was able to speak again.

"What do you mean, what am I doing?" Fletcher said, his brow furrowing.

"Marion getting off early, at request of Fletcher? Then Marion coming in late tomorrow, also at the request of Fletcher? Upton's gonna think…"

Fletcher blinked a couple times, then his face transformed into one of his charming, you're-at-the-center-of-my-world smiles. "And what's wrong with that?"

"Fletcher!" I straightened up and threw the bar rag onto the drainboard by the sink. "How am I supposed to… I don't want people to think I got this job because I am sleeping with the boss!"

Yeah, I know it's the 21st Century. But a girl's gotta still keep her pride. AmIrite?

Fletcher regarded me thoughtfully for a second.

Then: "Upton!"

Oh no.

Upton reappeared.

"Marion and I are not sleeping together," Fletcher said, his eyes not leaving my face. "Tonight is a business meeting. And Marion has requested tomorrow morning off for unrelated and personal reasons."

"Sure," Upton said. Face still unreadable. "Got it."

"So are we good?" Fletcher said to me in a quiet voice.

And then I made a tactical error.

I let myself actually meet his eyes. As in, look at them, directly.

At what they were saying.

Fletcher's eyes were brown. Light brown. And they were such intelligent eyes. So sweet. So pleading…

150

"I just want to talk," he said, his voice just above a whisper. "It's been so long..."

And you know where my head was going then.

That he was going to explain everything.

How he'd never gotten over me.

How after the young Prince had been parted so cruelly from his young Princess, he'd searched and searched, searched high and low.

But he hadn't been able to find me. And he'd finally given up (he needed an heir!) and married a Princess from the neighboring kingdom, and she'd turned out to be as evil as his evil mother, and now?

Now, he couldn't believe his luck, he'd found me again...

No. Stop it, Marion Flarey. Just stop it.

"Please?" he said to me, pleadingly.

And I straightened my spine.

I hardened my heart.

Because whatever fairy tales are, I'd seen enough to know how little you can actually trust them to play out in real life the way they do in the stories.

"Fine," I said. "Dinner. This once."

Because okay, I'd have dinner with him. But only because it would give me a chance to set some highly specific and rigorous guidelines with regard to his current and future behavior.

No way was I going to get involved emotionally or otherwise with a married man.

• • • • •

"Do you mind if we drive for a bit?" Fletcher asked as he pulled out onto the road in front of the brewery.

That was my first clue that "out to dinner" didn't mean grabbing a slice of pizza in Tibbs. Or a burger at Dingo's, Tibb's local watering hole.

So I felt my body stiffen in alarm, because I wasn't exactly looking forward to this, thank you very much, and the last thing I needed was a long, drawn-out evening versus a quick slice of pizza and an equally quick conversation that I would control, establishing that under no circumstances would Fletcher Beal and Marion Flarey become romantically involved.

Or sleep together.

Even though I felt a little warmth in the vicinity of my lady parts as that forbidden possibility crossed my mind.

Note to self. Gonna need to de-program my Pavlovian response to being anywhere near Fletcher Beal.

Steady, Marion. Focus.

"Uh, what do you mean," I asked. "Drive for a bit?"

He cleared his throat. "It probably wouldn't be a good idea for, uh, for me to be seen…"

"Ah, of course. The whole 'wealthy adulterer out on the town in Tibbs with his paramour' angle might not be great for business?"

"Marion. No. No. It's not like that. It's…complicated."

I sighed. Isn't it always? "Whatever, Fletcher. Pick a spot. Just, please, let's not be out too late. I told you. I have to be up very early tomorrow."

"We'll go to Cortland," he said. "That's not far. Okay with you?"

Not far.

Over an hour round trip.

But I'd started down this path, might as well finish. "Yeah. Sure. Fine."

And hey. Being annoyed would keep me safe, right? If I was annoyed, I'd be immune to the man. I'd be immune to the effect the man was having on places that I'd thought were probably atrophied, by now, like say the inner parts of my thighs and you need to get a grip, Marion, he's that incredible gorgeous *married* man.

21

He took me to a bar and grill in the middle of town. The kind of place with dozens of beers on tap and a menu geared toward college kids. Burgers and chicken wings and wraps and chili.

The kind of place where couples conducting an affair can slide into the dining room with their heads down and sit at a table along a wall and nobody will pay any attention to them.

Hopefully.

I ordered a chicken sandwich and a side salad. And an IPA, because frankly I needed a little bravery juice, and it didn't seem like the sort of joint where you do the wine.

Fletcher asked for an IPA, too. And then when the server left to put in our orders, he kind of leaned forward over the table. "Thanks for doing this."

I made a face. "Against my better judgement, you know."

"It's been a long time."

Ha. Where had I heard that before?

Oh yeah, that's it.

It's what RB had said. Exact same words.

How the heck did I end up in these situations?

I tried not to visibly squirm.

"What've you been up to?" he said. "Tell me everything. Starting with—"

"Starting with when you moved away?"

Ha. Take that.

But his shoulders slumped a little, and I felt a twinge of guilt. When will I learn to pull my verbal punches? Seriously, Marion Flarey. Stop it.

Because it hadn't been his choice, to move. To move away from me. It was his mother's doing. And they'd come from a different world. Tibbs is not a place of rich people, connected people, social climbers. So Fletcher had been on loan to us from the start, right? And of course his mother wanted to get him out of there before the place got ahold of him for real.

Before I got ahold of him for real.

The server returned and handed us our beers, and I lifted mine and said, "Cheers," and we tapped glasses and I took a deep breath.

Truce. Reset.

"Okay," I said. "I'll give you the run down."

He smiled. A sad smile on that beautiful face.

"It's not really all that interesting," I said. "I finished high school, obviously. Then went to college. Got a four-year degree. English degree. Then I wasn't quite sure what I wanted to do next, but since I have my thing about fairy tales, I thought maybe I'd go for my master's in folklore or something similar and maybe teach…"

I trailed off. This is the problem with telling people my life story. A. It's dull. And B. It's the story of how Marion Flarey can't seem to get anything quite right.

"A master's," Fletcher said, encouraging me. "Nice."

"Right. Only I, uh…I'm on a break from it. At the moment. I, uh, got nervous about the debt I was taking on and everything." I was avoiding his eyes, now. Looking down at the surface of the beer in my glass. Because I hadn't really thought this through and now my story had gotten to money. "Anyway, it seemed like a good idea to pull back and, you know. Take a little time, refill the coffers. You know."

Ugh. Because of course he didn't know. And so there I was, talking about my money problems, and money problems were completely alien to Fletcher, he must think… He must have been looking at me like, poor little Marion, struggling with her student debt, I wonder what that's like?

And good job, Marion, making a great impression on your ex-Prince.

So I suppose my next words were a bit rushed. I just wanted to get to the end. "And I moved to Rochester and I'm getting myself settled there. And then the folks called me up and asked me to come to Tibbs to help out with a couple things and, well. Here I am."

Ugh.

It sounded vague and stupid and I knew it.

"And how's your family doing?" Fletcher took another sip of his beer.

Wow, he had a way of looking at me that was so intense… *Focus, Marion.* "They're fine. You know. Same as before."

Not entirely true, if by "before" I meant fifteen years ago. Fifteen years ago, Winchell was still riding his MLM get-rich-quick scheme, Mom staunchly at his side. Ace was still a sweet little boy. And me and Candace were still friends although maybe not so tight as we were before because, you know. Puberty and realizing we had absolutely nothing in common.

But of course all I said was, "Mom's selling her pottery. And Winchell…well, you know what he's up to, right? That trucking thing."

"Right," Fletcher said. "That's how you got connected with the brewery."

I nodded. "Only I didn't know, at the time, you owned it."

Another potentially awkward line of conversation.

Fortunately, the server chose that moment to walk up and set our food down on the table. And she asked us if we needed anything more, and Fletcher asked for hot sauce, and she left again.

"And how's Candace?"

"She's good. She works in the office at the high school." I decided to omit the part about her leaving her husband. Let alone the soap opera about her son.

"And your little brother? Sorry, I forget his name."

"Ace?" I felt a flood of unexpected emotion, for some reason, and set my sandwich back down.

Fletcher picked up on what I was feeling, to his credit. Well. Maybe not exactly what I was feeling, but enough to know this was a bit of a painful subject.

"Sorry," he said. "I don't mean to pry."

"No, it's okay. You know he was always a bit…wild. Last any of us knows, he's out west. Vegas or something, I guess."

"Yeah." Fletcher made a face which I supposed meant he knew exactly what I meant, referring to my little brother as wild. Euphemistically. "But it's not a bad place to be, Vegas. Lots of jobs."

"Right."

I looked at my sandwich. And why did I feel so sad, suddenly, about Ace?

I really needed to eat. No matter how my stomach felt.

"So, your turn," I said. "What have you been doing with your life?"

And I picked up my sandwich, and at least it smelled good—chickeny—while Fletcher talked. He started with prep school, and then on to Yale (of course) and then he'd gone to work for his dad who owns some sort of investment firm, and then he realized he needed to get out from his father's shadow…

"So you re-connected with your father, then," I said. "That's nice."

"Yeah. Once I hit 21."

He meant: once he hit 21 and his mom couldn't run his life, anymore.

I thought about asking about his mother, but I decided it was a subject best avoided. And at least I'd put away a good percentage of my sandwich and most of my beer, so I was starting to feel a bit more settled.

And then Fletcher continued his story, focusing, the way men do, on business. First his dad had funded a little company that invests in start-ups. Then Fletcher had taken it over, and he'd decided to focus on breweries. He owned a handful of craft beer breweries, and then about a year ago decided to branch out into kombucha and hard seltzer.

"We have a little team of consultants, like Upton. They come in, set things up, establish best practices, that sort of thing." He paused. "You like beer, then? IPAs?"

"Sometimes."

He nodded. "Craft beer is more of an M&A play right now. You know. You try to get the brewery established as a national brand, lots of cachet or whatever, then offer it up to one of the big guys and cash out."

"Ah." I nodded. "Is that your plan with the kombucha place, too?"

"Oh no. No," he said quickly, shaking his head. "Well, maybe. But the objective there is a little different. You know, I always had special feelings about Tibbs…"

My antenna stood back up. Tibbs? Or…Marion Flarey, perhaps?

No. No. Do not go there! Do not go there… He is married. The man is married.

I refocused on what he was saying.

"It's about jobs, really. About finding ways to bring jobs into areas that need them."

"That's nice of you, Fletcher," I said. "Admirable."

He gave me a sharp look. I think he was checking to see if I was being sarcastic. I wasn't, though. It *is* admirable. Tibbs needs jobs. Every little town these days needs jobs.

But I was prepared to lob a little bomb over at him. And now was the time. "And of course, you're married," I said. "Got any kids?"

I took a good swallow of beer after that one.

"No kids."

I pretended not to care about those amazingly interesting words. In fact, on the contrary, I was not going to let him off the hook about the whole marriage thing. "And what does your wife do?"

"She runs a boutique in Manhattan. In Chelsea."

157

"Very nice," I said. Trying hard to really mean it.

"About her—" he started.

But I cut him off. "It's okay, Fletcher. Really."

I did not want the man to start talking to me about his marriage.

"Please, Marion. I just want you to know…I'm not 'that kind of guy.' I'm not—"

"Geez, Fletcher," I interrupted. "What exactly do you think is going on, here? We're not… This isn't a date."

He looked away and his cheeks colored up a bit, I could see it, even in the dim light of the bar.

And I was like, holy crap. He knows that, right? He knows that no way was this at all in the same universe as an actual date, right?

"Fletcher," I said. "If you think, for one freaking second, that…"

I didn't know how to finish. I really didn't. I stood up, pushing the chair back as I stood, and grabbed my bag from where I'd hung it on the back of my chair. Because I needed him to know. I needed him to realize I was perfectly capable of walking out of that place and finding some other way to get back to the dome, even if it meant I had to walk or hitchhike or hope some Uber driver would agree to rideshare me from Cortland to the middle of nowhere at 9:30 at night.

"Marion, please." He was standing up, too, and fixing me with a look of genuine shock and remorse. "Please sit down. I apologize if…if I've given you the wrong impression."

OMG how gorgeous he was…

I sat back down. "This'll sound old-fashioned," I said. "But I am not that kind of girl."

"Of course not." He sounded sincere. He sounded…anguished. If I'm being perfectly honest. "It's just that…it's just that…it's complicated."

That word again. Complicated.

"We can be friends though, right?" He looked up at me again as he spoke, and the look in his eyes was piercingly sad.

I heaved the biggest sigh of the night so far. "Yeah, sure, Fletcher. We can be friends."

"Because that's what we are. Old friends."

Old friends who have to drive 45 minutes to grab a sandwich, so nobody will see them together.

My phone buzzed and eternally grateful for the interruption, I fished it out of my bag. "Can we get the check?" I said as my fingers closed around my phone. "I have to be up tomorrow at the crack of freaking dawn."

And he looked around the room to flag the server while I swiped the phone screen to wake it up and oh, crap.

TweedleRoommateDum.

didn't u say u were getting ur shit out of the apt today

Oh. My. God. That idiot. She knew I'd requested a one-day-more extension and...

I typed as fast as I could. *no!!!!!! tomorrow. tomorrow morning*

Then a quick addendum:

first thing

Oh. My. God. Please, Tweedles, don't lose the plot now, please please please. Not when I am so close.

My books my books my books...

"Everything okay?" The server had already run Fletcher's credit card and he looked up, now, from signing the slip.

"Yeah, uh, all fine," I said in a false-sounding voice as I put my phone back into my bag even though what I really wanted to do was hold it in my hand until a Tweedle texted back.

There was no moon, that night. So the pitch black moonless night pressed in on the windows of the car as we drove back to Tibbs, everything around us black except for the beams of his headlights, and once in a while big pale moths swooped through the beams, and a couple of times Fletcher tapped the brakes because there was a big pale deer standing by the side of the road. And the last thing you want to do on one of those country roads in the middle of the night is broadside a deer.

"Everything okay?" Fletcher asked again because I kept checking my phone.

And then finally I got my return text. A little *k*.

"Yeah, everything's fine," I said.

And then we'd reached the dome, we wove back and forth up the driveway, and are you kidding me?

RB's truck?

What was RB doing there at this time of night?

"Thanks for dinner," I said in a false-sounding voice as I opened my door, and the overhead light came on and I avoided looking directly at Fletcher because if I saw that same pleading look in his eyes again I didn't think I'd be able to stand it.

And then I stood there listening to his car crunch down the switchback, and then he got to the road and gunned it and sped away.

Oh, gawd.

And of course the Weekes-Flareys hadn't thought to leave an outside light on, so I stood there for a moment in the dark.

I could hear the television from inside the dome. And voices.

I stood and listened.

I heard Mom say something. And Winchell…

But I couldn't hear RB.

Or Candace.

And I was gripped suddenly by an awful thought.

I looked over at the camper.

It was completely dark.

Is RB in the camper?

With my sister?

And what the exactly-in-hell was I doing?

Because if there was anything I needed less in my life than Fletcher Beal, it was this. Having to relive the whole Candace+RB thing.

And okay, so one of the things about fairy tales is that there are a lot of broken marriages and bad marriages and ended marriages. Because life is messy. And people make bad decisions. They jump to the wrong conclusions and ruin their lives and the lives of everyone around them. And so the stories play out, and the heroines and heroes learn their lessons and get to their happily ever afters.

But when you're living it, well, that's different. When you're living it, the messiness is all that you can see, all that you can know. Because life isn't a fairy tale, and I had no idea what lesson I was supposed to live or how to get to my HEA.

All I did know was that I didn't want to walk into the camper and turn on a light to see my ex-boyfriend and my stepsister doing the horizontal bounce-around on the day bed. Or worse yet, walk into the camper and before I could hit the light switch, trip on them! They were on the floor, doing it on the floor because they couldn't wait to get to the bed, they wanted their hands on each other so much, and cah-rash goes Marion Flarey on top of them. Breaking someone's collarbone again, probably. Which shows you that I couldn't trust Candace to, you know, put a sock on the door handle or something, and shouldn't I just accept that they were right for each other? That RB and Candace were a wonderful match, and Quill obviously worships his daddy, and it's not like I was in love with RB anymore. Right?

And all I wanted to do was go to bed, but how could I?

I turned toward the dome. Dragging my feet. Telling my stomach to just be cool, it was fine, if they're in the camper making baby Quill number two you can handle it, Marion Flarey. Somehow. You'll be fine.

I peeked in through the screen of the front door...

And: what a relief!

There they were.

All of them.

Mom, Winchell, Candace, Quill, RB.

All sitting there in a wonderful little Happy Home Tableau in front of Winchell's flat screen.

I could smell popcorn. They'd made popcorn!

"Hey," Candace waved at me when she heard the door open. "Come join us."

And I was so relieved that I actually hung out with all of them for a while. I ate a little popcorn and watched their TV show, telling myself that hey I didn't need to be up at four the next morning, only six, which was basically the same as sleeping in.

Quill fell asleep on the floor.

We were watching another Bachelorette.

Don't ask me why The Bachelorette seemed to be on all the time, isn't it a once-a-week show? And must be it was Candace's all-time fave. And as the wine began to ooze into the folds of my brain, I started thinking to myself about how, if I go back to finish my master's, maybe I could do some thesis about how in these reality shows they subliminally recreate fairy tale courtship rituals. Or maybe it's not subliminal, maybe it's overt, intentional. You know how the production people for these shows go out of their way to evoke exotic locations, and dress the Bachelorette in expensive gowns, and this whole thing about presenting the rose.

Thinking about the rose presentation reminded me that I needed to refresh the water in the bud vase in the camper. And again how weird it was that Winchell had given me that rose. How it echoed in a weird way the giving-of-the-rose ritual in the TV show, which then kind of creeped me out, and anyway Candace was Winchell's favorite...

Of course she was, she was his blood daughter. I was the add-on. The price he paid for getting Mom. And so of course Winchell would choose Candace, if it came down to it. Not me. Candace or Ace, my little brother. Mom's and Winchell's love child. Born when I was eight. Born the year Mom moved us into the dome.

Blood figures a lot in fairy tales, too. A lot of times it is magical. It talks. Drops of blood tell secrets that people want to keep hidden—like that they've murdered someone—or are used to do magic, like when the queen pricks her finger and drops of blood drip down and she sees them and wishes for a daughter with red lips. Red as blood.

Now we get blood-red lips with lipstick.

I was feeling pretty drowsy.

I stood up. "Well that's enough for me for one night," I said. "I'm going to bed."

"But there's fifteen minutes left," Candace said. "She still has to pick her next date."

"I'm about to fall over." I looked at the boy. "Want me to take him to the camper?"

"I'll carry him." RB stood up.

Oh, no.

"I can do it," I said, but it was too late and to be honest I might have looked a bit unsteady on my feet, standing up like that after an evening like I'd just had.

RB knelt and gathered Quill up into his arms.

The boy's eyelids fluttered but he nestled against RB's chest and fell back asleep.

"Thanks, RB," Candace said, her eyes still on the screen.

So. Okay. Not exactly a ton of sparks flying between them.

Maybe RB was there only to be with his son?

I held the door to the dome open for him, and then the door to the camper.

"Over there," I said, pointing to the day bed, and RB carried Quill over and laid him down and pulled a sheet over him.

"Night," I said, just above a whisper so I wouldn't wake Quill.

And RB sort of paused for a minute like he wanted to say something, but tell you what. The last thing in the world I wanted right then was a conversation with RB.

"Night," I repeated, but a little louder this time, and pointedly.

And it worked. He said, "Night," too, then, and left.

I watched through the screen door as he went down the concrete block steps and crossed the yard back to the dome, thinking to myself well, they're probably getting back together, but at least they can't have sex in the dome with my mom and dad right there.

And honestly, I needed to get to bed and get to sleep and get up on time and get my stuff from Rochester.

22

The good news is that since Fletcher had told Upton I needed the morning off, I didn't have to get up at four. I was able to sleep till six, which compared to getting up at four was almost like sleeping in, right?

Modified schedule: sleep till six. On the road by 6:25. Empty the apartment by 9:00. On my way to work at 11:35 to be easily on time for my noon arrival.

And why was the alarm on my phone so ever-freakingly piercingly loud?

Note to self. Find an alarm ring tone that doesn't cause muscles in jaw to spontaneously clamp into painful spasm.

Ugh.

I crawled out of bed, by which time I was already ten minutes behind schedule, so instead of showering I ran a wet comb through my hair and daubed my pits with a little more deodorant, wondering if I wasn't now colonizing the surface of the deodorant stick with microbiome critters that would soon be breeding a new, deodorant-resistant strain of super-stinkers.

I lurched out of the camper and up the slope to the dome, fumbled around in the grayish light to get the coffee started, pawed through the cupboard in a time-consuming but ultimately fruitful quest to find a decent travel cup—insulation being top consideration for a 2+ hour morning drive—slumped down at the table to wait for the coffee to finish brewing, poured coffee. Took a sip, scalded my tongue. Located truck keys on the counter (thanks Winchell), lurched back outdoors, yanked on handle of door not realizing it was locked (thanks, Winchell—not), rebound from tugging on un-responsive door latch caused me to loose balance slightly, sloshing coffee which thanks to inadequate design of lid splashed up into air and onto left hand, scalding hand to match tongue.

Unlocked truck door.

Climbed in.

Started engine. Sounded crazy loud in the morning air.

And I was finally on my way.

And then as soon as I got to the end of our road and started down into the valley, I hit fog. And it was thick. It was like driving inside a white blanket. I turned on my lights and drove at a crawl, hunched over the steering wheel with both hands gripping like it was a life preserver and I was about to drown, keeping the truck as close to the edge of the road as I dared because I really didn't want to wander accidentally into a ditch but I also didn't want some reckless idiot to come flying over a rise from the other direction and smash into me head on.

These roads, out there in Tibbs. They don't always have lines painted on them. They're country roads.

They aren't made to be driven in fog as thick as freaking cheesecake.

I finally emerged from the worst of it and reached the four-lane.

My coffee was, by then, tepid.

And I was way way WAY behind schedule.

Also, I forgot, in my calculations, that if I left Tibbs at six I'd hit Rochester at rush hour, and chances are someone has pulled off onto the shoulder which meant everyone else slows down causing a major traffic delay.

Seriously, people. You do not need to slow down to microscopically examine every detail of a car pulled off on the shoulder. It is a boring, boring object. Even more boring than the interior of your own live-in-this-thing-for-hours-every-day vehicle. I promise.

And then I noticed the analog clock on the dashboard and that could not possibly be the correct time? Little hand on the twelve and big hand at about 11:50?

Gah.

The boxes were heavy.

Why oh why do I collect books.

Back and forth, back and forth. I was hot and sweaty and vowing to never buy another book ever again in my whole entire life.

I'd allocated fifteen minutes to load my stuff into Winchell's truck. It took over a half hour.

I checked my phone and it was already down to 30 percent power and I hadn't brought my charger cable, and maybe I should stop at the CVS or somewhere to pick one up, but did Winchell's truck even have a USB port?

I crammed the last box into the truck bed between the pipes and the buckets of rusty tools and plastic bag of clay and other unidentifiable junk. I dropped my keys on the kitchen counter and texted the Tweedles.

apartment empty. keys inside

Okay. I should have felt relief, I suppose, as I sat for a second, taking another sip of my coffee, which was by then stone cold. Which brought out all the off-flavors you'd expect from store brand pre-ground coffee brewed in a 30-year-old drip machine.

I glanced at my phone again.

10:15.

I should really head back.

But wow I was so tempted to make a quick side trip to peek at my Tower. Because sure, it was in the wrong direction—west—versus Tibbs which is in the east. But if winning the Tower was my quest, wouldn't it be proper for me to rest my eyes, even for a moment, on my prize? The reason I was doing all this, the reason I was making all these sacrifices?

And I'd hurry. And maybe it wouldn't take that long.

I nosed Winchell's truck out into the morning commute traffic and a few minutes later I was in the Park Avenue neighborhood and turning down what would soon be my street, mine mine mine...

And there it was.

That beautiful Tower with its huge beautiful windows, standing in stately splendor at the corner of that beautiful old Queen Anne home…

I drank in the sight…

And checked my phone again.

Yikes.

I felt a little sick to my stomach as I pulled back out onto the street.

· · · · ·

Back on the highway. The hands on the dashboard clock had still not moved, apparently stuck in perpetuity, so I tapped my phone, breaking the law against operating a cell phone while driving but only slightly, to check the time.

Ugh.

It was already 10:37.

Seriously?

It occurred to me that Winchell's broken analog clock was obviously mocking me with its evil reminder of what time I was supposed to be at work.

I needed to phone Upton. I needed to tell him I was going to be late. On this, my mere fifth day of work. When I'd already been given the morning off by the boss who Upton hopefully did not believe I was sleeping with.

On the other hand, maybe Fletcher would be at the brewery, proving to Upton once and for all that my being late this morning was not because I was lingering with my boss's boss between luxurious satin sheets, somewhere. And as much as I hated to admit it, I could probably count on Fletcher to protect me from getting fired or whatever. So that was in my favor. Not that I planned to flaunt it. But I was being practical, here. And I really really needed the job.

On the third hand, my coffee had turned into a bladderful of pee with alarming speed…and there was a rest stop not far ahead.

· · · · ·

"Upton," I said from my safely parked truck. "I'm so sorry but I'm running late. I'll be there at one. I promise."

"Sure," he said.

He sounding annoyed but what could he do?

Hah.

I ducked into the service station and bought a Starbucks coffee and pulled back out and was back on my way, only now I kept my speed to the formerly-agreed-upon rate of only 7-9 mph over the limit, reducing chances of getting a speeding ticket to its usual low-risk level.

And sure, Upton would probably resent the fact that I was under Fletcher's protection, but so what? It wasn't as if I was going to keep the job long term.

And then something else occurred to me.

Today was payday.

My first paycheck was probably already direct-deposited into my bank account.

In other words, an amazing milestone day. A day that proved that Marion Flarey was Doing It. She was on track, exactly as planned, to make her next Venmo installment to Vicki against first month's last month's and security deposit. Only one more payment after that and I'd be moving into my lovely Tower.

And so I drove, headache completely gone now, yay, sky overcast but no rain in the forecast, the books in the back of the truck safe and dry, and I began to feel almost happy about life for the first time in I dunno how long.

And then...you know how sometimes when you're driving, you suddenly get a brilliant inspiration? Like something about the effortless way you're moving, the slightest pressure on the gas pedal and you're zooming, and the big semis rolling along in their glorious and mysterious business of transport, and the campers like big white turtles bolloxing up all the other traffic on their way to some glorious family holiday exploring our amazing national parks, and the guys with trailers hauling bass boats or four-wheelers on their way to some glorious boy-trip exploring our amazing public waterways. And the dark sedans with their sunglass-wearing drivers and suitcoats hanging in the back seat, sales guys on their way to make the deals of a lifetime, and the pimply teenagers weaving back and forth in their parents' cars on the way to a job interview at the Denny's up the road...

And you're sort of watching it all, driving defensively and everything, and your mind is wandering here and there, not really thinking about anything at all except what could that vanity plate on the car ahead of you possibly mean.

And then I had an idea so obvious that I couldn't believe its brilliance had never occurred to me before.

My mom's a clay artist.

She makes pots.

I could ask her to make me a Pot with a Golden Star.

Why hadn't I thought of that before? Doh! Doh!

I'd ask my mom to make me a Pot with a Golden Star, and I'd take that to Effie, and then Effie would have to grant my wish, and who knows how she did those things but she'd get the cat back.

And that's how I would make good on my promise to Quill.

23

I pulled into the driveway and parked Winchell's truck and ran into the dome and asked him if he would be driving me to work or if I could just keep the truck and drive myself (he said sure, keep the truck for the day, yay) and then I said, "Also, where's Mom?"

And he had no idea, but she obviously wasn't in the dome. And damn my phone was almost out of charge, I needed to remember to grab my charger before I left for the brewery, but first I ran back outside and around to the back of the dome to Mom's workshop.

I've mentioned she's an artist. So she's got this little shed around the back of the dome. Winchell built it for her not long after she moved in, I expect from salvaged lumber and windows, but he'd insulated it and painted it and it wasn't all that bad.

And that's where I found her.

Quill, too. He was sitting on an old kitchen chair in the corner of the shop. Giving the distinct impression that he hung out there often enough to feel pretty comfortable.

"Hi, Aunt Marion. I made a cat," he said when he saw me, and he jumped down and led me over to a bench along the back wall.

It wasn't bad. A little lopsided. But identifiable as a cat, for sure, albeit the color of brick red clay.

"Grandma says it has to dry, then she'll cook it in the kiln, so it will be hard and last forever, even if it gets wet."

There was a big kiln outside, next to the shed.

"Nice," I said.

I was looking a bit closer at the cat.

The reason it was lopsided is that it had only three legs.

Ugh. Way to restart the inner fountain of guilt, kid.

"Grandma says I can paint it, too," he was saying. Then he glanced at Mom and corrected his vocabulary. "It's not real paint. It's called glaze."

"You're lucky." I nodded with my lips pursed wryly, like I was a sage old adult, while in truth my aim was to deftly change the direction of our conversation before the boy raised a broader subject related to missing cats and related sad aftereffects. "Grandma never let us kids in here, when we were little."

"I did, too," Mom said. So she was listening.

"Not very often." I looked at Quill. "We were okay with that, though," I explained, defending my mother in the generous spirit of female careerists everywhere. "We knew it was her job. She needed to be left alone to work."

The walls were lined with shelves. She used them to store inventory. And I scanned them now, hoping that against all odds that I'd see a pot. With a gold star on it. So I could grab it and run up to Effie's tomorrow, and close things out on her bring-me-this-and-I'll-do-that story.

I frowned.

There wasn't a single pot on the shelf.

"What are these, Mom?" I asked as I peered at whatever-those-were lining her shelves.

"Wind chimes," she said.

"Ah," I said, like her answer made sense even though it didn't.

I picked one up. It was a flat disk with patterns cut into it. The patterns were glazed in deep colors, greens and blues and reds and yellows. And there were holes in the disk, and leather straps were run through the holes, and the straps were attached to what I realized now were the chimes: long unglazed clay rods.

I moved the disk so that the chimes tapped each other, clinking.

"Pretty," I said. "How long you been making these, Mom?"

"Few years."

"Hey," I said. "Okay if I hang one by the camper?"

Wanting an artist's art is the sincerest form of flattery.

"Sure. Help yourself," she said. She was bent over the end of the workbench, pressing a wooden modeling tool into the soft red clay of an unfired disk.

Then I did a double take on the windchime I was holding. Because I'd suddenly noticed something peculiar about the shape of the chimes. "Mom," I said. "The chimes. Are they...bones?"

Ugh.

Ever heard the expression, "to ask the question is to answer it"?

Because the chimes were bones, all right.

Femurs.

Little red clay femurs.

But Mom didn't exactly give me a straight answer. "They're whatever you want them to be," she said, without looking up.

Typical artist answer.

I put the thing back onto the shelf. Thinking to myself well okay, maybe they aren't really bones, maybe my mother wasn't making beautiful little wind chimes that were actually dangling bunches of bones.

But you're getting the idea, now, about my family. Right?

And I needed to get to work.

"So, uh, Mom," I said. "I was wondering. Do you have any pots lying around by any chance?"

"No. I don't think so." She looked up, distractedly, I could see her mentally reviewing the places in the dome where she might have stashed one of her old projects. "Maybe I have some around, somewhere. I haven't done pots in years."

She bent back down over her bench.

"Uh," I said. "So, could you, uh, possibly, make one? For me?"

She didn't look up. "Not really," she said. "The wheel's broken. What do you want a pot for, Marion?"

Are you kidding me?

I peered, now at her potter's wheel over in the corner. And suppressed a groan. Sure enough, the thing had been out of commission for a while. There were cobwebs hooking it to the wall and the surface of the wheel itself had been commandeered as storage space for tools and—oh gawd—were those more piles of little red clay femurs?

"What about a pinch pot?" I said. "Could you make me a pinch pot?"

"What's a pinch pot?" Quill asked.

"The chimes are selling real well on Etsy right now," Mom said. "And I have a show coming up." She reached for a jar of glaze. "If you really want a pot, I could do something next month."

Next month?

I wasn't going to be here, next month. Next month, I was going to be back in Rochester, living in my Tower.

And what was it about my family and Tibbs and all of this that made things so much more difficult than they needed to be?

I'll tell you what it was. It was that I'd succumbed to my past. Ever since I'd agreed in the first place to come back to Tibbs.

I looked at my phone. It had three percent charge and OMG, it was now 12:50 pm which meant that I was really depending on Fletcher to protect my job, and you know what? Depending on Fletcher to protect my job was another entanglement that I should have avoided at all costs.

This needed to end. I needed to put an end to my past reaching out and entangling me like this.

24

I pulled into the brewery parking lot, finally, at 1:14, i.e. only a short fourteen minutes after the one p.m. arrival time I'd promised Upton on the phone.

Fletcher's Audi was not in the lot.

I wasn't sure how I felt about that. Because on the one hand if he wasn't there, I wouldn't have to feel awkward and deal with the stress of trying to avoid him all day.

On the other hand, without him there, Upton might be mean to me.

So I did the smart thing. I pretended I was on time, even though I wasn't.

Upton was behind the bar.

"Thanks so much for being flexible," I said in my coolest and most professional tone of voice as I strode across the tasting room. "I had to drive to Rochester to get my stuff. Moving, you know. Traffic there was horrific. Tibbsters have no idea how great they have it, commuting around here!"

Bonus: he would now believe I was honestly relocating to Tibbs. Versus the truth, which was that I intended to cash out of my short-term seventeen-dollar-an-hour windfall in a few short weeks to move into my glorious Tower. I mean, apartment.

Upton, naturally, pulled out his phone and looked at it, making sure I knew that he knew that I had not made it by one p.m. But he didn't say anything. He disappeared into the back office and left me to manage the bar.

Perfect.

· · · · ·

Things were pretty slow for the first couple hours, and then around three oh joy oh rapture, in strolled an entire wedding party. They were on their way from downstate to the Finger Lakes, three carloads of them (each with designated drivers, yay) and they'd heard about how good our kombucha is (we'd been getting some very nice Yelp reviews, thank you, kind Yelpers) and I snapped into my best customer-service-behavior self, super attentive, fawning all over them so every time Upton peeked out to see how I was doing he could notice how terrific my customer-service skills were.

And when they finally left, laughing and happy and paired off two by two, there were a couple tens mixed in with the fives and ones they left on the bar.

I scooped up the bills and the change and dropped them into the tip jar, mentally tallying up my take for the week so far.

Ka-ching! Went my Tower fund.

And I started to feel like maybe this was going to work. Like—I did the math again—and are you kidding me?

I'd be able to Venmo that next $625 I'd promised. Like, tomorrow.

Worth a text to Teagan, don't you agree?

T! you won't believe this, am gonna send next chunk of $ tom!

And—because success breeds success—not ten minutes after those wedding party people left, what was that?

More cars?

I shoved my phone back into my handbag and my handbag back into the cupboard, and began collecting the glasses left over from the wedding party people and sloshing them, two at a time, down over the bottle brushes submerged in the sink and then dipping them in the disinfectant-treated rinse basin and then setting them on the drainboard to dry.

Thinking to myself that maybe things weren't as bad as they'd seemed. That maybe I really could carve out a temporary home in Tibbs without my past plaguing me all the time.

"Welcome!" I said chirpily as I heard the door open.

And then I straightened up, and...

Candace.

With a gaggle of other gals who I supposed were people from her office.

"Marion!" she says. "Here's my sister Marion, everyone!"

Of course my first instinct was to say something along the lines of, "What are you doing here?" but I controlled myself because, you know.

Tips.

"Hey, Candace," I said instead. "Who are your friends?"

"We're here for after-work cocktails," she said, rattling off their names, which I immediately forgot. But I smiled and complimented their hair, and they ordered tasters and cooed over how delicious all of the flavors were, except the ones they hated.

And I thought well, okay, so maybe once in a while Candace would stop in. That really wasn't so bad, was it? I could deal with her here as coolly as I deal with her back at the dome, and if she and her friends tipped okay it was a net positive for me, right?

They settled into their seats, smoothing their blouses and hanging their purses on the little hooks beneath the bar.

And then I noticed a big white Ford truck sliding into the lot.

Good, more customers!

I turned my attention back to washing glassware.

And a minute later a couple walked in, and I called out, "Welcome to Booch4U."

And the couple reached the bar.

And then:

"Marion Flarey," said the woman. "Is that you?"

25

So see how it worked? No sooner had I reconciled to having Candace show up at the brewery once in a while, and here it was.

Yet more People from My Past.

"Shari?" I said to the couple. "Alden?"

"Oh. My. God," Shari said.

Oh. My. God. I thought to myself. They are still together.

Shalden, we used to call them back in high school.

I circled around to the customer side of the bar for the obligatory how-long-has-it-been old friends hugs.

I noticed that he was wearing a gold band and she was wearing a diamond the size of a small planet.

"Wow," I said to Shari, "you look great."

And she did. But then she'd always looked great. Taller than me by at least five inches, and that long curly hair and that fabulous figure and her red polished nails that looked like they'd been done in a salon only btw there were no salons anywhere near Tibbs, which meant she'd either done them herself or had spent the morning in Syracuse or someplace.

She was dressed in an elegant white buttoned blouse and shorts and leather sandals and was wearing bangles with stones on them that were probably real gems.

"You look great, too, Marion," she said back.

Yeah, right. Scrawny little Marion Flarey with the flyaway hair that won't stay out of my face and my on-sale-at-Target V-neck tee shirt and my plain nails and alarming lack of jewelry.

At least I wasn't still wearing my mother's clothes.

"What brings you here?" I said, combining my best customer-service manners with a keen desire to understand what, in fact, might bring Shalden to a kombucha brewery on a weekday afternoon.

"Date night," Shari smiled, eyes moving smoothly from me to Alden and back to fully impress upon me the fact that he was Hers and Hers Alone.

Not that she had anything to worry about. I wasn't one of the girls who, back in high school, lusted after Alden.

I suppose Fletcher had immunized me against that.

Candace, on the other hand...

"You know we don't serve food," I cautioned Shari, thinking to myself ooh maybe they will realize they can't eat here and need to move on?

But Shari smiled. "We have reservations in Syracuse. We were hoping to say hi to Fletcher but looks like he's not around."

Oh gawd. "Haven't seen him today," I said, keeping my voice as natural-sounding as possible. Because okay, Alden and Fletcher had been buds back when Fletch was living in Tibbs, so of course they'd re-connect now.

Alden pulled a stool out from the bar and gestured in a gentlemanly way for Shari to sit. Which gave me time for a little pep talk. Like: okay, Marion. It's fine. Obviously Shalden is going to be parked here with you for a while and obviously they'd renewed their friendship with Fletcher, but you can deal with it. High school is ancient history and any friend of Fletcher is a friend of mine, and I'm sure they are very nice people, they were always nice people, and wouldn't it be nice to maybe have a couple friends in Tibbs, as long as you're here anyway. Give you someone to hang out with besides Candace.

Also they probably tip well. Notice how I was all about the tips.

And, speaking of Candace, she was now waving over at Shalden and saying hi. And they both said hi back although if I wasn't mistaken, Shari was a bit cooler toward Candace than she'd acted toward me.

"I'd like an 8-ounce of the lemon-thyme," Shari said as she settled daintily onto her stool.

I poured her drink, and then washed more glasses while Shari commenced to conduct a three-way conversation during which she was the only person who actually spoke.

"Alden. Seriously! Alden, can you please put your phone away for two seconds at least? He's always on that phone, you know, it's people from work, he's in sales, med device, I shouldn't complain, he's doing very well, they love him…"

I noticed that Alden didn't appear to be terribly chastened by Shari's scolding about his time on the phone. No doubt he'd long since learned to tune it out.

"…Alden, are you finished? Do you want the Mosaic hops thing? He likes the ones with hops. He's really a bourbon drinker, kombucha's not his thing, I enjoy a glass because it's so low alcohol, but of course we're doing it to support the place. We love that Fletcher opened the place. Tibbs needs the jobs, you know. But of course you know. When did you get back?"

Alden set down his phone on the bar. "Yes," he said. "Pint for me, Marion."

I'd been smiling and nodding throughout Shari's soliloquy, and now I nodded again and stepped over to the taps and poured Alden's drink, my mind running almost a bit too fast for me to keep up. Because okay, exactly where did things stand between Alden and Shari and Fletcher?

"So," Shari said as I set their drinks on the bar. "What do you think of our beautiful Fletcher?"

Our?

That was not a random "our." Because of course Shari knew our history—Fletcher and me—and how lovestruck I'd been, and the tragedy of our being torn apart.

Everyone in Tibbs knew.

What they say about small towns and other peoples' business is one thousand percent true.

"I don't see much of him, to be honest," I said.

Shari leaned forward in a "just between us girls" sort of way. "You know he's getting a divorce," she said.

"I'd heard something about that," I said. "Of course, we don't discuss personal business at work."

Oh gawd. Had Shalden really just exchanged glances just then?

I bent back down to wash some more glassware. "How about you two?" I said in my best hiya old friends plus excellent customer service voice. "What are you up to?"

"Well." Shari smiled. "We've got three little ones, of course."

Of course.

"Eight, six, and four. Two girls and a boy. The boy's the baby."

"Gonna be a ball player," said Alden.

Shari, ignoring him: "And we bought that big Gothic Revival just past the Tibbs four corners. You know the one, right? With the gables? The Moreland house?"

Okay, so, give me a break. Of course I know the house. It was like the stone house, you couldn't not know it, if you were from around here. Built in the 19th Century by the founding family of Tibbs, enormous, fabulous. Of course it was looking pretty shabby the last time I'd seen it seven or eight years ago, but...

It suddenly hit me.

The Moreland house? It had a tower. On the back.

Right? I was remembering that right?

OMG. I *was* remembering it right. I could picture it now, perfectly.

Shalden lived in a house with a Tower. Are you kidding me? Life is soooo not fair. That was a so-not-fair coincidence and I could NOT stand it.

Ugh.

Hang in there, Marion. Two-and-a-half weeks of this, that's all you have to put up with. Then you'll be outta here...

"Excuse me," I said with a nice smile, and went over to Candace's flock o' workmates to check on their drinks.

One of them ordered a pint and then Candace said, "Oh why not" and ordered another as well, and kind of smirked at me like "wasn't it nice of me to bring you business," which it was, I admit. Assuming they tipped okay.

I crossed back to the Shalden end of the bar.

"Alden has done an amazing job restoring it," Shari continued on about her house as if I'd never left. "It is positively gorgeous. In fact, we're having a party tomorrow night and you really should come by. Nothing fancy. Burgers and beer." She giggled and took a sip of her drink. "Or kombucha if you want. Will you come, Marion? We'd love for you to come."

Honestly, her chatter was making me almost dizzy. But I must have nodded because she said, "Oh good!" and told me what time to be there, and I warned her that I couldn't be there until after work and she was saying, "Oh that's fine."

And meanwhile what I was really thinking was whether their good friend Fletcher would be at the party.

I didn't dare ask. Because there was no way to ask without giving Shalden an extremely wrong impression. I.e. the impression that I cared one way or another. Which accounts for the kind of dizzy feeling because I swear, I wanted nothing to do with Fletcher. Nothing.

And then Shari, like magic, actually answered the question I hadn't asked. "I doubt Fletcher will make it. But you never know."

"He'd probably come if he knew Marion was there," Alden said.

I may have accidentally made a small choking noise in my throat.

"Alden!" Shari said, looking at me in alarm, and then at Alden in equal alarm. "What makes you think…?"

Alden shrugged. "I dunno. You were close with him, right, Marion? And he's going through a tough time, right now." He shrugged again. "I dunno. I just think he might like having a friendly ear. Ya know?"

Ugh. Was it possible that Alden knew about me and Fletcher and our not-a-date?

Ugh.

Shari, having apparently recovered herself, proceeded to redirect the conversation into a more reasonable track. "His wife is perfectly lovely," she said. "And to be honest, Marion, I'm not saying you would, you know, consider dating Fletcher, but if that has crossed your mind?" She lowered her voice. "You should probably guard your heart, as they say. I wouldn't be a bit surprised if they ended patching things up."

"Not if he's smart, they won't," said Alden, picking up his phone again.

"Really, Alden." Shari turned her face back to me. "Just be careful, Marion, that's all I'm saying."

Oh, I'm being careful.

"But you'll come to the party, right? We'll expect you. Bring Candace."

Oh, no.

"I'm not sure," I said.

But too late. Eagle ears over there had heard her name and her head swiveled immediately in our direction.

"We're holding a little party on Saturday night," Shari called over to Candace. "You'll both be there, won't you?"

"Just so happens I have a sitter!" Candace gushed.

"Oh, you can bring your boy if you want. Quill, right? It's a family-friendly thing. Nothing fancy."

"We'd love to come." Candace. Grinning ear to ear.

"I have to work," I mentioned again.

"Oh, just show up whenever you can make it," Shari said. "Oh, here's Upton, hi, Upton!"

More hand-shaking all around. Me, watching them because clearly there was this whole Tibbs social scene that I had not until this afternoon begun to suspect. Involving Candace as well, possibly, although I got the distinct impression that Shalden didn't normally socialize with Candace, which may account for her so quickly accepting that lobbed-across-the-barroom party invite.

And—I may have been imagining it—but it also seemed like Alden wasn't all that warm toward Upton.

So maybe the Shalden-Upton connection wasn't so much evidence of a Tibbs elite clique as the revolving satellite of Friends of Fletcher.

By then it was getting on toward dinnertime, and some more locals came in carrying pizza boxes and filling the room with the smell of tomato sauce and pepperoni.

And Candace's flock was getting happy, and I admit I kind of enjoyed, in a way, how Shari kept her eye on all the females. Because Alden had been a hunk back in high school and—receding hairline aside—he was still a good-looking man. You know, 6 foot 3, built, obviously took care of himself. And dressed all Urban Sophisticate, short-sleeve windowpane check shirt and perfectly cut slacks. Yeah, the kind of husband who exuded that triple charm: money, sex, and commitment. The kind of husband you'd want to keep a close eye on, if a single woman entered the room.

Which reminded me how completely single I was, and how long it had been since I'd even had a decent boyfriend prospect, let alone a Prince.

Ugh. Stop it, Marion.

I'd fix it. I'd find my Prince. As soon as I got out of Tibbs.

26

Home from work.

I still hadn't unloaded all my boxes from Winchell's pickup.

And naturally nobody was around, so I lugged everything into the dome without any help, and then as soon as I was done and rooting through the fridge for some cold cuts voila, Winchell materialized from the master bedroom, his hair sticking up on top and his face sleep-looking like he'd been napping.

He settled into his chair—one of those oversized faux leather creations that looked, after oh-so-many years, exactly as you'd expect an easy chair to look when it's spent its entire life supporting a guy who is borderline obese—and began flipping back and forth between one of several baseball games and a fishing show.

I sat in the couch with my turkey sandwich.

"That all your stuff?" he said.

"You and Mom said it was okay for me to store it here, for now," I reminded him.

"Yep. That's fine with us," Winchell said.

I swallowed a bit of sandwich. "Where's Mom?"

"In her shop. She has a show coming up."

"Yeah, she mentioned that. She said she does pretty well, selling on her Etsy shop, too."

"Yep," Winchell said.

A commercial had interrupted one of the several baseball games, so he flicked back to the fishing show, where a guy in camo was extolling the virtues of a lure that mimics exactly the gyrations of a badly injured but still delicious minnow.

And I suddenly had another inspiration.

Etsy.

Of course.

I could *buy* a Pot with a Golden Star.

I reached for my phone, but then stopped, because dealing with the interwebs on a tiny little phone screen is such a PIA, not to mention my tiny little screen was crisscrossed with toothpaste-enhanced cracks.

"Winchell, okay if I use the computer?"

It was an ancient desktop computer set up on a student desk along the wall. They didn't use it much, although sometimes Mom sat there for a little while in the morning, presumably to manage her Etsy-based wind chime empire.

So it was clearly operational.

"Sure. Go ahead," Winchell answered.

The desk was one of the ones that have painted metal frames and laminated blonde wood tops, and an opening in the front, which was stuffed with papers.

I cracked a knee against the frame when I pulled the chair in.

"Ow."

I took another bite of my sandwich while the computer booted up.

I was still waiting when I finished the sandwich. I mean, the operating system had been discontinued at least six or seven years ago, at that point. That's how old the thing was.

Then finally it stopped churning and the welcome screen came up, and I opened the browser and went onto Etsy.

Surely someone on Etsy had created a Pot with a Golden Star...

I searched, and scrolled, and changed my search term, and scrolled some more.

Damn it.

There had to be one, somewhere?

Try searching on planters...

The screen door clunked. Candace. Since there were no more boxes to carry.

"Whatcha doing?" She stood behind me, looking over my shoulder. "Shopping for more crap?"

"None of your business." I minimized the screen. "And do ya mind?"

"When are you gonna open that Cabernet I bought you?"

Ooh. Truth was, I'd completely forgotten about that bottle of Cabernet. "Where is it?"

I got up and she followed me to the kitchen, a path which now required that we circle around my piles of boxes.

"Here, I'll open it," she said, taking the bottle from me.

I felt a twinge of suspicion. "Thanks?"

She yanked the cork free and poured some wine into my glass. "So wasn't that nice of Shari to invite us to her party?"

"Right," I said. "Only no way am I going to a party at the Shalden's. Cheers." I lifted my glass.

"Aw, come on! I'm going. It will be fun. And aren't you dying to see their house? I've heard it is amazing inside."

Right. Because although on the one hand, I admit I was a tiny bit curious about their house, on the other hand if it was as beautiful and costly as all that, it kind of showed me up for what I was. The lowly servant class person. Lucky if I was permitted to peek around the doorway at the royalty twirling around the dance floor in their sumptuous finery.

And why did Candace bug me about everything all the time? "Thanks again for the wine," I said. "Now, if you don't mind, I'm gonna finish up over here..."

And she seemed to take the hint. And she'd noticed the television station. "Hey, Dad, okay if we switch to Married at First Sight?"

"The Braves just tied it up," he muttered and I felt a tiny bit of empathy all of a sudden, since clearly I wasn't the only one who had to deal with Candace trying to get me to do things I didn't really want to do.

I sat back down at the teensy desk, cracking my knee against it again in exactly the same place I'd cracked it before.

"Damn it," I muttered.

I scrolled some more...

Really and truly, nobody in the entire Etsy community had been gripped by an amazing and inexplicable compulsion to make for sale a Pot with a Golden Star?

I sipped a little wine, then a little more, hoping that the alcohol would kick in quickly because I needed something to offset my growing and increasingly sour attitude of resentment toward the entire Etsy community.

planter+star

Maybe that would work. Maybe the Etsy-community-member-of-my-dreams had made a Planter with a Golden Star, but simply forgot to tag it properly.

Ugh. No good.

There were about 50,000 Death Star planters, revealing to me for the first time that Star Wars aficionados apparently all have, in secret, greens thumbs and an abiding love for plants from planet Earth.

And there were planters with brown stars, planters with red stars...

There was a blue planter with a gold triangle painted on it and a blue star painted on the triangle.

Oh, so close!

I considered buying that one.

Hovered the cursor over it.

Took a sip of wine.

Would Effie accept it?

Grrrr.

Who was I kidding?

I could hear her. "Oh come on, Mayfly," she's say to me. "That's no Golden Star!"

Ugh.

I poured another few swallows of wine.

Hopeless.

I stood over next to the couch for a couple minutes. There was a gal on the screen sobbing about how her husband hadn't come home the night before.

"Fletcher at work, today?" Candace said, as if for some reason the bereft young wife reminded her of my long-ago ex-boyfriend that had been torn from my arms by his evil mother.

I pretended I didn't hear the question and returned to the desk, managing this time to sit down without jamming a kneecap.

I pulled down the browser history to remind myself what terms I'd searched on.

Brought back one of the first searches.

The simplest one.

Golden+star+pot.

And then… How could I have missed it?

There it was.

It was a glass coffee pot.

One of the retro Pyrex coffee pots like you see from the 70s or so, with mid-century designs stenciled on it.

And the designs were stars.

Some of them were black, but—I blinked my eyes, hard, just to make sure I was seeing it right—some of them gold.

So I'd been thinking a clay pot, like a planter or something. And my eyes had completely skipped over this little beauty.

I smiled.

There it was.

I'd show Effie. I'd play her game. I'd complete the task she'd set for me.

Kinda steep, at nineteen bucks. Plus tax.

But okay, nineteen bucks plus tax wasn't going to make that big a difference in how fast I'd be able to come up with the rest of the money for my beautiful Tower. Right?

I clicked on the icon and added the coffee pot to my cart.

And then I looked at the shipping costs.

And damnit. I really didn't want to wait 7-10 days for shipping. This cat thing needed to be fixed sooner rather than later, so that when I gave my notice at the brewery and fled back to Rochester and took possession of my beautiful Tower, I'd be doing so with my conscience nice and clean. Not that I believed that it was going to work. That if I showed up at Effie's with this coffee pot in hand, somehow she'd materialize Surprise.

But I owed it to the boy to try. Right?

So I winced and clicked on expedited shipping.

Ugh. The shipping was more than the coffee pot... It was close to fifty bucks once they added in the sales tax...

But the pot would arrive on Monday.

Fingers crossed tomorrow would be another good day for tips.

I stood up. "Okay," I said to Winchell and Candace. "Been a long day. Bedtime for me."

I noticed that the television was on the reality show instead of Winchell's ball game.

"And you're going to the party with me, right?" Candace said, looking up at me.

And I guess I was tired or something, or maybe she'd just worn me down, or maybe it was because I'd found that Pot.

Because I didn't say no. "Maybe," I said. "We'll see."

27

I lived to regret it, that I let myself give in a little bit about attending the Shalden party. Because the next morning, when I made my usual pass through the dome for my coffee, Candace brought it up again and kept going on and on about the house, and how she'd never seen it, and how everyone raved about the interior. And listening to her chat on and on, it was pretty clear that this wasn't about the house, it was about Shalden, the "it" couple of Tibbs, New York, and also that Candace knew damn well she'd never have been invited to that party, if she hadn't been sitting there in Booch4U when Shari invited me.

It was an opportunity Candace was determined not to miss.

She was actually planning to go shopping. To buy something to wear for the thing. Seriously. Outlet mall. Halfway to Rochester, she was going to drive. While RB took Quill fishing, again.

Oh, well. If the stupid party meant that much to her, I could stand it for an hour or so. I'd have a drink and ooh and ah about the house, and then I could coolly take my leave and be done with it.

And hour or so is all it would take.

So we agreed that Winchell would drive me to work, and Candace would pick me up at 9:00 and we'd go from there to the party.

"It might be 9:30 before I can get out," I said. Depending on how busy we got.

She made a face and I made a face back.

Not my fault, Candace. That's life.

"Well," she said. "I guess that will give me time to take a nap before I pick you up. Okay!"

• • • • •

It turned out to be another great day for tips. Upton had persuaded a BBQ food truck to come up from Binghamton and park in the Booch4U lot all day, and he'd pushed things hard on Instagram and Facebook. So he actually had to join me at the bar for a couple hours to keep up with the crowd. They were two-deep for a while, waiting for drinks. Which made me wonder if maybe Booch4U wouldn't be smart to hire more help. Upton was planning to move onto his next project pretty soon, and clearly there were going to be days when one person pouring wasn't going to be enough. And also of course in the back of my mind I was increasingly aware that I secretly planned to quit, and if they had someone else trained to manage the place, they wouldn't miss me.

But of course I couldn't mention that, and I pushed it out of my head before I started to feel guilty.

Pushed it into the back of my mind where I was also storing Fletcher.

And why hadn't he shown up again at the brewery?

Maybe he'd left Tibbs. Maybe he was back home, back in Manhattan.

With his wife.

A pop-up thunderstorm hit late afternoon. Total downpour. The noise of the rain on the metal roof was deafening and water came off the roof in sheets, and then one of the lightning strikes must have hit the weathervane. The crash was ear-splitting, and the lights blinked off for a few seconds, and a couple of the customers squealed.

Adrenaline rush, for sure.

And I was thinking, well so much for a record day at Booch4U. But then the storm passed, and the sun came back out, and the air was all sweet and clean, and the customers had bonded so they ordered more rounds. And then even better here came another little rush, and everyone was ordering kombucha and then heading to the food truck for paper plates of ribs and brisket and the place smelled deliciously like barbecue sauce.

And I smiled and grinned and nodded and poured and kept an ongoing mental tally of my tips.

And by six o'clock I'm thinking, Marion!

If you get these tips in the bank?

You can send Vicki the money today.

· · · · ·

Of course, the last thing Candace wanted to do was swing me by my ATM before heading to the party.

"Can't it wait, Marion?" she whined.

But I was not going to back down. No way, no how. Because Venmoing Vicki her next $625 chunk o' change would dispel any lingering doubts she might have about Marion Flarey's commitment to moving into that beautiful Tower. Apartment.

That next-in-line apartment candidate could go right where she belonged: the discard pile.

"No, it can't wait," I said firmly. "It will only take a minute."

So she drove to the outskirts of Tibbs, where a regional bank had a little brick office with a drive-through ATM. And she parked and I got out and stood in her headlights, depositing my tip money, and putting a little hex on the regional bank for charging me a $3.99 fee.

Greedy bastards.

And then I got back into the car and tap, tap, tap on my phone: off went the money to dear, dear Vicki.

So I was feeling pretty good as we wheeled around and headed back toward the middle of Tibbs.

Candace parked on the street. About five doors down from the Shalden house, because that was the closest she could get, their driveway was full of cars and there were cars galore parked on both sides of the street in both directions. And because the party was outside—lucky for Shari that line of t-storms had passed through so fast—we heard it as soon as we got out of the car. Music, some 90s hits Pandora or Spotify station from the sound of it. And people shouting and laughing the way they do when they've had a couple hours of social drinking under their belts.

And then we walked to the house, and I saw, immediately, that Shari wasn't exaggerating when she said they'd fixed it up. I mean, like I said, the last time I'd seen the place, it was looking pretty dumpy. The bricks were crumbling, and those lacy carved cutouts around the gables had gotten dry rot and were broken in places, and the plantings around the foundation were all overgrown and shaggy.

Now, I had to grudgingly admit, the place looked like something out of a fairy tale book or would have if there was such a thing as a fairy tale set in the mid-1800s. Immaculate. Enormous. Up lights on the front so you could see the immaculate paint job and the perfectly restored gables with their finials spiking up from their peaks, and the gorgeous pointed-arch gothic porch columns. And the lights inside were turned on which showed off the gorgeous pointed-arch windows with their leaded glass panes.

I refused to look toward the back of the house. Where the Tower was.

We threaded through the cars parked bumper-to-bumper in their driveway and reached the back yard.

It was strung with party lights. The air was kind of humid like it gets in that part of the world after dark on summer nights when there's been rain, which meant that the lights cast a serious glare. I couldn't make out anyone's face and was suddenly, inexplicably glad that Candace was there so that I could mask my nerves by pretending she and I were buddies.

Ugh. Nothing worse than walking up to a party that's been going on for hours already when you don't know anyone who's there.

Then Shari must have spotted us.

"Marion!" she said, striding over. "Candace. You made it!"

28

Shari, like fine hostesses everywhere, fetched us drinks, first. She walked us over to a table set up under a party tent along the back of the house, and I asked for a vodka soda because if I was going to medicate myself I might as well go for the hard stuff. And she gave me a generous pour, too, Tito's, in a plastic cup and then squeezed a lime into it from a little bowl on the table. Me, meanwhile, looking around surreptitiously because of course I'm thinking is it possible Fletcher is here? And telling myself of course not, don't be silly, and you don't want to see him anyway, Marion...

"Ready for a tour?" Shari chirped as she filled a plastic wine glass with Chardonnay and handed it to Candace.

"Absolutely," I said because you can be sure Shari was dying to show off her house, and also I was becoming increasingly nervous, standing there, that Fletcher was going to emerge without warning from the impenetrable curtain surrounding us, that mix of glarey white light and impossibly dark shadow, and the last thing in the world my nerves needed was to find myself face to face with *him*.

Ugh.

Whose idea was it to come to this party, anyway?

"This way," Shari said. "We'll go in the front door, so you get the full effect."

Phew. "Front door" meant away from the backyard which meant away from the party guests.

And maybe he wasn't even there.

Most likely he wasn't even there.

· · · · ·

So Shari led us into her house and… Okay. In fairness to Shari, it was incredible.

Stepping inside was stepping into a story. How Once Upon a Time, Shalden bought a huge, partially rundown but salvageable old house that had been built by the town founder in what was, at the time, a bit outside Tibbs proper but as the town took off it became part of the village. And such a shame it had fallen into partial disrepair but hooray! The Shalden had always adored it and they probably spent too much to buy it, but hey, if they had to do it all over again, they would still jump at the chance.

And meanwhile Shari was walking us around, pointing out as she did all the work she and Alden had done, layering the story I'd built in my head with her own little stories, the kind people tell on tours like this. About how awful it had looked when they started (that entire wall was ready to collapse; you should have seen the carpenter ants, it was horrible, I had nightmares for weeks; they had to jack the foundation up in that corner to rebuild it) and how as soon as they pulled this apart or that off they discovered things were in even worse shape than they'd realized and were going to cost even more to fix.

And Candace and I were oohing and ahing, of course. And it really was extraordinary. High ceilings, polished oak floors in the foyer and the library a.k.a. home office and black and white tiled floors in what Shari called The Grand Room. Tiled, Shari told us, because the Moreland family was so rich, they could afford tiles.

Who knew?

We paused to admire the huge wooden mantle over the fireplace with its Gothic arch motif. Shari pointed out the furnishings, told us stories about how they'd found each piece. Massive furniture to fit the space, some of it antique but a lot was modern re-interpretations, because have you ever sat on a Victorian-era chair? Giggle giggle.

She led us next to the kitchen, mentioning apologetically that you can only take the restoration thing so far, with three kids you need a modern kitchen. But it had one of those stamped tin ceilings.

Right, apologize for a kitchen with granite countertops and stainless-steel Viking appliances and pendant lights with opalescent shades hanging like pearls from the ceiling, because it's not all vintage 19th Century.

Ooh. Ah.

We walked to the front of the house again, Shari ahead, pointing at the art on the walls now, too, "Do you believe we got our hands on this piece from the Hudson River school? The appraiser says it's museum-quality."

And the more I saw, the more I was thinking: there's another story playing out here, and I'm not sure exactly what story but I know what part Marion Flarey is playing: the goose girl. Meaning, the impoverished but dignified gal in the ragged clothes who lives out in the shed with the geese and the chickens and the goats and the milking cow—goose girls smell kinda ripe btw—while inside the Moreland house, Shalden argues about whether to buy and refurbish the obscenely expensive antique tufted settee or merely invest in the obscenely expensive reproduction tufted settee and be done with it, and then jumps into their expensive motor car to attend the art auction because you can't have too many Hudson school paintings. And one has to think it's the sort of art Caleb Moreland would have hung here, don't you agree?

I was about to interrupt with something about how goose girls are incredibly content, watching butterflies and sparrows from their comfortable straw beds in the shed.

But I caught myself.

And Shari was still talking. "Would you like to see the upstairs, too?" she asked, and I opened my mouth to say "no" but Candace answered "yes" and I lost my vote in the matter.

We started up the stairs. Me trailing my hands over the smooth wood of the handrail and thinking: sheds are only one story. Not two.

And then into the bedrooms, the kids' rooms and then the master (another fireplace in the master bedroom, of course) and there it was.

Figures.

The Tower was in the master bedroom.

Of course.

And they'd knocked down the wall between so that the bedroom extended into the Tower, making the Tower an alcove furnished with cushioned benches. A reading nook.

I walked over.

"Beautiful, Shari," I said, temporarily forgetting that I was goose girl and should speak only when spoken to.

The three windows in the tower were enormous. They started at the floor and reached almost to the twelve-foot ceiling. Gothic arches, naturally, with leaded panes in a diamond pattern.

Enchanting.

I stepped up to one of them to look out.

Of course I did.

That's what you do, in a Tower.

The party was stretched out below. And since the strung lights crisscrossing the yard were now pointed away from my eyes—pointed down—there was no glare. I could see everyone perfectly. Well, the tops of everyone's heads. The baseball caps and French knots and bald spots. I could see the drinks in their hands and their movement as they got up and walked around and found a chair and sat down, and there was a table I hadn't noticed before, the food, bowls with the remains of salads and a platter with a few burger rolls, plastic sheet over them to keep them from drying out, and...

An upturned face.

Someone was looking up at me.

OMG.

Had he seen me?

I stepped back quickly from the window, my heart hammering.

"Oh, is that Fletcher I see?" Shari had joined me and stood now in the spot next to the glass where I'd just been standing, only she was smiling and waving. "How nice he could make it."

And I felt Candace jab me with her elbow, and I shook my head violently and mouthed a "NO" at her that would have been on the violent end of the spectrum as well, if it had been accompanied by actual sound.

"Shall we go down and say hi?" Shari said, turning away from the window.

And what could I do?

I couldn't just pretend I needed to use the bathroom and then slink away from the party unnoticed.

I was stuck.

I had no choice but to go back down to that party and find some way to pretend all was perfectly fine while I avoided the one guy I really, really needed to avoid, and somehow the evening would finally be over and I could escape.

"We'll use the back door," Shari said. "Through the kitchen."

And then a moment later as she held the door open and I stepped out into the cool air, "Marion," she breathed into my ear. "Just remember what I said. Guard your heart."

Like I needed any encouragement on that. Like I had any intention of getting close enough to Fletcher Beal that heart-guarding would even be necessary.

29

Right. So much for my plan.

He was waiting for us, of course.

For me.

Or at least, that's what the little voice in my head was whispering.

"Marion," he said.

"Hi, Fletcher." I was trying to sound natural and I think I was going a pretty darn good job. "You remember my sister, Candace?"

"Of course."

"Oh, I've seen Fletcher around town, ever since the brewery opened," Candace said. "Right, Fletcher?"

He smiled.

His eyes were on me.

"Candace," Shari said. "There's still plenty of food left..."

No! Please don't! Please don't leave me here alone with... Weren't you just warning me to guard my heart?

Aaaand there they went. Shari dragging Candace by the arm.

Leaving me with...him.

I snuck a look.

And oh! My heart! He was a delicious-looking man... And why was he looking at me like that?

"I knew it was you," he said. "Standing up there, in the window. Come here."

And now he was steering me by my elbow, guiding me past the other partygoers, past the lawn chairs, past the last of the strung lights, across a bit of dark grass and then we reached a little garden on the far side of the lawn. I could make out a semi-circle of flagstones with rose bushes planted in an arc along the outside.

And a bench.

But we didn't sit. Instead, he turned and pointed back at the house. "See?"

I looked back, looked up. The arched windows in that Tower were amazing, tall, glowing cut-outs of warm light against the dark brick and the black sky now pricked with twinkling stars.

"You were standing right there. Marion. You looked... You looked exactly like one of those princesses you always talked about."

"I'm wearing jeans," I said in a voice that sounded wispy and strange, like it had gotten stuck in my throat.

Because everyone knows that wearing jeans cancels out a girl's princess-ness.

"You could be wearing rags and I'd know who you really are."

"Fletcher," I said.

I don't know what I was planning to say next. A thought was forming, for sure. Something cliched but true. Like, "you know this is never going to work," or, "what's in the past is past."

But we'll never know. Because whatever words I was trying to string together in my swirling head, the man knew exactly what I was really feeling. And he was Fletcher. And Fletcher being Fletcher, he acted on what he knew. He took a step toward me—invisibly and instantaneously, thanks to his sexiness superpowers—and then one arm was around my back and the other one was cupping the back of my head, and I was melting into the world's most incredible kiss.

"Marion," he breathed a moment later. "I have been trying to tell you. I have never forgotten you. I have never gotten over you."

OMG.

That kiss. So familiar—how many times over the years had I re-imagined Fletcher's kisses?—and at the same time unlike anything I had ever experienced, that intoxicating scent of his skin and his breath, the bewitching touch of his warm lips brushing mine and then joining mine, searching me, pressing me gently into him…

Fletcher…

Fletcher…

I've never gotten over you, either.

Yep. That's right. One little kiss and I forgot everything. Forgot Shari's warning. Forgot my own precious promise to keep my heart securely locked away and out of reach.

Forgot everything except my first Prince.

Our lips parted.

I caught my breath.

We were standing so close. I could see his eyes. They seemed lit up, like there was a light inside them shining out…

Shining into mine…

I ran the tip of my tongue over my lips.

I opened my mouth.

"Fletcher," I whispered.

"Fletcher!"

Huh?

A woman's voice.

Like an immediate echo of my own, only: yikes.

Her voice was…loud.

Shrill.

And it was coming from the other side of the yard.

Our heads turned toward the direction of the voice, and "Oh, shit," Fletcher said.

"There you are!" came the voice again, and now a woman was striding toward us, emerging from the glare of the party lights.

I swear if you were making a movie and wanted to depict a Dark Fairy materializing in the night you could film it just like that, the effect was spot on.

And I'm thinking, it can't be.

But it has to be…

"It's my wife," Fletcher muttered, and his arms fell away as he took a step back.

30

I got myself out of there, somehow.

Sputtered a lame, "Nice to meet you," and, "really must be getting home, have to work tomorrow," to the stately woman with the glowery eyebrows who was married to Fletcher-who'd-just-kissed-me and who had almost certainly seen the kiss.

Fletcher, shifting his weight from one foot to the other, clearing his throat, "Marion works at the brewery, couldn't run the place without her."

OMG.

I was mortified.

I was beyond mortified.

I was the goose girl who just got caught kissing the prince, and this was no fairy tale which is good on the one hand because I would likely escape with my life but very, very bad on the other hand because no, folks, I am NOT a goose girl who is actually a princess in disguise.

I am an actual goose girl.

I kind of backed away, of course, during the lame "nice to meet you" business. And then I turned and ran. Figuratively speaking, actually more like walking as fast as I could without literally running. And thinking to myself, just get back across the yard without tripping,

Marion Flarey. That's all you have to do. Do NOT trip, do not face plant, just find Candace and…

Candace was sitting on a lawn chair not far from the food table, empty paper plate on her lap, talking to a heavyset man I'd never met. I caught a little snatch of their conversation, they seemed to be agreeing whole-heartedly about what a terrific thing it was that Shalden had saved this old place.

"Candace," I said. "Need to talk to you." I nodded at the man. "Can you excuse us, please?"

Goose girls, even very distressed goose girls, do remember their manners.

And thankfully Candace didn't argue. I suppose she didn't dare. I suppose despite my excellent manners I sounded a bit unhinged. She stood up and set her plate on the chair, and I grabbed her arm and yanked her through the partygoers, *nod nod smile smile,* and around the corner of the house and threading back through the cars parked bumper to bumper in the driveway.

She hit her brakes. Dug her feet in and broke loose from my grip.

"Marion! Wait a minute. Are we leaving? We just got here! What is going on?"

"We gotta go," I choked out the words.

"Oh my God. What happened?"

"I don't want to talk about it. Please."

I turned and started walking out to the street, her following me.

I waited by the passenger door of her car and she finally caught up and unlocked the doors, and I got in, and then she got in.

"He's married," I said to her. "Married."

I slouched into the car seat, staring at the black, black world outside.

"And I don't want to hear the name Fletcher Beal ever again."

31

Candace went to the camper to check on Quill.

I didn't go with her. I was still shaking a little and felt adrift and lost and was sure I wouldn't be able to sleep for hours. So I headed the other direction, to the dome.

Inside, Mom was emptying a plastic bucket into the kitchen sink.

Apparently, there was a leak in the roof, and she'd put a bucket under it earlier when the storm had come through.

And then I saw the boy. He wasn't in the camper, asleep, like Candace had expected. He was on Winchell's lap, surrounded by popcorn kernels and holding a bowl of what had been ice cream and staring at Winchell's baseball game. And I thought, ooh boy, Candace was already pissed that I'd made her leave the party, she'd be livid when she discovered that Grandpa and Grandma hadn't put her son to bed like they were supposed to.

And sure enough, a second later she stormed through the door, and at first her face was anxious but then she spotted Quill and yelled, "Mom! Dad!"

But because I felt bad for spoiling her evening, I intervened and played peacemaker and told her I'd get him ready for bed so she could just relax.

And she scowled but relented, and I led the boy to the camper.

And he asked me to read him a story.

"Well, it's late." I wondered how much Candace would mind. "One story. Put on your PJs."

And I stepped into the tiny little bathroom and flicked on the light, and: my face. My eyes!

I looked like hell.

I smeared make-up remover over my eyes and rubbed it around, then splashed my face over and over with cold water—and it's cold too, it's well water—in the hopes that it would calm my eyes and they wouldn't look so swollen and red.

So that took a couple minutes, so by the time I'd finished Quill had already fetched a book and gotten up onto the bed, plumping the pillows up to make a backrest like he'd seen me do.

And maybe—just *maybe*—I was a little bit glad he'd asked me to read a story. I mean, it was a distraction, right?

And I needed a distraction.

I looked at the book he'd picked. The Grimm, again. He liked the Grimm.

But I wasn't in a Grimm kind of mood. "We're gonna read out of a different book, tonight," I said, taking the book out of his hands and opening the cupboard at the foot of the bed.

And I took out my Norton editions fairy tale collection—the costs-its-weight-in-gold thing I'd bought when I was a student with student loan money—and flipped to *The Merchant*, by Giambattista Basile.

Because I wanted a story with some bite to the language.

"Once upon a time there was a very rich merchant," I began, and lost myself in the reading for a couple of minutes. It's a funny scene, the first scene, the conversation between the merchant and his son, Cienzo, after Cienzo makes the unfortunate mistake of bashing in the head of the king's son…

Yeah. Bite to the language, like I said. Basile stories tell it like it is. Basile stories are not, strictly speaking, fairy tales. They are satire. Which means they are reminders that fairy tales aren't real.

I skipped over the part where Cienzo soliloquizes about leaving Naples, since I figure that bit would be boring for Quill. Although it's quite hilarious, Basile lays it on so thick. Saying good-bye to all those different kinds of food. Funny. But it would have bored Quill, so I skipped ahead. Which got us to the forest. Cienzo going his way and evening came and he arrived at some woods...

And then Quill, who had been very quiet and attentive until then, broke in with his first question. "Aunt Marion," he said, putting his hand on the page to show that I was to pause reading for a minute. "Why do fairy tales always happen in forests?"

"We talked about this one other time," I answered. "They don't. Some of them take place in cities. Or castles. Or near mill ponds..."

I trailed off because I had just noticed the word "tower" a couple lines below the sentence I'd just read.

Argh.

I'd forgotten there was a scene in this story that took place near a Tower.

Argh.

Too late to pick another story, though...

I started reading again. Got as far as the place where Cienzo finds the gnomes' treasure but instead of splitting it half and half with the owner of the Tower says, "You can have it all" and walks away.

And Quill piped up again. "Why'd he leave the treasure?"

"He knows he's better off without it," I said grimly. "Sometimes it's better to just walk away from something even though on the outside it looks valuable."

"Oh." He didn't sound convinced.

And naturally, the very next thing Cienzo does in the story is arrive at yet another forest, this one "so gloomy it made you want to writhe," a sentiment to which I could certainly relate at that particular moment.

"See?" Quill said. "It's a forest, again."

I glanced down at him. And he looked up and...he was smiling?

The kid was teasing me.

My re-hardened heart softened a wee bit.

"Okay," I said. "I'll give it to you straight, kid." I took a breath. "Forests are a symbol of the unknown. And especially when they are thick, wild forests, they are places where things can hide. Bad things, like man-eating wolves and bears, and evil witches, and gnomes. And giants." I wondered briefly in the back of my mind whether Quill believed in witches and gnomes and giants. "Although all those things aren't real," I said. "They're symbolic, too."

He didn't seem particularly bothered. He was looking at the page and nestled up against me, his bony little shoulder tucked under my arm.

"So in fairy tales," I continued, "forests represent times in our lives when we have to face unknown, hidden dangers."

"There aren't any wolves in *our* forest," Quill said.

"No, there aren't. Although there used to be in the olden days. Now we only have coyotes."

"Mom says a coyote is big enough to eat me if it wanted to. If I see one, I'm supposed to yell for help."

"I suppose so."

"Are you afraid of coyotes?"

"No," I said. But the truth is I wouldn't want to run into a pack of them, if I were alone in the forest at night. Just saying.

He'd looked up at me again, like he does, watching my face while he asked his question to make darn sure I answered truthfully. "Are you afraid of ghosts?" he asked.

Ghosts. Right. Like the kind that haunt you when you fell in love with a boy when you were fifteen and thought you were over him and suddenly everywhere you look a translucent image of him rises in front of your eyes?

"No," I answered nervously. "I don't believe in ghosts."

He shook his head impatiently. Like I hadn't answered his question. Wtf?

"I didn't say do you believe in them," he said. "Are you *afraid* of them."

I stared.

It had never occurred to me before that maybe you might not believe in something, but still be afraid of it.

"I guess I am, come to think of it," I said. "To be perfectly honest. Yes."

"Then you believe in them," he said triumphantly.

The little imp.

"Never mind about ghosts," I said. "Can we please finish the story? You're already up way past your bedtime. Your mother is going to holler at me."

I started reading again, while in the back of my mind I'm thinking holy moley.

I believe in ghosts?

I got to the end of the story, which being a Basile ended with a proverb.

"It is the crooked ship that goes straight to port," I read.

And Quill looked up at me, his eyes all lit up, and laughed. And then climbed down off the bed and skipped away.

Leaving me with my ghosts.

32

Sunday.

Sundays are not a day off, when you work at a kombucha brewery and tasting room. Quite the opposite. When you work at a kombucha brewery and tasting room, Sundays are a day when you can expect to work a full shift, serving loads of happy smiley people as they tumble into the door with their friends and wives and husbands and kidlets and parents and cousins.

And wives.

So if you've ever been emotionally involved with a guy at work—or to be more precise, The Absolutely Wrong Guy At Work—you'll know exactly how I felt when I crawled out of bed that morning.

"Dread" doesn't even begin to get it.

"I can't do this," I whispered, sitting on the edge of the bed. "I can't do this."

• • • • •

I took a walk. To clear my head and put courage into my heart. Up the road, past Effie's.

Thought about dropping in to see her but decided that what I really needed was time alone.

So I trudged along the road.

A car passed. I raised my hand in a quick wave because that's what you do to every single car on a country road like ours.

I was thinking about fairy tales.

I was thinking, okay, suppose there is a lesson for me here, one that I am extraordinarily equipped to learn because of my lifelong lesson of fairy tales.

Trudge trudge trudge.

And for crying out loud, was that a rain drop that just hit my face?

I looked up and noticed for the first time that the clouds overhead had that heavy look they get when they are way too full of water.

And I thought, okay. Fine. I'm going to get soaked, then.

Bring it on.

Trudge trudge trudge.

Raindrops hitting the pavement now, making little dark marks that soaked in and disappeared almost immediately because the pavement was so warm.

Trudge.

Rabbit ran across the road.

I was thinking about beasts.

Fairy tale beasts.

Like in Beauty and the Beast, which is a story you know. So you have probably thought about one interpretation of the story: that it is about how in the olden days, when you have a woman who is young, unexperienced a.k.a. virginal, and she finds herself suddenly betrothed to a man—it's the olden days, she's in her young teens maybe, creepy by today's standards, but leave that aside for now—and think: What if he was a manly man?

You know. Beard and gruff and swords hanging from his belt.

Well it would have seemed pretty horrifying. To the woman. Like here's this guy. I hardly know him. And he's big and hairy and scary. So how do I know he'll be nice to me? How do I know he won't beat me up or worse?

Which of course was a real possibility. Probably all too real.

But what the story says is, look, it's possible this man is a Beast, but it's also possible that he's actually a gentle and mannerly Prince. That under that beastly façade, there's a really nice guy. Give it a little time.

But in my story—my flarey tale—what if the opposite were true?

What if there was this guy, call him Fletcher Beal, who on the outside was a gentle and mannerly Prince. Handsome, excellent dresser, wealthy, and a most excellent kisser, as I had so recently been reminded.

But under that princely façade?

You guessed it.

A Beast.

Trudge trudge trudge…

A Beast. Not in the hairy, sharp-toothed wild boar meaning of the word, but in the moral sense. The sort of Beast who gets married, but then the minute he sees an old girlfriend decides he loved her and not the wife all along. And then shows up at a party and tosses out some lines he probably practiced earlier in front of the mirror, and then kisses the old girlfriend, and then when he gets caught kissing the old girlfriend jumps back like he'd been zapped, looking guilty as hell, posturing like oh, no, nothing at all was going on here, when his wife sure as hell knew exactly what she'd just seen with her own two magnificent flashing eyes.

It started to rain a bit harder.

I turned around. The pavement was cooling off, so the rain wasn't evaporating as quickly, and the pavement was starting to look wet.

Trudge trudge trudge.

And it seemed to me, my flarey tale was a more likely candidate as Important Life Lesson in today's day and age, when we women are fully grown adults before we get married and men aren't running around in armor and swords and unwashed underwear and food between their teeth.

Beware the true Beast, girlfriends! The Beast who looks like a Prince on the outside, but on the inside, all he wants is to sink his teeth into your poor, unguarded heart.

OMG it was raining hard by the time I got back.

The tree trunks in the forest had turned black from the wet, and the leaves were dark green and flopping downward with the weight of the rain so that water poured in little streams from their tips.

And the little rivulets running down the driveway were now full of water, water cascading in streamlets between the stones Winchell had dumped on the driveway to fill in the washed-out spots.

I got to the camper.

Candace had shut the windows, so my bed was dry. Thank you, Candace.

I toweled my hair.

I changed into a dry set of clothes.

My only hope was that the Beast would feel enough shame to stay away from work.

· · · · ·

No Audi in the parking lot.

Phew.

I let myself in the back.

Tiptoed in. I dunno why, I guess in my mind I was thinking "hide from Fletcher." And my tiptoeing must have been extremely effective, because when I passed the office Upton looked up, startled.

"Geez, Marion," he said. "I didn't realize you were in."

"Sorry! I'll be up front."

I went to the tasting room and flicked on the lights and the sound system, then stood a while looking out the window.

It was raining pretty hard again. The puddles in the parking lot were sloshing from the impact of the raindrops.

And the lot looked so, so empty.

It looked like it was settling down into being empty for a long, long time.

So different from the day before.

Ugh.

I wanted to be busy.

I wanted to not think, and I wanted the hours to go by as quickly as they possibly could.

Upton seemed to feel it, too. All afternoon he kept pacing from the office to the bar and from the bar to the front door. He'd stand and look out at the rain for a few minutes, then turn around and come to the bar and straighten the stacks of cardboard coasters for the fiftieth time that day.

"Enjoy the party last night?" he asked when the stack of coasters at the far end of the bar were at long last really and truly and impeccably straightened.

"Party?"

How had he known I was at the party? He hadn't been at the party, had he?

But I recovered myself. After all, what with the glarey lights and me all nervous about Fletcher maybe Upton was there, and I'd just missed him.

"Uh, it was great. Shari's and Alden's house is beautiful," was my half-stuttered answer-not-answer. "They did, uh, an amazing job. Restoring their place."

Upton nodded like he wasn't really listening.

Which was probably a signal from somewhere—my fairy godmother, if I'd had a fairy godmother—for me to let the subject drop.

But I'd never liked the fact that Upton might think Fletcher and I were a thing.

We weren't a thing.

We'd never been a thing.

So yeah. I went there. Kind of blurted it out, actually: "Upton. We're not a thing."

He gave me a what-are-you-talking-about look.

"Fletcher and I," I said, feeling my face start to get hot. "We're not a thing. We're not seeing each other."

"Oh, really," Upton said, and seemed to study me for a second. Then he looked away. "Well, whatever. It's none of my business."

"It kind of *is* your business," I said. "I mean, from a workplace relations point of view. He's the big boss…"

"Yeah, I get that," Upton said. "But if there's nothing going on, there's no problem, right?"

He sounded kind of short-tempered about the topic for some reason.

On the other hand, Upton was a short-tempered kind of guy.

Which was all the more reason for me to drop the entire subject. "Right. Exactly," I said quickly. "I just wanted to make sure…"

Ugh.

I checked my phone.

It was only three o'clock. Five more hours of this.

Please, customers. Please come to the Booch4U tasting room, have a drink, and rescue Marion Flarey…

• • • • •

Another hour passed.

I started to relax a bit. I started to think that maybe Fletcher had realized how horrible it was to put me in the sort of position I'd been in, last night, and he'd learned his lesson and was now going to do what he should have from the start.

He was going to leave me alone.

Upton paced by and scanned the parking lot again.

I understood why he kept checking. Booch4U hadn't been opened that long. And we'd been doing pretty good. We'd done a ton of business the day before, for sure. But when you have a new venue like this, you're going to put every twist in clientele ebb and flow under your business analytics microscope. I imagined that Upton was wondering if this was an anomaly or if maybe the business had peaked and was already starting a protracted and ugly decline. And he was probably brainstorming what do to. You know, how to fast-track some sort of Inclement Weather social media flash campaign, get some bodies in the door.

"Kinda slow day," I said.

"Yeah," he muttered, looking out at the sodden lot with its gradually enlarging puddles.

"But that's understandable, given the weather," I added encouragingly. "Are you thinking of pushing something out on Instagram?"

He didn't look at me. "Instagram," he said. "Yeah, that's probably a good idea."

Okay, so that was a bit odd. After the bang-up job he'd done yesterday, promoting the food truck.

He paced back past me toward the office.

"I'm gonna do the windows," I called after him. Thinking to myself, stick to your lane, Marion. The man is obviously just distracted about something, this afternoon.

I switched the Spotify playlist to grunge rock. Maybe that would put a little spirit back into the place.

I double-checked the windows. They weren't that dirty. But we have a row of stools along the front of the barn, and people who sit in them tend to touch the windows and smudge up against them, so I'd been cleaning them every other shift or so.

I saw a couple handprints and figured I might as well take care of them.

We kept the window cleaner on some shelves along the back wall of the barn.

It was dark back there. The only windows were high up, near the eaves, and it was a gloomy day, and Josh wasn't working. So we hadn't bothered to turn on any lights.

I mean, I could see fine.

It was just dark.

And so I reached the end of the corridor, past the brew tanks and all Josh's equipment and supplies and grabbed the window cleaner and turned around.

And I saw something move.

A person.

A man.

Ducking behind one of the tanks.

33

Okay, so I screamed.

A loud scream. Good and loud.

Which was the right and natural thing to do, when you are standing in a dimly lit industrialish storage area of a large building and lost in your thoughts, and it's been hours of you being under the understanding that there is nobody else in the building besides you and Upton, and OMG.

OMG.

I felt myself break into a sweat. Instantly. And my heart was banging. And my mind was racing in record speed through a what-now scenario that went something along the lines of: okay, Marion Flarey, you have two escape routes, you could run to the front, but that means you'd actually have to run past the Serial Killer's hiding spot and he would for sure leap out and grab you, or you could go the other way and hopefully get the door open before the Serial Killer leaps out and grabs you but then of course you'd be out in the rain and Upton would be alone in the barn with the Serial Killer and does he have just a knife or is it a gun?

"Upton!" I screamed.

I could see the Serial Killer's feet. He was standing behind one of the brew tanks, which are raised above the ground. I could see the Serial Killer's feet below the tank.

And then the feet moved.

And the Serial Killer stepped out.

And it was...

Fletcher?

• • • • •

"Jesus, Marion. What the fuck is going on?" Upton had materialized next to me, his face at first looking about like I'm sure mine had, i.e. highly alarmed, but now it looked like I'm sure mine also did the next moment.

Very, very pissed off.

Fletcher, meanwhile, looked about like he had the night before when his wife had caught him kissing his ex-girlfriend. Guilty. Only his hair was wet. And his shirt was soaked. Sticking to his chest, the wet tee shirt contest effect.

Don't, Marion. Do NOT think about how the wet tee shirt effect shows off Fletcher's chest and torso to an extraordinary advantage...

"I just came by to check on things," he mumbled.

Upton eyed Fletcher skeptically. "What did you do," he said. "Swim here?"

It was kind of a joke. Although neither of them looked like they were on the verge of laughing.

Nor was I.

Because I was suddenly angry.

Angrier than I think I've ever been before. Furious.

Because are you kidding me?

Fletcher is *stalking* me now?

This whole "we need to talk" thing had now escalated into: I need to sneak up on you because I know if you see me coming you'll refuse to talk, and I'm too deranged to realize that no matter how I spin it you are going to believe your own eyeballs which have made it abundantly clear that I am married and my advances are the advances of a cheating spouse?

And suddenly, I'd had it. I couldn't take it anymore.

"Look, you guys," I said. "I don't know if you realize this, but when I took this job, I didn't realize Fletcher was the owner. And yes, we have history. But that was a long time ago, and you'd think we could both just let it go. And I have been trying. But Fletcher..."

I trailed off, looked away, and even out of the corner of my eye I was aware that both men were staring at me. But I didn't let their man-gazes throw me off my train of thought. I straightened my spine and threw my shoulders back, feeling for the first time in a long time like I was not five-foot-one-inch goose girl Marion Flarey but more like seven-foot-one-inch someday-a-queen Marion Flarey. "What I'm trying to say, is: this is an unfair working environment for me. I mean, intolerable. An intolerable working environment."

I handed the bottle of window cleaner to Upton.

"And so, I quit." I delivered the words very dramatically.

And then I marched past them to the bar to get my handbag, and then marched straight out the front door, and the rain immediately started beating my face and I ran to the truck.

Two cars pulled in just as I was leaving, windshield wipers slashing at the rain pouring over the glass.

Customers.

But they were Upton's and Fletcher's problem now.

Not mine.

34

Okay, you go, Marion Flarey. You go, girl. You tell them.

That was what my mind was singing for, oh, maybe the first five minutes after I quit my job and dashed triumphantly through the downpour and opened the door of Winchell's truck and got in and started driving myself back to the dome.

And then it hit me.

OMG.

I'd just given up my Tower.

OMG.

My whole body started to shake.

I'd just given up my Tower. I'd effed up *everything.*

Because I hadn't worked long enough to cover first month last money security deposit, which meant I was going to have to make a humiliating call to Vicki and tell her I was backing out and please give my money back. Which she really didn't have to do and after all I'd signed the lease, and I had no place else to move to and all my stuff was now in Tibbs and OMG could this possibly be worse?

I pulled off the road. I burst into tears. Sat there and bawled.

Pulled a tissue from my purse and wiped my eyes.

The windshield was all steamed up.

I turned the defrost on.

I watched the little clear spot near the dash slowly expand so that I'd be able to see, again.

The windshield wipers flashed back and forth.

Keeping time.

You. Are. An. Idgit.

You. Are. An. Idgit.

You. Are. An. Idgit.

35

Monday.

The brewery is closed on Mondays. So if I hadn't quit my job, it would have been my day off, and I would have spent the day hanging around the camper. Which meant that it wasn't necessary, strictly speaking, to mention to the family that Marion Flarey was no longer employed.

So I didn't. I hid out in my bedroom.

Well, except for one foray to the dome to fetch a mug of coffee and a blueberry muffin, which I was unable to eat, because I took one bite and then realized that my stomach was in knots.

I'd lost my Tower.

I counted the cash money I had in my purse, on the outside chance that my mental tally was off and by some miracle I'd actually be in possession of the final $625 installment I owed Vicki, but of course my mental tally had been accurate.

Ugh.

I sat on my bed with my back against the camper wall and my legs pulled up against my chest, drinking coffee.

What the heck was I going to do with my life, now?

I could, of course, crawl to Mom and Winchell and ask them if I could please stay in the camper for some reasonable period of time.

Six months, say. To keep my living expenses down while I figured out what to do, next.

There were two problems with that idea.

One: jobs in Tibbs, New York, are not exactly plentiful. Especially when word would quickly spread that Marion Flarey was a person who had just quit a perfectly good job less than a week after her start date, owing to some crazy thing having to do with possibly conducting an adulterous affair with her boss.

Problem number two: it would mean I was back living with my goofy family, which I had sworn I would never do again, and if I broke that oath not only would I be breaking an oath, I'd be setting myself up for probably losing my mind.

Nope. My best course of action would be to head back to Rochester. Throw myself on the mercy of Vicki. Tell her of course I'd help her find a new renter and hope that she'd refund the money I'd sent her so far so that I'd be able to afford some non-Tower apartment somewhere. And Winchell had said I could take my time paying him back, right? Because he'd have to wait. And I'd get a job, somehow. And I'd muddle through.

I heard Candace's car, which was good, it meant she was on her way to work, and Quill was probably still eating pancakes in the dome.

Funny how Mom was never a fix-dinner-for-the-family sort of person, but she was making Quill breakfast every morning like that...

I began to pack.

No point in taking any of my old fairy tale books. They'd have looked fabulous in the Tower, of course. Curved bookshelves lining the Tower walls, full of fairy tale books...

Could you imagine?

But in the cheapo apartment I was going to no doubt have to settle for, they'd just look stupid and sad.

• • • • •

What with my Fletcher drama and my Tower drama and my surreptitious packing, I'd almost forgotten about that glass coffee pot

I'd ordered. But I heard a truck growling up the driveway and peeked out, and it was a UPS delivery truck.

I ran out and intercepted the UPS guy before he reached the dome and told him the package was for me.

I saw Mom looking out the door, but I waved her off and then when she'd disappeared again and the UPS truck was gone, I headed down the driveway.

• • • • •

"Good morning, Marion," Effie said. "You have a package."

"It's for you," I said.

I carried the box into her kitchen, set it on the table, took a paring knife out of the drawer, and began cutting through the packing tape. And inside the coffee pot was wrapped in about fifty layers of newspaper that were held into place by another three rolls' worth of packing tape. So it took me awhile to free the thing.

But I did, finally, and then I held it up to show her.

"My," Effie said. "That is lovely."

Yeah. I was feeling pretty damn proud of myself. A three-day string of failures but I'd finally gotten something right. "It's the Pot with the Golden Star!" I said.

"Mmmm," she answered.

Worrying, that mmmm.

And where was she going?

"Effie," I said, following her as she made her way toward the front door. "It's the Pot with the Golden Star. See?" I pointed to the stars printed on the pot. "Like you asked. I've succeeded in my task."

She sat on the little chair next to her front door, where she kept her gardening shoes. Black leather shoes with thick soles that looked like they were about a hundred years old. She was slipping them on and winced a bit as she freed her left arm from her sling so she could tie the laces.

"I have just the spot for it," she said. "Carry it for me, will you, dear?"

"Effie," I said. "The cat."

She smiled.

I didn't like the looks of that smile. Not a bit.

I followed along one of the little footpaths she'd worn between the clumps of junk and flowers, to a spot along the edge of the yard where she'd clearly been digging recently. There was a hole maybe a foot across and three inches deep, and a pile of soil next to it, and a pile of stones that she'd sorted out of the soil.

"Right here," she said.

I handed her the pot and watched her set it into the ground and use her trowel to fill in the hole around the pot's base.

"I need my potting soil," she said.

"Where is it?"

"On the porch. In a pail."

I fetched the pail of potting soil from the porch and watched her fill the pot with soil, and then she took some seeds out of the pocket on the front of her overalls and made a few little depressions with her finger and pressed the seeds into the depressions.

"There!"

"Effie." I was starting to feel anxious. And not a little irritated.

"Marion, dear. Be honest with me, please."

Honest? I wasn't sure what that meant.

"If you think carefully, you'll realize. It's not the right pot," she said.

I felt my jaw drop open. "What do you mean?"

She was kidding. She had to be kidding.

But she shook her head and stood up and started back toward the house. "It's not the right one," she said over her shoulder. "You haven't brought me the *real* Pot with the Golden Star."

I could have about screamed.

In fact, I did raise my voice a bit. "That's not the way it works, Effie!" I wailed. "I brought you a pot, like you said! And look! It has stars. Gold stars!"

I followed her into the kitchen.

"Tea?" she asked.

I didn't answer. Because, the fact is, I like Effie.

I probably actually love Effie.

But this was too much.

"Marion, dear. You seem a little low."

Yeah, low is right. Maybe because on top of losing my Tower and the awfulness with Fletcher and messing up my entire life, my brilliant plan to get Effie's help with Surprise had also just crashed and burned.

But for some reason my mind suddenly went, not to the cat, but to Fletcher Beal.

I slumped onto a chair.

Effie set a porcelain cup in front of me.

"I don't understand," I said as my eyes welled with tears. "The pot..."

"Never mind the pot right now." Effie sat down, and then leaned over to pour my tea. "What else is going on?"

"I did something I shouldn't have, Effie." I dropped my face into my hands. "A Beauty and the Beast thing. And I really should know better."

"Ah. Beauty and the Beast."

Her voice sounded almost musical as she said the words. Wistful, but musical.

"Only," I said, "instead of a guy who looks like a Beast but is actually a handsome Prince, it was the other way around."

"I see." Effie picked up her cup and took a sip. "Although one of the most important lessons from Beauty in the Beast is that when we get mixed signals, we have to pick and choose which ones we ought to read."

I sighed. "I dunno about mixed signals," I said.

"You're trusting appearances," Effie said. "Well, my dear, ninety-nine times out of a hundred, that's a very good thing to do."

"Exactly," I muttered.

"Now, for example, sometimes when you're looking for something, like a Pot with a Golden Star, and you see a thing that looks like a Pot with a Golden Star, you might jump to the conclusion that you've found what you're looking for."

Ugh.

Seriously.

How was I supposed to take any comfort in this?

And weren't we talking about men, and Fletcher Beal, and Beasts?

"You don't understand," I said miserably.

"Marion, what did the fox tell the king's youngest son, about the cages and the Golden Bird?"

I looked up at her. "Don't put the bird in the fancy cage."

Effie nodded. "Same thing with the magic horse. Use the plain leather saddle, not the golden one."

Okay, I got her point. Sometimes in these stories, the hero is supposed to ignore the glittery thing.

The glittery thing is a trap.

So I understood what Effie was saying.

She was saying that the real Pot with the Golden Star might not look all that special.

It might look pretty dull.

It probably wouldn't cost me nearly $50.

I looked up from my tea.

"I gotta go, Effie," I said.

36

Trudge trudge trudge.

Picking my way along Effie's driveway.

Pushing through the weeds and stepping around the puddles.

And at first, I felt a bit better. Like, somehow, Effie's words had comforted me.

But the further along I went, the more that feeling faded.

I mean: come on, Marion Flarey.

You don't live inside a fairy tale.

That's just nuts.

You're letting your crazy family and this crazy Fletcher thing and your crazy old lady friend get to you.

You don't live inside a fairy tale.

I stopped walking.

Because of course Effie would say the opposite.

She'd say I was wrong, wouldn't she?

She'd say I *do* live inside a fairy tale. She'd say we all do. Not literally, perhaps. Not with literal witches and castles and talking cats and kings hunting in forests and stumbling onto sleeping maidens...

She'd mean something else.

Only what?

I started walking again.

And, okay. Theory.

Maybe, in some bizarre way, maybe everything our ancestors observed and recorded by weaving them into these innocent-sounding little stories.

Maybe all those stories were made up of fragments of things that have an energy of some kind. Maybe after centuries of being shared and told and re-told so many times, they'd taken on a life of their own. They are living fragments. And they are everywhere around us, wafting over our heads and down around our ears. Invisible but there. Only if you pause a second and really pay attention you can detect them, or maybe what you detect is how they've worn patterns. They've worn channels. And sometimes the channels affect certain aspects of your life. Like, aspects of your life get caught up and tugged and start to flow in them.

So it might seem like your life is a crazy mixed up mess, but if you look closely the mess is actually mixed-up pieces of…fairy tales.

OMG, Marion Flarey. You are losing your mind.

Fairy tales are stories.

Just stories.

A subset of literature. Low literature. Folk literature.

Created by uneducated storytellers to entertain people during a period of history when you couldn't just swipe a screen every time you had some idle time on your hands.

That's all.

Right?

Right?

And could I be any more mixed up about any of this?

I looked around, suddenly aware again of where I was standing.

I was about halfway down Effie's driveway.

Surrounded by forest.

And then I knew, suddenly, what I had to do.

Of course!

What every fairy tale hero does when there seems to be no way to solve an awful problem.

I had to get lost in a forest.

37

I didn't let myself think.

Because at times like this, when you are quite possibly losing your mind but on the other hand nothing you've tried so far has even come close to working and so why not do something completely crazy? Well, it's best not to let yourself think.

And hey. What else did I have to do, other than put myself in a story that—if my theory about fairy tales was true—would lead me to my happy ending?

So I did it.

I crashed through the brushy stuff bordering Effie's driveway and there I was.

In the woods.

And I started to walk.

With purpose and determination.

The purpose and determination of a noble and courageous heroine who was now purposefully determined to get herself completely and utterly lost.

• • • • •

Real-life forests, unlike fairy tale forests, have ticks.

I remembered this after maybe ten minutes.

I checked my bare arms—no ticks, phew—and double-checked that my jeans were tucked into my socks.

Onward!

• • • • •

Real-life forests, unlike fairy tale forests, have a lot of tangled up spots. Places where it's brushy and you can't get through, so you have to turn around and try another way.

Also gullies.

Ugh.

I suppose fairy tale forests have those things, too, only the fairy tales don't mention them. But when you get to a tangled spot and have to turn back and try getting through in a different way, or you get to a gully and you need to follow it a while to find a place you can climb through that's not so steep that you're risking life and limb? Well, that's how you get lost, right?

• • • • •

Real-life forests, unlike fairy tale forests, get HOT.

Steaming hot.

Almost as if it had rained all day yesterday and now the sun was high and beating down and all the moisture from the forest floor that had been sponged up by the ground and leaf litter and was now evaporating into the air, turning the place into a huge green steam room.

Ugh.

I was so hot and sweaty...

And thirsty.

And in real fairy tales, the heroine—if she's a smart heroine—brings along a little loaf of bread and little jug of water and a little stool to rest on if she gets tired.

Marion Flarey, turns out, wasn't a very smart heroine...

Ugh. Another gully.

Could they not make forests flat instead of all hilly and full of stupid gullies?

· · · · ·

Real-life forests, unlike fairy tale forests, are full of deer flies.
And mosquitoes.
And did I mention they are HOT.

· · · · ·

Tfw you've set out to get lost in a forest and then realize, oh shit.
I'm lost in a forest.

38

I sat down on a rock and flailed at yet another deerfly buzzing around my head, trying to figure out what the hell I was going to do, now.

In the plus column: this wasn't a very large forest. It couldn't be. It was the 21st Century, and granted, Tibbs, NY is a small town in a relatively unpopulated part of the state, and the road we lived on was heavily forested. But it's not what you'd exactly call a vast wilderness. There were other roads out there, a lot of them, in every possible direction I could walk. And roads equal houses. And also kind strangers in cars, who I could flag down to ask for help.

In the minus column: I had no idea which direction was which.

And I had a sneaking suspicion that I'd been doing exactly what they say people do, when they get lost in the woods. I was going in circles. Although I should note not very perfect circles or you'd think I would have ended up back at Effie's driveway, which I had not. And I should also note that this forest struck me as far too chaotic for any of its features to stand out as familiar, so I couldn't be sure about the circles thing, because the trees around me at that moment looked exactly like all the other trees I'd been wandering past for however long I'd been wandering around.

Okay, more in the minus column. My cell phone was back in the camper, and oblivious to my plight, because as usual I'd had to leave it to charge. And, I might have mentioned, I was hot. And tired.

And I was feeling pretty foolish and sorry for myself. And wondering what had possessed me to think this was a good idea. That deliberately fairy tale-ing myself was somehow going to solve my problems, when in fact all it did was create new ones.

I looked around.

I said, "Help?" in a little voice. Because obviously there was nobody anywhere around who would hear.

· · · · ·

Okay.

I really am an idiot.

The sun was out.

And I might not be Marion Flarey, Expert Backwoodswoman, but I know the sun rises in the east, and I knew it was still morning.

So okay. Got it. I had a general idea of the directions, after all.

All I had to do was pick one of them and walk in as close to a straight line as I could, and sooner or later I'd come out on a road.

Got it.

I picked west, so that I could just follow my shadow.

And since the Earth is round if I kept going west, I'd end up east of the sun and west of the moon, right? Hahahahaha.

· · · · ·

Okay, so now that I'd solved the direction thing, and actually had a plan for how to come out, eventually, on a road, I no longer felt lost.

Instead, I felt more like: Marion Flarey, you are a stupid idiot for thinking that deliberately getting lost in a forest was an actual solution to your problems.

And also? Just like how people lost in forests go in circles, guess where I was, all over again? I was where I'd started. Where the only way to save my beautiful Tower was to do it like normal people. Get a job, get your hands on the money you need for first month's rent, last month's rent, security deposit.

And ugh, the ground was so uneven and strewn everywhere with rocks and roots and fallen logs and branches. I had to pay attention to where I was stepping to keep from getting my foot tangled in a vine or stepping into a hole or something. So step over this, step around that, look up again to make sure my shadow was still more or less in front of me, now step around something else.

And then finally, finally, finally, I looked up and the forest had that more thinned-out look that means you are almost to the end of it.

I started to see glimpses of blue sky through the trees.

I heard a car!

My plan had worked!

There was a road up there. I was saved!

I picked up speed.

Around this, over that, moving faster now, more blue sky visible between the trees...

And then I saw it.

Through the trees.

· · · · ·

And so that's what happens when you make yourself loony toons by deliberately getting yourself lost in a forest because you had some cockamamie idea that you live in a fairytale.

After wandering about in said forest actually lost for what seemed like days, and feeling a bit dizzy from all that stupid walking in the steamy forest-y heat, plus you're probably also dehydrated, and you finally reach a clearing and OMG, there's some sort of building in the clearing and you can't see more than a little slice of it through the trees, but that's enough that you can tell it is the top of a wall, and that the wall is built of stone.

Gray stone.

It's...a *castle?*

I've come to...a CASTLE?

I grabbed a tree to steady myself.

Because it couldn't be.

No. No. Freaking. Way.

39

Okay. So maybe you're thinking right now: Marion Flarey, it wasn't a castle. You were having an episode and need psychiatric help...

Well, you are on the right track.

You are almost right.

It wasn't a castle.

It was worse than a castle.

Because I took a few steps, and one of the windows came into view.

And then I realized what I was looking at.

It hit me like a plank across the forehead.

It wasn't a castle. Not at all.

It was the stone house.

That stone house.

The stone house that Fletcher Beal's mom had bought when she'd split from his dad and decided to move herself and her kid to Tibbs.

A little sound escaped my lips.

Somehow, in my ridiculous I'm-lost-wandering-through-the-woods, I'd managed to walk straight in the direction of the stone house that, as Fletcher had mentioned, his family still owned. The house where he stayed, when he was in Tibbs.

Which meant there was a very good chance he was there, right now, and any minute he'd look out a window and see someone lurking in the trees next to his lawn, or maybe he was outside strolling the grounds and he'd come around the corner of the house and see me and not only see but also recognize me and OMG think I was spying on him?

And so, yes. I did what any sensible young woman would do if she found herself in my position: a few yards away from walking out onto the lawn of a man she was trying with all her might to avoid.

I turned and ran back into the woods.

40

Only I didn't run very far.

Because as addled in the head as I was, at that particular moment, I wasn't so addled that I forgot how hot and tired and thirsty I was, and how completely sick I was of wandering through that stupid forest.

Also, running through a forest is not an easy thing to do. I have mentioned the rocks and roots and fallen logs, right? They're hard to walk through. So running through?

Oof.

So after maybe three or four highly dangerous hops over rocks and roots and fallen logs, somehow avoiding falling and breaking an ankle or worse, I stopped and thought to myself, Marion Flarey, you don't need to go back into the woods.

Just go way way way around the house.

To the road.

Stay hidden in the forest and you'll be fine.

Okay. So I had a plan.

A sensible plan.

Of course it turned out that the bits of the forest near the road weren't so much forest as a briar thicket. And maybe I should have retreated and tried to find another way to the road, but by then I was past caring, and a thorny cane dragged across the back of my hand, leaving a line of bloody dashes, and its thorny cane friends were grabbing at my clothing so that now I had little pulls in my jeans and little runs in my tee shirt.

So you know what? If I had been a Prince going after a Princess, and needed to work my way through that thorn patch to win her hand?

Hah. I would have been like: never mind.

I'll stay a bachelor.

But I was an until-recently lost unemployed homeless Millennial, and it was going to take more than a few briars to keep me away from a shower and a fresh cup of drip coffee…

I finally made it to the road.

I was maybe a quarter mile away from Fletcher's mother's stone house.

Far enough that if he was there and happened to look out of a window, he wouldn't see hot sweaty red-faced Marion Flarey thrashing through the undergrowth.

And I knew the way home from there. From all those times when I used to walk this way as a lovestruck teenager hoping the exact opposite of what I was hoping today.

Hoping to catch a glimpse of Fletcher Beal.

And you know all that stuff I'd been thinking about? About how I was living in a fairy tale, blah blah blah?

Well I wasn't. And I never had been.

I was living in a nightmare. A weird nightmare woven by my subconscious that was trying to tell me some message about Fletcher Beal, only I didn't want the message. I didn't want anything to do with him.

I didn't want anything to do with any of this.

I had to get out of Tibbs.

This thing had to end.

I had to get out of Tibbs, and I had to do it immediately.

Today.

• • • • •

I headed to the camper, first, to shower. So that when I walked into the dome I looked as fresh and calm and natural as could be.

Winchell was in the kitchen buttering toast.

"Hey," I said as I took a mug out of the drainboard. "Just a heads up, Winchell. The job didn't work out. So, sorry, but I'm gonna need a lift back to Rochester. Where's Mom?"

Winchell gave me a studied look for a moment before answering. "In the shop."

"Right," I said.

"You're bleeding," Winchell said.

I looked down at the hand holding the coffee pot. Drops of blood had re-formed on the skin where one of the thorns had snatched me.

"I went for a hike and got a scratch," I said calmly and coolly. "What time can you drive me?"

"I can't do it today. I have deliveries to make."

Argh. So much for getting out of there today. "Tomorrow morning, then?"

"I suppose," Winchell answered, and I smiled calmly and went to the shop to find Mom.

She was sitting next to Quill at the bench in the back. Helping him with another project.

"Look, Aunt Marion!" he said when he noticed me standing there. "Grandma's helping me make a pot. It's for you. It's a pinch pot. She said you wanted a pot."

Oh, geez.

"Yeah," I said. "That's right."

He held up his creation for me to admire. "See?" he said. "I drew a picture of our family on it."

Gah. Double geez.

"This is Grandpa and Grandma an' me," he said, rotating the pot in his hands as he pointed. This is Mom and Dad and you an' RB and here's Surprise."

"Beautiful," I said on the outside, while on the inside I was thinking ouch. Did you really have to do that, kid.

242

"And I made a sun. And that's a tree and that's grass."

There wasn't a lot of empty space left on the side of the pot. "Can you add a star?" I asked.

He shook his head. "Stars don't come out in the daytime."

"Good point," I said, thinking to myself what difference would it make, seeing as there's no way the pot will be glazed and fired before I leave.

I could feel Mom looking at me and I looked at her and her face had the same expression Winchell's had a couple minutes ago.

"Quill," she said, "you want to rinse your hands off in here or use the hose?"

"Hose," he said.

She knew full well that would be any kid's choice.

She waited a minute until he was out of earshot.

"Okay. What happened?" she said.

I admit, this threw me for a bit. I'm so used to my mom being off in her own world. And I'm sure she wished I was a normal person, that I was more like Candace. But on the other hand, she was also a bit like me. Being an artist. And a reader. Poetry, though, not fairy tales.

And also, I may have looked less calm and cool than I thought.

"I have to go back to Rochester," I said. "I can't do this anymore."

"It's that boy, isn't it," Mom said. "Fletcher."

Boy? Really, Mom?

I took a swallow of coffee to force the lump in my throat back down. "Sort of."

"I wondered if there wasn't something going on," she said. "Quill is going to miss you."

I noticed the pot again, with the stick figures encircling it.

"I was thinking," I said. "Since I'm here until tomorrow…maybe I could cook dinner tonight. You know, a real dinner. Where we all sit down together and eat."

She nodded, thoughtfully. "That would be lovely, honey."

Lovely…

Lovely, like a clay pot encircled with a family of stick figures?

I went back to the dome and asked Winchell if I could ride along with him to do a little shopping.

And then I invited Quill to go along, too.

And that's how I spent my last day in Tibbs. Riding with my stepfather and my step-nephew from farm to farm, picking out fresh vegetables and potatoes and then a beautiful grass-fed roast.

And then back in the kitchen I pecked at my phone for instructions on how to do a beautiful grass-fed roast, and then Candace got home and a few minutes later I saw from Quill's face that his mother had told him the news.

They said the food was great. But the dinner was kind of quiet. And to be honest, I was glad when Candace offered to clean up.

I wanted to say good-bye to Effie, too.

"Hey, I'm gonna take some of the leftovers up to Effie's," I said as everyone began standing up and leaving the table, the way families do after a meal.

Hopefully she hadn't eaten her dinner, yet.

41

Effie was standing on her porch, watching as I crossed her yard.

"It's roast beef," I said, holding up the two containers I was carrying. "With mashed potatoes and vegetables, and this one is gravy. It will need to be re-heated."

"Lovely," Effie said.

"Have you eaten?"

She hadn't.

I followed her in, and she put a couple pans on the stove and peeked inside the containers. "There's enough here for four people!"

I wasn't hungry. But I pretended I was, because I knew she would want me to join her. "Shall I set the table?"

"Yes. And get some fresh flowers, won't you?"

I picked out a vase from the shelves in the front hall, and then wandered for a few minutes in her yard, choosing wildflowers and arranging them as I went.

She was turning the burner off under the pan when I returned, and then she ladled the gravy into a deep little bowl and set it on the table.

We sat down.

"Oh, look at that," she said.

She pointed.

I followed the direction of her finger.

Effie had set the bowl of gravy right near the vase of flowers. And one of flowers I'd picked was St. John's Wort, which has little butter-yellow flowers, and one of the blossoms had dislodged and fallen into the bowl of gravy.

"So pretty, floating there," Effie said. "Like a little golden star. Floating in a pot of gravy."

Oh, no.

Freaking coincidence. That's all it was.

And not even a very good coincidence. "A bowl isn't a pot," I muttered.

I reached over and plucked the blossom out of the gravy and set it on my napkin.

"And you forgot to ask about the cat," Effie said, helping herself to a slice of beef, and then calling over her shoulder, "Kitty kitty!"

And I dropped my fork and looked in the direction she'd called.

And there came Surprise, trotting with her funny three-legged gait through the kitchen, and Effie bent over and let the cat take a bit of roast beef out of her fingers.

42

So there you have it.

I got the cat back.

And don't ask me how. Do not ask me how it could have happened like that, a coincidence like that. Because it sure felt like it was something Effie had made happen, I also know that's impossible and I really, really didn't want to think about it.

I carried Surprise down the road and up the driveway to the dome. Everyone was watching TV.

And I walked over to the couch and handed the cat to Quill. And he gasped and yelled MY CAT! but fortunately Surprise is pretty mellow and didn't jump down from the boy's lap but arched her back and purred and pressed herself against him.

And there they sat, Mom and Quill and Candace, petting the cat and telling me I knew you could do it, Mayfly. With Winchell looking on and nodding and then switching the channel to a ball game to check the score.

Quite the scene...

It kept flashing through my head the next morning, as I finished packing.

But I'd made my decision. So sure, maybe there were some aspects of being around my family that weren't so bad. They were family, after all. I couldn't help feeling a little bit attached to them, no matter how annoying they were most of the time. And it was nice to see them like that last night and know I'd done my part to fix something in their lives that had been broken.

I took a final look at some of my favorite books.

Could I really leave them all here?

Because I was back at square one. Well maybe square two, because assuming Vicki would refund my money, I'd have enough to find me some crappy room somewhere.

But at least I'd have a place to stay.

A place for books.

I poured myself a glass of water in the camper kitchen and noticed the rose that Winchell had given me. Odd that it still looked pretty fresh.

I changed the water.

Candace would enjoy having it there, right?

I went to the bedroom to collect the books I'd put in the cupboard by the bed, and when I turned around there was Quill.

I hadn't heard him come in.

"Hi," I said.

He looked small and forlorn. "Thanks for finding Surprise, Aunt Marion. Was she with Effie?"

"Something like that." I sat on the bed and patted the mattress to invite him up. "Look at this book. It has really cool pictures."

It was an old collection of English fairy tales, illustrated by Arthur Rackham, who is pretty famous if you are into illustrators. I flipped to one of the color plates and looked down at Quill, watching him as he gazed at the image.

"It's a very, very old book," I explained. "But because of these pictures, it's worth a lot of money."

"How much?" he said. "A million dollars?"

I laughed. "No. Not that much."

"A hundred dollars?"

"Could be." I picked up my phone and opened my browser. "Let's see what the internet says." I typed the title in and +Arthur Rackham, and a couple sites came up. AbeBooks and eBay. "See this? It's the same book, only my copy isn't as nice. The cover is a little worn on the edges. So you're right. My copy is probably worth about a hundred dollars."

He nodded. "Are you going to sell it?"

I shook my head and opened my mouth to answer.

No.

Of course not.

I loved these books.

I'd never sell these books.

But then it hit me.

A hundred dollars.

I was holding a hundred dollars.

Here. In my hands.

And I had other books—quite a few other books—that were probably worth something in that same range.

I could sell a dozen or so of these old books and I'd have enough money to get my Tower after all.

My heart started hammering.

"Okay, sweetie, I gotta finish packing," I said, left Quill to look at the Rackham illustrations while I started quickly sorting through my books again, only this time checking the titles on my phone, until I had a stack of the ones that were most valuable.

And I put them in a box and carried it out to Winchell's truck.

43

And a few hours later, Winchell was driving me to Rochester.

I navigated him straight to my favorite second-hand bookstore.

The owners knew me pretty well. I'd spent a small fortune there, over the years. And they were very fair as they priced my books. And they paid cash.

I stood inside the shop door for a couple minutes before going back to the curb where Winchell had parked, taking deep breaths because even though this was the right thing to do, I really really hated to sell those books. And I wanted to cry.

Tower, I reminded myself.

This is how we do things in the real world.

I texted Vicki.

got the rest of the cash. can I meet you and get key

She texted back, said she was at work but would meet me at the apartment on her break.

• • • • •

Winchell helped me carry my boxes of stuff from his truck and stack them on the porch of my about-to-be-new-home.

Nice of him.

"A new beginning is the elixir of life," he said.

Right.

He hugged me and I stepped back, thinking that of course now he would go down the porch steps and back to his truck, but he hesitated and shifted his weight back and forth and it suddenly dawned on me what he wanted.

"I don't have quite enough money to pay you back," I said. "I need a little for food, right?"

He was looking longingly at my handbag where he'd seen me stuff the wad of bills I'd gotten for my beautiful books.

"I'll need a few weeks. That'll be okay, won't it, Winchell?"

And I am sure he knew as well as I did that it might take more than a few weeks. Considering that I was pretty obviously unemployed at the moment and it's not like I had second copies of all those books he'd just seen me sell.

But he said "sure." So he was being nice.

And he left.

And a minute later another car pulled up to the curb.

Vicki.

She got out of her car.

She was holding a bouquet of roses.

Pink tea roses in a clear plastic vase.

"Hey," she said, handing me the flowers. "I came from work. Housewarming gift."

Roses, again. Seriously? And wasn't that odd? The synchronicity, because of how Winchell had given me a rose too and I'd left it in Tibbs and now here I had pink roses here, too?

Odd.

Or maybe not.

We went inside.

I gave Vicki her cash, and she gave me the keys, and she left.

I set the vase of roses on the counter.

And what was funny was, there I was, in my Tower. And I walked around and looked out of the windows and told myself how great this was, I'd gotten what I wanted, and how much more happy could I possibly be?

But something didn't feel quite right.

I knew what it was. I was tired and hungry, and the last few days had been so stressful, of course I couldn't feel a thousand percent happy, what with all that family drama and the Fletcher drama etc. etc.

And yes, I needed to be very careful with my spending until I got myself a job, but there were a million restaurants within walking distance of my new place. And it wouldn't hurt to treat myself to a dinner out, right? Not a huge dinner, but I could go to one of those cool restaurants on Park Ave. and have an appetizer and a glass of wine and groove in the vibe of my new neighborhood and all of the cool people I'd be around, now, all day every day, and maybe I'd learn about a job opening, and maybe I'd make some new friends.

Maybe I'd meet my Prince.

• • • • •

So I ended up ordering a charcuterie plate and a glass of house Cab and I didn't meet my Prince. But eating made me feel better.

I walked back to my Tower.

It was sticky hot, humid.

A robin was singing in the tree in front of my new apartment.

The key to the door on the porch stuck a little but I got it open.

And I thought, okay, Marion Flarey. You sold some of your favorite books. And now you're feeling the aftereffects. Now you're feeling the hangover.

My boxes were in a cluster in the center of the room, where Vicki's bed had been. And I still didn't have a bed, of course, so I found the box with my pillow and blankets and made a bed on the floor.

I plugged in my phone to charge and surfed the net and thought about how maybe I should just break down and try a dating app.

I thought about unpacking books.

I listened to some tunes on my phone.

I lowered the window blinds and laid down.

There was a streetlight right outside. Its light shone through the blinds, so that as my eyes adjusted, the room was still pretty bright.

I'd get drapes. That was the plan. Drapes would look gorgeous in that room.

The floor was hard.

I couldn't help thinking that although this wasn't the Tweedles' apartment, how ironic it was that I was back sleeping on a hard floor, in an apartment empty except for the boxes of my stuff.

There was quite a bit of traffic noise.

At one point a siren started squealing and got really loud before it finally died away.

And later I woke again because there were people yelling and laughing as they walked by on the sidewalk outside. They sounded like they had been drinking. They sounded like they were having fun.

44

Sleeping on the floor like that meant I woke up the next morning with a little headache.

I dug out some ibuprofen and went to the little kitchen to see if maybe Vicki had left a glass in the cupboard. Or a plastic cup. Something.

Or I could just hold my mouth under the faucet.

It was early, still, and dark in the kitchen so I fumbled on the wall until I found the light switch and flicked it on.

And there were the roses Vicki had given me.

And they were dead.

45

Okay. So they weren't completely dead.

But they were on their way. They'd wilted, badly. And mind you, they were buds, still. Babies. They shouldn't have wilted. They should have been standing up, tall and proud, and maybe starting to unfurl a bit, to reveal their rosy petaled faces to the world.

But instead, they were all sagging. Their little necks were all bent down almost 180 degrees over, like they were hanging their little heads, and the edges of the petals had started to turn brown. Like they were beaten and had given up. Had given up and were hanging their heads and weeping.

I checked the vase. It had plenty of water in it.

I looked at the buds again, the way the brown-edged petals looked limp and soft.

And then it hit me.

OMG.

OMG.

Marion Flarey: you'd banished yourself to a Tower.

You'd banished yourself to a Tower. And your father brought you a rose and said it was your favorite flower, even though you didn't think it was your favorite flower, that is exactly why Beauty's father brought her the rose. And the rose is from the garden of the Beast who is actually a

Prince, therefore if my roses are dying when they shouldn't be dying, it could only mean one thing.

I had to get to Fletcher.

I had to get to Fletcher before it was too late.

46

It took me all day to get back to Tibbs.

Because I couldn't quite bring myself to call Winchell and beg him to come get me and nobody would Uber me that far and anyway, I had a little money, so I could afford to rent a car, right?

So I cleaned up and walked to the bus stop and went to a rental car place to rent a car. And thanks a lot, rental car company. They wouldn't rent it to me. Something about needing a real credit card instead of a debit card. But they said I could try a competitor rental agency, we believe they accept your inferior kind of card.

So this time I Ubered, and I even asked the driver how he felt about a five-hour round trip job which he couldn't do because he had to pick up his kids from his ex's. So he dropped me at car rental place number two, and I was just about ready to cry when the agent nodded. Turns out this agency really was more sympathetic to struggling Millennials who only have debit cards.

I got my car. Yes, me, dead-broke Marion Flarey spent $80 renting a car.

I drove straight to the stone house.

Fletcher's Audi was not in his driveway.

I pulled in and ran to the door and rang the doorbell.

I stood there, waiting.

I rang the doorbell again.

I banged on the storm door in case the doorbell was broken.

Nothing.

The place was deserted.

Well. Hopefully it was deserted. Hopefully Fletcher was not stretched out on the floor, dying and unable to come to the door.

I decided to try the brewery.

. . . . .

Fletcher's car wasn't parked at Booch4U, either.

In fact, the parking lot was empty except for Upton's car. And that BMW SUV his girlfriend drove.

I considered my options.

Upton would know where Fletcher was, right?

I got out and went around to the back door.

It was locked.

I knocked. Waited.

Nothing.

I walked around to the front.

Odd.

The front door was actually unlocked. Upton must have let his girlfriend in the front.

I stepped inside.

There were no lights on.

But there, near the bar, I saw two figures.

Upton and his girlfriend.

They were standing together near the bar, only when they'd heard the door shut and realized I'd come in, they'd kind of jumped apart.

And then I saw who she was.

But before I had a chance to even process what was in front of my eyes, another movement caught my eye, and from the dim recesses in the back of the brewery—over by the brewing vessels—a figure emerged.

He was holding a phone out in front of him, clicking pictures.

Fletcher.

"Well," Fletcher said as he clicked the button on his phone camera. "My best friend."

He paused.

"And my wife."

47

Okay, so let me just tell you that the next few minutes were pretty awkward.

Upton got pissy.

Fletcher's wife got even pissier. She accused Fletcher of being an S.O.B. who had no business harassing her like that.

And meanwhile I stood there, watching the whole scene unfold and wondering what the hell, exactly, was going on?

"And don't think I don't know who *she* is," Fletcher's wife said, pointing at me.

"She's an old friend," Fletcher said. "Drop it, Linda. You're busted and you know it."

"Uh," I said, "I'm gonna head out, now. Bye, all."

But before I made it to my car, I heard the tasting room door slam behind me and footsteps, and then Fletcher had caught up to me and was touching my arm.

"Marion, please. I'm parked down the road," he said. "Please walk with me?"

I hesitated.

"Please, Marion?"

And so we walked.

And he talked.

He told me about his pre-nup.

"After what my parents went through, I was a bit skittish about marriage." This was a country road, so there was no sidewalk. Just a gravelly shoulder. And he was kicking at stones as he walked. "I guess that's why I didn't argue too much when my lawyer advised we do a pre-nup."

He told me that the pre-nup had a clause in it called a Lifestyle clause, that meant they had both promised they wouldn't cheat on each other.

He kicked a stone. "It's got nothing to do with money," he said in a low voice, his head bowed and he kicked another stone, hard, so that it flew into the air and bounced onto the road and then bounced to the other side. "It's a pride thing. It's about her making me look like a fool."

"You're not a fool," I said.

"You see, I've suspected something was going on for months. But she denied it."

I nodded.

"We have mutual friends. Mutual business contacts. The Lifestyle clause... The point is that we both promised each other that we wouldn't do anything to damage each other's reputation."

I was thinking, of course, about the Shalden party.

About Fletcher kissing me...

And as if he was reading my thoughts, he turned his head toward me, and touched my arm, and we stopped.

"I told you it was complicated," he said. "She's been cheating on me. Which wasn't a huge surprise. Things have been breaking down for a long time, between us. And then I started hearing rumors. And I kept asking her, do you want a divorce, and she kept saying no, no... And finally I asked her flat out, 'Are you sleeping with Upton,' and she denied it." He shook his head. "But I didn't believe her. The rumors... I knew they weren't just rumors. People had seen them out together."

Ugh.

"And then Upton tells me that he's hired a manager, and he says your name, and it hit me right here..."

He tapped himself on his chest with the flat part of his right fist.

"And then I saw you and...Marion. I didn't know what to do."

His eyes met mine.

"It's pride, Marion. I didn't want her to turn to me in front of our lawyers and say, 'Oh, but Fletcher was having an affair, too!'"

"So that's why you pulled away, at the party, when you saw her coming..."

He dropped his eyes, nodding. "I wanted to explain everything to you..."

He touched my elbow and turned, and we started walking again.

We reached his car.

"I'll drive you back to the brewery," he said.

But when we got into the car, he sat without pressing the start button. As if he'd forgotten I was there.

I watched him as he sat. His profile. The way his mouth moved from time to time, like he was trying to put some words together that he could say aloud.

But when he spoke, all he did was repeat what he'd said a few minutes before. That he'd drive me to the brewery.

I reached over and stopped his hand before he started the car. "Listen, Fletcher. Just tell me one thing."

He nodded, waiting.

"What's next?" I asked quietly.

He looked at me.

Then he looked at his left hand, where it rested on top of the steering wheel.

His left hand, with its silvery wedding band.

And he pulled the band off and dropped it into the cupholder between us.

"What's next," Fletcher said, "is that I am getting a divorce."

He reached over, now, and picked up a bit of my hair that had kind of fallen across my cheek and tucked it gently behind my ear.

I swallowed. "And...anything else? I said, my voice cracking a little bit.

His hand, gentle behind my head...

"I kiss you, Marion Flarey," he answered.

"Oh," I whispered.

And he kissed me.

And it may not have been a happily ever after. Yet.

But it certainly was a happily ever next.

Pssst ... Marion's adventures aren't over...

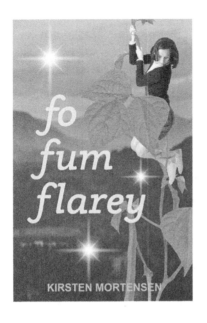

Fo Fum Flarey

She's got her prince, at last. If she can keep him.

Happily Flarey...Ever?

She's lost two princes. Is number three the charm?.

Made in the USA
Monee, IL
06 January 2023

24486649R00148